THE
EMPRESS

THE
EMPRESS

GIGI GRIFFIS

zando

NEW YORK

Zando
zandoprojects.com

First Edition: October 2022

Text design by Pauline Neuwirth, Neuwirth & Associates
Cover design by Evan Gaffney
Cover photo © Thomas Schenk

Bird © val_iva / Adobe Stock
Knife engraving © channarongsds / Adobe Stock
Botanical engraving © OlgaKorneeva / Adobe Stock

LCCN: 2022939803
ISBN 978-1-63893-016-7 (Paperback)
ISBN 978-1-63893-017-4 (Ebook)

10 9 8 7 6 5 4 3 2 1
Manufactured in the United States of America

For my sisters, by blood and choice:
RJ, Natalia, Sarah, and David

On the wild waves of the North Sea
Beloved,
You lay stretched out;
I have consumed you bit by bit,
Covered in salt and foam.
—THE DIARY OF DUCHESS ELISABETH OF BAVARIA

1853

PART I

ONE

E LISABETH'S MOTHER WAS PANIC AND FURY, A WIND-
storm of skirts and schnapps, rampaging through the
house loud enough to wake the dead.

"Sisi!"

Elisabeth hated that nickname, and her mother knew it. It was
a child's name—and her mother's excuse to treat her like one.

"Sisi, where are you?" Mother's voice was closer now.

Elisabeth was hiding behind an elegant sky-blue floor-to-
ceiling curtain. The curtain matched the rich blues of the plush
chairs in the sitting room where she was hiding, which in turn
matched the rich walnut of the wood floor, which matched the
richness of her mother's tastes. The rest of the house was similar: baby-blue archways and doorways, jewel-toned bedcovers,
warm wood floors laid with rugs, everything swirling with flowers or twining with vines.

Elisabeth's eight-year-old sister, Spatz, slipped behind the
curtain beside her, conspiratorial. Elisabeth wiggled her eyebrows at her tiny, wide-eyed sister and pressed a finger to her

lips. But Spatz didn't need to be told to be quiet. She knew the hide-from-Mother game well by now. They all did. Only Helene had recently become very serious and stopped playing.

The thought made Elisabeth's eyes close involuntarily. Her sister had scolded her just yesterday that she needed to grow up. "You sound like our tutor," Elisabeth had replied, unable to keep her disappointment from spilling out. Now Helene had given her the silent treatment for half a day.

"Si-si!" her mother shouted again, pronouncing each syllable of her name separately as if that would draw her out of hiding.

Elisabeth knew Mother wanted to do something with her hair. She could picture the next two hours of her life: *Sit still, Sisi! Don't fidget, Sisi! Let us yank your head in every direction and stab you with pins, Sisi!* Even when she tried to do what her mother wanted, it was never enough. Every breath was a fidget. Every accidental wince a complaint. Elisabeth had tried—*really tried*—the last time a duke came calling about an engagement, but in the end, it still turned out the same: with her mother angry and the duke gone.

Today, she'd rather hide.

Elisabeth rubbed a thumb against the thick, silky fabric of the curtain, a breeze tickling at the back of her neck through the open window behind her. All three girls had climbed out that window time and time again in games of hide-and-seek—and whenever they needed a fast escape. Though she supposed Helene wouldn't stoop to climbing down the trellis and into the grass any longer, now that she'd lost her sense of adventure. Now that she was supposed to marry the emperor.

It was worse than that, Elisabeth realized, because Helene would be unadventurous and distant *and* gone. Marrying the emperor meant moving to Vienna. And leaving Elisabeth behind with—

"Where are you?" Her mother's question was followed by a frustrated, almost animal noise, and it was so startling, so close, that Elisabeth jumped and Spatz put a hand over her mouth to stifle a giggle. Mother had managed to come into the room without them hearing—a feat with her normally heavy footsteps.

Elisabeth regained her composure, winked at her sister.

"For heaven's sake, Sisi. The duke will be here any minute!"

The duke. Mother's great hope for Elisabeth's future and one of the most pompous humans in existence. Mother was hoping he'd propose today; Elisabeth was hoping he'd fall off his horse on the way.

Another set of footsteps rushed into the room. A maid, for certain. Helene wouldn't stoop to rushing anymore.

"She isn't even dressed yet? That can't be!" Mother said.

Elisabeth rolled her eyes. *Any minute* was an exaggeration. The duke wasn't due for several hours. She smiled at Spatz, raising an eyebrow. Neither of them were anywhere near dressed— both in white nightgowns, bare feet, hair wild and not yet brushed.

Emboldened, the sisters peeked around the curtain. The maid was holding Elisabeth's dress for the day—ruffled and glamorous, decked out with ribbons, but so stiff with starch that it looked like it could stand on its own. Perhaps that was the answer to the day's woes: the dress could stand in for Elisabeth. She doubted the duke would notice if it didn't have a real woman in it. In fact, he might think it an improvement.

They watched as Mother clutched dramatically at her side and leaned heavily on the poor, put-upon maid, who struggled to support both her and the stand-alone dress.

Despite her nerves, Mother looked perfect, as usual, her own dress a deep shade of green with a plunging neckline and puffed sleeves. A floral necklace drew the eyes to her delicate throat and perfect bone structure. Mother's hair was honey hued and her features elegant, a stark contrast to the dark locks and playful faces of Elisabeth and Spatz. Helene, on the other hand, had inherited her mother's golden tones and graceful movements, and she had also now adopted the propriety to match.

Sensing that Mother might turn at any moment and catch them, Elisabeth and Spatz darted back behind the curtain. And as the older women took their conversation into another room, Elisabeth turned to Spatz, clutching her side in an exaggerated impression of her mother. "I'm bleeding to death on the inside, and all because of that child! Bring me some schnapps!"

Spatz giggled, hand to mouth.

They could still hear Mother's shrill voice, farther away now, this time pointed at Helene, who must have chosen this unfortunate moment to leave her room and come into the hallway. "I won't allow things to go wrong—not again, not at the last minute."

That was the problem, though: the duke had been wrong from the very *first* minute, his attentions unwanted before he stepped through the door. But no matter how nicely Elisabeth said so, no one seemed to hear her.

Spatz looked at her older sister, curious. "Mother says he wants to propose to you."

"Well, he can propose all he likes," Elisabeth answered, leaning in, conspiratorial, "but I don't want him."

She smiled wryly, ruffling Spatz's mussed brown hair. Spatz looked like Elisabeth had at her age: aquiline nose, pale skin, cheeks rosy with mischief. The only difference was their eyes:

Elisabeth's a mysterious color somewhere between blue and green, Spatz's the liquid dark brown of a forest floor after the rain.

"But why not?"

Elisabeth poked her sister and whispered in mock horror, "Did you see how he dresses?"

On their first meeting, over a very awkward dinner, the duke had worn a collar so ruffled that it made him look like a turkey. Of course, much worse was the way he'd gone on and on about himself through dinner and then placed a proprietary hand on Elisabeth's knee under the table. But Spatz didn't need to know that part. The costume would be what was memorable to the youngest duchess.

Spatz rolled her eyes at the reminder.

Then, more serious, Elisabeth brushed a loose lock of hair from her sister's face. "I don't love him, and I want to make my own decisions."

Spatz nodded sincerely, but before she could ask another question, the telltale noise of a carriage rattled across the gravel drive and through the open window behind them. Elisabeth's eyebrows rose in surprise. She'd thought Mother's wails of *any minute* had been hyperbole. As usual. But now the duke had arrived—and was descending from his carriage. Elisabeth could see flashes of him through the trees between the window and drive. Her supposed beloved: his skin pale, his mustache curled, his expression ridiculously self-satisfied for a man dressed in the largest plumed hat Elisabeth had ever seen. She watched him until he disappeared around the corner of the house.

Elisabeth turned away from the window, took her sister's little face in her hands, and leaned down to look straight into her inquisitive eyes. "I want a man who satiates my soul. Do you understand?"

Spatz nodded, then shook her head and giggled.

"I want that for you, too—one day." Elisabeth kissed her sister on the forehead, Spatz's skin warm and dry and scented with the honey and tea their soaps were made with.

"Sisi!" Mother's voice was closer again. Too close.

And so, before her mother could find her and march her to her doom, Elisabeth lifted her skirts, climbed over the windowsill, and dropped into the dew-cold grass.

As she slipped around the corner of the house, she heard her mother screech again. "Where is she?"

And Spatz, dear, lovely Spatz, answered so seriously: "She said she wants a man who satiates her soul."

Yes, little sister. Elisabeth would have a great love or no man at all. It was the line she'd drawn in the sand, and she would not cross it.

TWO

F RANZ LOVED EVERYTHING ABOUT FENCING: THE COLD
air raw on his throat, his shoulders drawn tense as a bow-
string, the sweet smell of the wet grass, and the way the
world narrowed in on itself until all that was left was focus—
movements and countermovements. It was the one time he felt
completely right in the world, completely certain. The one time
he wasn't surrounded by people asking him to consider this alliance or that nobleman or some pretty girl who would make a
quiet, obedient empress. Everyone needed something from him,
and Franz was exhausted.

Fencing was how he forgot about all that, how he could—
for a few moments—be simply Franz. Not the emperor. Not
a Habsburg. Not a source of money, support, heirs. Just a man
with a sword proving himself with his wits and training against
the backdrop of a royal garden—all tall shrubs and bright white
stone paths. Alone except for his opponent and Theo, his
personal valet, standing to the side.

"Ah-ha!" His opponent made a triumphant noise, lunging
into an opening Franz had left him. But as usual, the opening

had been by design. Franz parried the blow and went in for the kill.

"Ah-ha yourself," he returned, confident that his sword was about to hit its target.

But no. His opponent blocked the blow easily, attacking back with vigor. "What now?" A familiar voice rang through the other man's mask. "Can't win them all, can we?"

Surprise and irritation flinched through Franz, bunching his muscles. He'd thought he was practicing with the fencing master—the lack of conversation a normal part of their peaceful routine since Franz had asked him to skip the formalities. But this voice was not the low, calm cadence of the fencing master. It was too sharp for that. Sharp enough that it could only belong to Franz's little brother: Maxi.

But since when was Maxi back at the palace? The least reliable Habsburg had been away for months doing who-knows-what with who-knows-whom. Franz had sent him on a scouting mission to Italy, but he'd neglected his correspondence again, so there was no telling where he'd actually been.

Franz tightened his jaw. Of course, Maxi would come out to needle him at the one time Franz could just *be*. Maxi couldn't just leave him alone. And today of all days—when Franz needed his composure more than ever.

Franz's feet moved urgently, almost without permission, as he lunged forward. Maxi would be unbearable if he won the match. Winning was suddenly more important than good form.

The swords clashed, the two brothers locked in a complicated dance: two steps forward, back, back, forward, back. Franz pushed, attacked, almost stumbled. And then—

He had him. Finally, Franz's épée found its mark at Maxi's heart, the dulled tip denting the cloth on his brother's chest.

"Match." Franz stepped back, breathing hard, and lifted his mask.

Maxi's shoulders dropped and he let his mask fall to the grass, casually running a hand through his sandy-blond hair. Maxi appeared unfazed, and Franz wished that he could look so carefree. If Franz didn't know Maxi better, he'd think his brother didn't care about the loss. But Maxi always cared. They both did. Competition was the lifeblood of young men. That's what their mother believed, and it's how she had raised them. Now neither of them could stand to lose.

"You haven't been neglecting your training, Brother." Maxi's smile didn't reach his eyes. "I see rumors of your demise were overblown."

"It's nice to see that those rumors sent you rushing back in concern for my health all those months ago." The edges of the comment were sharp. Franz knew better than to be hurt by Maxi, his unreliability all too familiar. But he *was* hurt. Franz had been on his deathbed, and his brother hadn't come home.

Maxi waved a hand, dismissive. "Alas, I was delayed, and anyway, you rose from the ashes like the damn phoenix, like I knew you would."

It was true. The doctors had been shocked by how quickly Franz recovered. A knife to the neck, yet he'd been out of bed, walking, exercising, and governing long before the doctors thought he would.

The truth was he'd had to. If he hadn't gotten out of that sickbed, he would have fallen apart. The skin at his neck may have stitched itself back together, but the tears in his mind hadn't. A noise or smell, a trick of the light, could send him straight back to hell. Every day he felt the blade go in, felt the life leaving his body, felt the hate behind the act. The only cure was constant motion, perfect control.

Franz rolled his shoulders, shaking the thoughts away. Today of all days, he couldn't afford to dwell. He hoped it looked like he was just stretching. He couldn't let Maxi see any hint of weakness.

"Your Majesty. It's time."

Franz turned to face Theo—in the past few months, his confidante—the one person in the palace who knew his secrets and laughed at his jokes. They didn't do more than exchange a small nod now, but even that action made Franz feel steadier, supported. He didn't know how he would have gotten through those months without Theo.

Franz let his eyes wander past Theo to the palace in the distance. The white facade had softened to gold in the early morning light, the rooftops a metallic green: a beautiful exterior that hid something colder and harsher inside. He clenched his fist.

Maxi was watching him closely, so Franz shook his shoulders again, tried to smile. It felt wrong, his face out of practice.

Maxi retrieved his mask and turned to follow Theo up the hill. Franz walked close behind—slowly, reluctantly. Leaving the garden set his heart racing, his sense of danger spiking. He reached down to run his fingers over the silk-soft petals of a rose to remind himself where he was.

You're not dying, Franz. You're not in danger.

You're only going to an execution.

THREE

N OW ELISABETH WAS THE WINDSTORM. WILD AND free, her horse, Puck, gaining speed beneath her, breaking into a gallop. Her nightgown clung to her sides, and her hair bounced with the rhythm of the horse's movement. Riding away from self-important dukes, away from mothers who tried to pinch her into a smaller shape—lacing her soul into a corset. She would not shrink, not for anyone.

She knew she would fall in love one day, and that love would make her more expansive, not less. She'd written poems about it, her favorite lines etched deep in her soul. As she and Puck cantered through the forest and leapt over meandering streams, she recited them to herself:

In deep, rocky gorges
In bays wreathed in vines
The soul always seeks
Only him.

Only *him*. Elisabeth knew with her whole heart that she would know him when she found him. Her soul would reach across the gap and recognize his right away. She knew he was not the pompous duke, so now, she rode. Away, away, *away*. Windstorm, hailstorm, tempest. Climbing up into the hills where low shrubs, rolling fields, and mirror-bright lakes spread out below her in every direction.

She only wished she could take Helene out into these hills with her, bring her back to herself. They could forage for berries, soaking their dress hems in dew. Lay out under the stars at night. Live, breathe, and stop trying to fold themselves into some other shape—and for what? There was nothing worth losing yourself over: not your mother's whims, not even an emperor. That's what Elisabeth had told her sister last week after Helene accidentally mislabeled the forks during etiquette lessons: *If he doesn't love you for you, then he doesn't deserve you.* If you had to be prim and proper all the time, know every fork by name . . . wouldn't you just suffocate in the box they forced you into?

Besides, Elisabeth had heard the talk. There'd been an attempt on the emperor's life. Her heart twisted in her chest at the thought that the engagement might put Helene in danger too.

Elisabeth urged Puck on faster, tightening her hands around the reins. She was a wild thing, untamable in the way of a storm or a fire. She'd never let herself become what Mother wanted her to be: a girl without hope, without dreams, without love. She would find her great love one day, and they'd be untamable together.

Today, Puck was the only one who understood that feeling. Her beloved horse was the only one who truly knew her, knew what it was to be free. She felt a rush of affection for him as they crested a hill, and she softened the pace. She was on a ridge, a steep, rocky drop on either side, the sun a pink-yellow orb in the distance.

She closed her eyes, reveling in the tickle of sun on her skin, the smell of forest pine in the air, the strength of Puck beneath her. If only all of life could feel like this—so lived in, so real.

But then, unexpectedly, the world tilted. Puck bucked beneath her, and Elisabeth flew through the air, righting herself just enough to fall on her hands and knees. She gasped at the impact, her knees throbbing with it, hands clutching at the grass as if those fragile green stalks could anchor her to the earth.

When she looked up, Puck was disappearing down the ridge path, wild from whatever spooked him.

And then she saw it: a grass snake. This one wasn't poisonous, but Puck didn't know that. He hated snakes like she hated dukes. They'd both flee before the bite came.

"Puck." Her voice was resigned. He was far away now. But never mind that. What mattered was that they were unhurt. She'd retrieve Puck, and all would be well. Better yet, she'd have quite the excuse for why she wasn't at the house for the duke's visit.

"All will be well," she repeated quietly to herself as she followed the horse's path down the hill. There Puck stood, on the edge of a pond with the sun gleaming off his chestnut coat. How beautiful he looked. How she loved him.

But then he turned—and all was not well.

Her father was asleep when she walked into his bedroom—but he wasn't alone. Not one but *two* women lay beside him, neither of them Elisabeth's mother. The room was elegantly decorated, like every room her mother had touched, but strewn with wineglasses and empty bottles. As she slipped into the darkness, Elisabeth stepped gingerly over the clothes that should have been on the two women—but were most certainly not. Her father was entangled in arms and legs, breasts, and the contours of exposed thighs. The hills and curves that comforted her father were not the same ones Elisabeth sought out.

The room smelled of sex, stale wine, and cigar smoke. Elisabeth's nose wrinkled involuntarily as she stepped up to the foot of the bed and was greeted by the nipples of a third woman she hadn't immediately seen.

And this was why Elisabeth refused to marry for anything less than love. She didn't want a life like her mother's, pretending not to notice that her husband was entertaining other women in her own home. And she didn't want a life like her father's, constantly seeking comfort from outside his marriage because he'd never loved her mother one day in his life.

It wasn't the sex that bothered her. She hadn't been with a man yet herself, but her father's reckless behavior meant that she knew a lot about it. She wasn't a prude; she wasn't afraid. She just hated the way it underscored the lack of love between her parents—two people who were supposed to love each other first and foremost.

But Elisabeth didn't have time to dwell this morning. Puck was injured. Besides, it wasn't the first time she had encountered her father in this state, and she knew it wouldn't be the last.

She spoke into the darkness. "Papa? I need your help."

Groggy, he opened his eyes. As usual, his look was brazen rather than sheepish. Her father, the rake.

"Puck's injured," Elisabeth whispered.

Her father didn't answer—only sat up and began to untangle himself from the snarl of limbs on the bed. Elisabeth turned away. She'd seen enough already.

When he moved into her line of sight, Father was dressed and carrying both a cigar and his rifle, two things he was rarely without. He motioned for her to lead the way out of the house.

"What happened?" he asked once they were outside.

"Something with his leg . . . he doesn't want to walk." Elisabeth was relieved to hear that she sounded steady. Certain.

"We'll have a look." Father picked up the pace, then smirked as he realized what day it was and turned to look at his middle daughter. "I thought you were getting engaged this morning. Aren't your mother and the duke waiting for you?"

Elisabeth gave him a sideways glance.

"I'm curious to see what absurdity he's wearing today." Father raised an eyebrow at her, and she laughed, if a little sadly. Papa was a strange and fickle ally, but he at least understood how ridiculous her suitors were.

"You could stop it, you know," Elisabeth replied. "You could send these dukes away."

He waved a hand, dismissive. "You know these affairs are your mother's business. Nothing to do with me." It was the same answer as usual. Sure, Father would teach them to ride and laugh heartily at their antics. But when it mattered, he never stepped in. Elisabeth didn't know why she kept hoping for something different.

Then, finally, they were there. Puck stood before them holding one leg up off the ground. He was breathing much heavier now, chest trembling, eyes wild. He looked much worse than Elisabeth remembered. She glanced at Father as his eyes narrowed, his lips turning down. Her heart trembled. This was her fault. She had taken Puck out to feel the freedom of wind on her face and now—

Now the foolish duke would be the end of them both.

Father stepped forward, examining Puck's leg.

"It's broken," he said, more irritated than sad. Puck might be a friend to Elisabeth, but to her father, he was property. Another thing to be replaced.

Tears brimmed in her eyes, but Father shook his head. "His leg is broken, Elisabeth. You know what we do when a horse breaks a leg. He won't be able to run; you won't be able to ride him."

Ride him. That was all Father saw Puck as: a thing to ride, a workhorse, nothing more.

When Elisabeth was little, he told her that you had to shoot a broken-legged horse because it couldn't live a full life anymore. But that was just an excuse, a dispassionate business decision. Why did Father get to decide how Puck felt about the fullness, the potential of his life?

Father cocked his rifle and handed it to Elisabeth, its weight heavy and familiar in her hands. "Do it," he said, nodding at the horse.

Elisabeth's skin went cold, and her hands began to shake. Puck had been her horse, her friend, her comfort for more than ten years.

"I can't," she whispered.

"You caused the damage; you pay the price."

Her father was so good at blame. Never mind his own flaws. Elisabeth bit the inside of her cheek.

"Puck isn't damaged goods to be thrown out. He's my friend." She knew what her father would say, but Puck was worth fighting for. Even fighting a losing battle.

"He's a horse, Elisabeth. Not a person. And you shouldn't have even been out here." He took the gun back, aiming it at Puck. Her poor, precious, wild, free Puck.

Elisabeth grabbed the barrel. "No, wait. It will heal. I know it." It was a hopeless plea, but still she made it. If she said it out loud, maybe there was some small chance that Father would believe her. Or just forget long enough to let Puck live out his life in a cozy pen eating apples out of Elisabeth's hands.

Father stood firm, his expression unmoved, and Elisabeth's breath wound tight in her chest, stealing her words. Time seemed to narrow in on itself, slowing, quieting. The birds went silent, the breeze stopped—even nature taking a moment of silence for her dear, sweet Puck.

She went to Puck one last time, pressed her hands to his soft face, then pressed her cheek to the top of his nose. She willed him to read her thoughts. *I'm sorry, Puck. I'll miss you.*

"Move, Elisabeth," came the words behind her.

So she did. And then she wept.

FOUR

I T WAS A GOOD THING THE HABSBURG UNIFORM WAS stiff as a tank, because Franz was shaking like a leaf inside it. He hated that he couldn't stop. His only hope for composure was that no one else noticed. The collar on his shirt rubbed roughly against the scar on his neck—a constant reminder, but at least it was covered. He wouldn't let those bastards see the marks their cause had left on him: the scar nor the shaking.

Franz was standing in his room, surrounded by an army of slick-haired, white-gloved servants who had spent fifteen whole minutes sealing him into his monstrous uniform. Out of the corner of his eye, he could see his reflection—elegant, regal—in the gold-rimmed mirror to his left. But the room around him felt as stiff as the uniform today: the wallpaper drab, the rich umber of the heavy curtains unyielding. It was amazing how a room could reflect his own mood back at him.

The only person in the room less comfortable than Franz was the new valet, standing at attention by the mirror. Was the man even alive? He looked as stuffed as the taxidermy bear in the corner, which had been delivered that morning, compliments of the Russian tsar—a reminder of yet another thing someone wanted from Franz: military support.

"Theo, do me a favor." Franz broke the silence.

"Of course, Your Majesty."

"Find out if the new guy is still breathing." Despite the deadpan delivery, Theo smiled at the joke, and Franz felt a little better.

Franz took a deep breath and adjusted his collar. The new guy looked a little like Maxi—something about the eyes, the jaw—and Franz wondered where his brother was and if their mother would try to bring him to the execution. After their match, Maxi had—predictably—disappeared. Franz could never get away with that, but Maxi was free as a bird. Freer, even. Birds still had to build nests and feed their young. Maxi's nests were built for him, and while Franz suspected there were a few screaming infants out there with his brother's eyes, Maxi definitely wasn't doing any feeding.

Franz could hear his mother approaching in the hall. She always walked with purpose, a habit he'd found useful when he was a boy trying to hide from his duties and that now gave him advance notice to stand up straight.

Countess Esterházy, his mother's favorite companion, was rattling off the schedule in her clear, cool voice. "There is a short audience with the Bohemian delegation after breakfast, then you have a fitting for the winter wardrobe. But first, the execution."

At that, the footsteps stopped abruptly, and Franz's eyebrows flicked upward in surprise. It wasn't like his mother to be hesitant in the face of an execution. Was she feeling some of the anxiety in his own heart?

But then the footsteps started again and the disgust in her voice aimed itself elsewhere. "Not another fitting. Postpone it."

His mother: Archduchess Sophie of Habsburg, the pragmatist. People called her the only man in Hofburg Palace. It was meant as a slight on Franz, but it never bothered him. They weren't wrong. She was the best strategist, the sharpest mind, in all of Vienna. She was almost psychic in her ability to know the right thing to do, to see danger before it struck. She'd even told Franz not to go out the day of the assassination attempt. She'd told him that there was unrest, that he was in danger.

It was his fault for not listening. For only taking a single guard. So, if his decision to listen to her made people gossip, well, he would bear it. He owed her that much.

Franz turned toward the doors as they opened, and his mother walked into the room. She was imposing as always, in a black dress with a tall, stiff collar. As usual, she filled every spare inch of space with her quiet power.

"Mother."

She hinted at a curtsy and a smile. "Your Majesty."

He stepped forward to kiss her hand, relieved that his own was no longer shaking.

"I hear you've been out already. Did you sleep at all, dear?"

He shook his head. He hadn't slept a full night since the day they gave him the scar. He wondered if he would after the execution, knowing he'd struck back at the revolution that wanted him dead. But no use bothering his mother with all that; she wouldn't understand.

"You look perfect, Franz." Sophie motioned to the door, and he fell into step beside her as they walked into the gleaming marble hallway, their feet tapping loudly, echo bouncing off the high ceilings.

Some days his mother would stop to admire the details of the palace—the portraits of their predecessors lining the walls, the intricacies of the stone columns—but not today. Today, she was all business. She turned midstep, looking seriously at her son. "This won't be a pleasant morning, but you will have to get used to it."

Franz held her gaze. "I believe there are things one never gets used to."

An hour later, Franz and his mother stood in a square fitted with gallows. Five men waited steel-faced and dirty on a rough wooden platform, nooses hanging behind them. Franz stared at their hands, the fingernails soot black and plum purple, some of them missing. Had they always been like that, he wondered, or had his guards done it? The thought turned his stomach. Didn't meeting suffering with suffering only yield more suffering?

"Show them your face." His mother's voice broke through his thoughts. "There are times when a ruler must show his strength."

Franz tried to keep his expression calm as he tore his gaze away from the men's hands and focused on their faces. Sweat beaded inside his collar, underneath his hat, and dripped hot and then shockingly cold down his neck and spine. He breathed in through his nose and out through his mouth, but the breaths still came quickly, and his heart beat hard inside

his chest. His upper lip was tingling again and he knew—
even if no one else around him did—that he was on the brink
of passing out. It happened sometimes, when the memory of
that day rushed in. The numbness would creep in, his vision
would narrow, and then: darkness. So far it had only happened when Franz was alone. *Please, God,* he thought, *don't let it
happen now.*

All around him, people jeered, their voices rising in an unin-
telligible roar. It was making the feeling worse, making it harder
to track his breathing. Beside him, his mother nodded at the
police chief.

"Nooses!" the chief shouted, and Franz nearly jumped as men
scrambled to place ropes around necks.

Franz reached up to his lapel and detached one of the medals
pinned there, slipping it into his closed fist, letting the jagged
edges push into his palm. *Focus, Franz. Feel the sharpness on your skin.
You're here now. You're not back there.* If he told himself enough times,
maybe one day his body would believe him and stop tingling
then screaming its way into the past.

"You have been sentenced to death on charges of lèse-
majesté and seditious conduct, theft, and high treason," the police chief continued. "Only His Majesty the Emperor has the
power to pardon those who have been condemned to die."

Franz pressed the medal harder into his fist, tightening his
hand around it, the sharp edges slicing through skin. He stared
straight into the eyes of the revolutionary in the center: a leader
in the movement that had tried to kill him.

None of these men were the one who'd plunged in the knife.
But they were all a danger. They had planned it. They had

sanctioned it. They were the unrest of the people sharpened into a weapon, striking at the heart of Habsburg.

Franz held his gaze.

"Do the condemned have anything to say?" the police chief asked, and the crowd went silent. Franz's heart shrieked in his ears.

"You sit in your palace while we live in *filth*." The man in the center was the one to speak. "We have no food. We have no supplies. We have no way to get the things we need. And you ignore our suffering. You ignore your people."

Franz forced his face to stay stony, composed.

"Your Majesty," the man added, mockingly, with a slight curtsy, awkward with his head still in the noose. "You can kill us, but it won't make a difference. The people will rise up against you."

A chorus of yeses echoed ominously through the crowd. Franz focused on his breathing, the feeling of pin against palm, blood pooling sticky where it rubbed too hard.

It was another confirmation of what Franz wished he could forget: *He was still in danger.* Another knife or, perhaps this time, a revolver, a sword, a hundred fists from a hundred angry men, their voices rising like the ocean. His mother exchanged a glance with the police chief and Franz knew she was as surprised as he was by the crowd's reaction. The crowd should have been on their side, but instead they were cheering *for* the men about to die.

The man continued, "I die for the people—"

The crowd roared its approval.

But then, midshout, the lever was thrown, the gallows opened, and the man's words were cut off with a crack. Franz tried not to flinch, but he could feel that noise in his bones, his toes, his fingertips. Attendants threw the other levers in turn, the other revolutionaries following their leader into death.

The crowd fell silent. The attendants stepped down from the platform.

It was over.

FIVE

BREATHE IN, BREATHE OUT.

Elisabeth stood outside the sitting room, repeating those words to herself and trying to calm her ragged breaths, the sick pounding of her heart. Puck was gone. Her nightgown was covered in grass stains and blood from holding him. Her face was tight with the salt of dried tears. And there was a ridiculous man behind this door who wanted to marry her. She'd started the day in good humor, despite it all, but she was too tired for that now.

Elisabeth stood in one of her favorite places in the house, all sweeping ceilings and stone steps stretching gently up to the second floor. The entryway was elegant in its simplicity, the one place her mother's heavy fabrics and gold leaf hadn't swallowed whimsy whole. The staircase's wooden banister was carved with vines and roses, and slightly imperfect knots dotted the wood. It was like the outdoors had come dancing playfully inside. It usually comforted her. But today it felt oppressive: the entryway to a life she didn't want.

She could hear her mother through the door. "Sisi will be here presently. Her morning prayers are so important to her."

If she had the energy, Elisabeth would have rolled her eyes.

"This last summer has made her blossom and become even more mature. She is ready for marriage . . ."

Mother was babbling, as usual. Elisabeth hated how she had been reduced to whatever her mother thought a girl *should* be, not what she actually was. She wondered what it would take for her mother to call Elisabeth witty or wild or spontaneous. That kind of truth would probably make her mother's ulcer explode on the spot.

"My daughter was blessed with a clever mind. But not *too* clever, of course."

Elisabeth let out a weak, rueful exhalation.

"Above all else, she's inconspicuous and will submit to your every will."

Elisabeth turned away from the sitting room. Her mother could keep lying, but that didn't mean she had to listen.

"Sisi!" Helene met her at the bottom of the staircase. "I think the duke is about to leave."

Elisabeth took her older sister in slowly: her light hair perfectly pinned, her skin flushed pink, her dress well fitted in a playful yellow. A few months ago, Helene had hidden Elisabeth in a trunk when one of the counts came calling. But now she was firmly on Mother's side. The side of duty, obligation. The loss carved into Elisabeth's heart.

"I don't care, Néné." She said her sister's nickname gently, her voice resigned.

Helene shook her head slightly. "But it's been arranged. He's here to get engaged."

"You take him then," Elisabeth replied, her words tired and thick with grief. She was a girl without a mother who loved her for who she was, without a sister to support her or a father who would intervene, and now no horse to escape with.

Before she could slip past Helene and up the staircase, the sitting room door banged open, and Mother and the duke spilled into the entryway.

Elisabeth turned to face them at the foot of the stairs, taking in the duke. Today he had chosen to match his yellow plume with yellow stockings, a yellow vest, and a purple coat. He looked even more ridiculous than last time.

Mother sucked in an audible breath at the sight of her, but Elisabeth only curtsied. "Duke."

"Oh, here she is." Mother's voice was shrill, her eyes bulging even as she tried to pretend that her precious, marriageable daughter wasn't covered in dried mud and blood and tearstains. "Sisi, you remember Duke Friedrich of Anhalt. The duke insisted on discussing something important with you . . ."

Mother motioned to the duke as if anything about this moment was romantic, as if he could possibly still want to propose. Elisabeth wasn't sure whether she wanted to laugh, cry, or scream.

The duke paused for a long moment, and then he started to laugh—full-belly, shoulder-bouncing, shocked laughter. Elisabeth supposed it was better than a proposal, but still, he had some nerve.

"You're laughing at me?" She couldn't help herself. "While wearing that hat?"

The laughter died in the duke's throat. His cheeks flushed with embarrassment, and—without even the slightest bow—he stormed away.

If looks could kill, Mother's would have put Elisabeth six feet under. But she didn't have time for more than a passing glare as she rushed after the duke, already spinning some story about how Elisabeth wasn't quite herself.

"You can't keep doing this, Sisi." Helene sounded tired behind her, and Elisabeth turned to face her sister again. "We all look bad because of you."

Was that all Néné cared about now? Elisabeth wanted her older sister to ask if she was all right, if she was in pain. To ask about what had happened this morning to leave her so filthy.

Elisabeth didn't understand how a duke she didn't want and an emperor Helene had never even met were more important than a brokenhearted sister in a bloodstained nightgown.

When Elisabeth stepped into the salon a few minutes later to face her mother, the room's bright white walls were a jarring contrast to her muted feelings. Helene followed her into the room, closing the door on Mother's command.

Standing off to one side, Helene was Elisabeth's complete opposite. No mud-caked bare feet. No words uttered in haste. Elisabeth's heart stretched across the space. *Néné, I miss you. Where did you go?*

Elisabeth opened her mouth to speak, but then closed it, not sure what to say. It was pointless, anyway. Mother had made it quite clear she had no interest in Elisabeth's opinions.

Mother was standing at the far window, beside the alcove where Elisabeth often tucked herself away to daydream and write. With its view over the grounds, it was the perfect place for verses about love and wanting, mountains and skies—but now it was full of her mother's anger. It beat off her like a glow-ing coal.

Mother turned sharply, crossing the room to Elisabeth and leaning in close. "That's two counts and two dukes you've driven away. They were very good men!" She practically spit the words.

No matter how many times her mother said things like that, the unfairness took Elisabeth's breath away. The first duke had undone his trousers while they were eating cake. The sec-ond count believed women should speak one word for every ten words from a man. Was that what her mother thought good men were? Mother condemned her own husband for be-ing just like the first duke. The hypocrisy—and the double standard—were stunning. Dukes and counts could behave as badly as they wanted; Elisabeth would be the one punished, the one blamed.

"I have an ulcer, you know," Mother continued, less state-ment and more accusation. "The doctor said it could burst and then I'll bleed to death on the inside. All because of you, Sisi." Mother stepped back and leaned heavily on the back of a chair.

Elisabeth was always the source of Mother's pain. For having the audacity to not want men who were rakes or self-important or twice her age. Perhaps also for not wanting what her mother wanted, for not being who her mother was. She'd had enough.

"My name is Elisabeth," she answered slowly, deliberately.

Mother stared at her, face shifting from shock to fury. She lifted her skirts and crossed the room in barely a breath, raising her arm. Elisabeth could feel the passion and violence of the slap before it came. As if Mother was slapping her not just for today, but for all the offenses Elisabeth had ever committed in her life. Elisabeth braced herself for not just the hand, but the disdain, the rage, the disappointment.

Except—

Helene stepped forward, her breath shaky.

"Mother," she whispered, holding out a glass of apple-red sherry. "A refreshment, perhaps?"

Mother lowered her arm, took the sherry, and pointed it at Elisabeth. "Why can't you be like your sister? If she's unhappy with something, what does she do?"

Elisabeth stared at Helene, willing her to say something, to give her the answer.

When Helene said nothing, Elisabeth turned her attention back to Mother. "I don't know."

"I don't know either! And that's exactly how it should be!"

Elisabeth took another slow breath and tried to share her truth again. "I want to make my own decisions. I want to live a full life. What's so bad about that?"

"What do you want to do with your life—*write poetry?*"

"Why not?" Why shouldn't she have her poetry, her dreams? It was better than Mother drinking her life away, Father wasting his on meaningless affairs.

Mother shook her head. "You don't know what the world out there is like."

"I know there's something waiting for me," Elisabeth whispered, almost to herself.

Mother paused, narrowed her eyes.

"Oh, my darling girl . . ." Her words a knife aimed at Elisabeth's heart. "Believe me, there is absolutely nothing—and no one—waiting for you."

Cold despair wrapped itself around her. They'd had similar conversations before, but something in Mother's voice was

different now. More certain, more disdainful. For the first time
in her life, Elisabeth wondered if her mother might be right—if
she was fighting, screaming, clawing at life for no reason at all. If
there was nothing out there for her but the loss of a horse, a
sister, hope.

But no. She refused to give up hope.

"You can't force me." Her words echoed in the silence. "I
won't marry these men."

Mother came toward her, her face serious and voice cold.
"You know, there are establishments for young women who
have lost their minds."

Elisabeth's stomach tightened. Mother had threatened her
with convents before, but never an *asylum*—and she knew why.
She could see the letter sitting open on the desk, where her
mother had clearly been rereading it. The letter that had come
only a couple of months before. The arrangements for Helene
to meet—and become engaged to—the emperor.

Now Elisabeth realized what that letter meant for her. Her
daydreams had no place at court, in the home of the future empress. Mother would send her away if she didn't force herself
into the shape of the imperial family.

Helene took a step forward, then broke her silence. "Not an
asylum, Mother. You're going too far."

Néné. The relief of Helene coming to her defense didn't untangle the knots in her throat or stomach, but Elisabeth was
grateful. Néné still cared.

"Enough!" Mother snapped. "Helene has a magnificent future ahead of her. You won't ruin that for us, Sisi. Do you
understand?"

Elisabeth reached a hand out toward her mother. "Please. I'm not insane."

It hurt when Mother ripped her hand away, hurt in all the places where the old wounds kept trying and failing to heal. "Then prove it to me."

SIX

"Sisi," Helene whispered, tapping lightly on her sister's bedroom door.

Silence.

"Sisi, please, can we talk?" Helene pressed her fingernails into the playful carved flowers in the dark wood of the door.

Silence again.

"Mother was too harsh." Helene bit her lip, glanced over her shoulder, as if Mother might have sneaked up behind her.

Perhaps Sisi had climbed out the window again. Her bedroom was on the second floor, but the tree outside it was sturdy. Helene wouldn't be surprised if she was talking to the air.

"Sisi?"

Helene pressed the door handle. Unlocked. She hated to violate Sisi's privacy, but she needed to know that her sister was all right. She'd never seen her mother threaten her sister quite like that before. If it had taken the wind out of Helene, what had it taken out of Sisi?

She gently pushed the door open and stepped inside. It was nearly lunchtime, but Sisi's heavy blue curtains were drawn and her room was dim. Clothes and books were strewn haphazardly across the settee. A pair of shoes peeked out from under the bed, where they'd clearly been kicked. A rogue sliver of light escaped around the edge of the curtain to fall, sparkling, onto the golden rug. And on the bed, lying on her side and facing away from Helene, was Sisi. She looked so small, like Mother's threat had taken away half her presence. Helene had been thinking of herself and Sisi as grown women, but in that moment, Sisi looked like a child again.

Helene took another step toward the bed, tentative, then stopped. Sisi hadn't answered or turned toward her. Maybe her sister wanted to be alone.

"Sisi?" Was her sister ignoring her because Helene was using her nickname? Helene wasn't sure if she was allowed to use the endearment anymore. Sisi had never minded before, but lately she'd been asking Mother not to use it. So was Helene forbidden to use the endearment as well? She wasn't sure. She wasn't sure of anything these days.

"Are you hurt?" she whispered, knowing it was a foolish thing to ask. Of course Sisi was hurt. Father had come in a short time ago and told Helene about Puck. If Mother hadn't done the damage, surely that had.

But maybe it was a good thing. Sisi couldn't keep up like this. She'd ruin herself, ruin her family. And a little hurt now might save her a lot later. A little hurt had forced Helene to grow up, and she knew she was better for it.

Then again, it hadn't been a *little* hurt for Helene. It had been the worst moment of her life that forced the change; it was a violent stripping of her confidence in the world she thought she knew.

It was springtime a year ago, and she and Elisabeth and Spatz were playing outdoors, loose hair dancing on the breeze, sun pinking their noses. They'd run all the way down to the river, and Helene announced that she was going to cross the water on a newly fallen tree. They'd never been to the far bank, and Spatz wanted to see if there were fairies living there.

"Let's see then," Helene said, balancing on the trunk five feet above the water, rubbing the soles of her bare feet on its rough bark and dancing across. She wasn't always the sister with the right thing to say, but she was the graceful one.

Spatz went next, scooting over on her hands and knees, too afraid to stand. And that was probably for the best: the rains had left the river rushing cold and wild and fast below them.

"My turn!" Sisi announced, balancing on the trunk with arms outstretched like a tightrope walker.

Helene laughed at her younger sister's antics, but the laughter died quickly in her throat.

She knew the moment before it happened that Sisi was going to fall. Helene could even feel her arm reaching out of its own volition, futile with her sister still so far from the bank.

Sisi's eyes went wide, her body tilted, and she went into the river. The river that had only been a little scary only moments before now sucked Helene's sister straight down.

Helene heard herself scream. Spatz pressed a tiny hand against her mouth, eyes wide.

"Stay here!" Helene shouted at Spatz, taking off down the riverbank, following the dark outline of Sisi under the surface, rushing so fast downstream.

Sisi surfaced once, sputtering, coughing, before going under again, her skirts swirling around her like a jellyfish. How long could a person hold their breath? Helene didn't know the answer.

Helene ran like the world was on fire, racing toward the bridge, rocks and sticks tearing into the bottom of her feet. If she could get there in time, she could reach down and grab Sisi's dress.

But when she neared the bridge, a man was already standing there, reaching down to haul Sisi out of the water by her hair.

By the time Helene got there, Sisi was vomiting water, coughing, crying.

It was Helene's fault. She'd suspected it then, and Mother made sure she knew it later. She was the oldest. She was the one who was supposed to be making adult decisions. She was twenty, for God's sake, and acting twelve. She'd almost killed her sister—looking for fairies, no less—and the guilt of it was heavy and sharp, even months later. It lived on in her gut and her headaches and the perpetual tightness across her skin.

Every time Helene went out with her sisters after that, her mother would remind her: the only way to keep them safe was to stop acting feral and start behaving.

Helene promised herself then that she wouldn't encourage childish behavior anymore, not in herself and not in Sisi. It was the only way to keep her sister safe. But no matter what Helene did, Sisi kept being wild. And every time she was, she got hurt. Proving Mother's point over and over, carving it into Helene's heart.

Now, that wildness was going to get her landed in a convent—or worse, an asylum.

Helene pressed her hand against her chest at the thought, as if she could crush the fear of it if she pressed hard enough. She took the last couple steps to the bed, climbed in, and put a hand on Sisi's shoulder, leaning over to try and look her in the eye. Sisi might be shutting the rest of the world out, but Helene needed her to know she was on her side. Sisi's eyes were closed, though, her lips parted slightly. Asleep in the middle of the day—a surprise. Sisi always slept like the dead, so she probably hadn't even heard Helene come in.

Relief loosened the knot in Helene's chest. Sleep was good. Sleep could heal so many ills. She lowered herself gently beside Sisi, curled around her warm back. *I love you, Sisi. I'm trying my best to look after you.*

She hoped that when her sister woke, she would finally understand. The more you fought, the more you hurt. But when you embraced life for what it was . . . well, Helene's life had become safer and her prospects brighter.

Her heart delighted in that thought. She still could hardly believe it. If all went according to plan, she was going to be *empress*. The foreign dignitaries: she'd be the one to charm them. The royal line: she'd be the one to extend it. *Empress* Helene. *Her Majesty* Helene. That's what life rewarded you with when you let go of childish things, learned to hold your tongue, and listened to your mother—however ridiculous she might sound.

The first letter, the first invitation to a new life, had come months ago now, not so long after Helene had started pouring her heart into etiquette lessons and French literature. Archduchess Sophie—the emperor's mother and Helene's aunt—had written to her personally. She said she thought it would be a perfect match, that Helene had blossomed into exactly the kind of person Habsburg needed. Helene's head was still full of the letter, each line read so many times that she could recite it by heart.

Helene held her sleeping sister tight. While Sisi wouldn't find as advantageous a match as Helene had—there was only one emperor, after all—she was beautiful and bright, and if she applied herself, Helene was certain a most hopeful match would land in Sisi's outstretched hand. She only hoped Sisi would open her heart to receive it.

In that moment, as her body warmed and she started to drift to sleep herself, Helene knew what she would do: she'd take Sisi along to Bad Ischl for the emperor's birthday. Perhaps one of the emperor's brothers might fall in love with her. Perhaps love would be the thing to tame her. And they could face this new phase of life together.

FRANZ TRACED A FINGER ALONG THE NEW SCABS ON HIS palm, carved there that morning as he clutched his medal to keep the darkness at bay. It was strange how comforting a scab could be. It was something he controlled in a situation so far outside his control.

Now another situation outside his control was demanding his attention.

"The people's anger, the unrest, the chaos . . . it will pass, Franz. It always does. Be patient." His mother sat across from him at the ornate dining table, soup spoon poised above a bowl of hearty goulash.

Franz could see himself reflected back at half a dozen angles by the brightly polished platters, carafes, and spoons organized across the table. They made him look pinched and small, in stark contrast to the rest of the room, expansive with its high ceilings, long mirrors, and tapestries so deep they felt like windows to another world.

The room smelled of paprika and slow-roasted meat, and if he didn't already know what his mother was about to propose,

Franz would be devouring the goulash like a last meal. But his stomach felt too tight for that now, ready for what came next. He owed his mother his life, and she was coming to collect it.

"You know what the people need . . ." His mother looked at him seriously for a moment, then snapped her fingers.

Two servants swept in with the portrait that'd been sitting, covered, in the hall for the last hour. Earlier, Franz had peeked underneath and—surprise, surprise—it was another pretty noble girl, presumably one his mother was suggesting as his bride.

She'd tried it several times before, and he'd always managed to evade the obligation. He was unwell. He was still learning. He was too new to being emperor and needed his wits about him. The idea of marriage felt as stiff as his military uniform. It was another obligation on a life already so heavy with them. One more might crush him.

He envied Maxi, not for the first time. His brother was so free, so unburdened by obligation. Even the duties he *should* take seriously, Maxi ignored. And their mother loved him for it, indulged him in a way she never did with Franz.

What would it feel like to be so carefree, to win hearts without even trying, even just for a day? Franz couldn't imagine it.

Even the small freedom of putting off marriage was over for Franz now. He couldn't delay siring heirs forever, no matter how little he wanted yet another person demanding his time and attention. His mother was right, he knew—right as always about it all—but Franz's heart was slow to agree.

At a raise of his mother's eyebrow, a servant unveiled the portrait with a flourish. "Introducing Helene of Bavaria." Mother was more forceful than usual.

Franz had already made up his mind to stop fighting her, but he couldn't help but temper his mother's enthusiasm. "She won't solve Habsburg's problems, Mother."

The people needed real solutions: food, work, thriving businesses, roads, rails. A wedding wouldn't solve an empty belly, struggling finances, a five-day carriage ride that could be a one-day train journey. The people wouldn't forget their hunger, their hurt, over a wedding. But now wasn't the right time to tell Mother his plans. Later, when everything was in place, he'd unveil them. Dazzle her. Make her proud.

"You are wrong, my dear." Sophie leaned in, her face certain. "The people will trust you again if you give them a bride. And an heir. Believe me. They have waited long enough."

She made it sound so simple. As if earning back the trust of thousands of people was a mere cough, solved by hot water with honey and ginger. Franz had real plans to earn back the people's trust, even if he hadn't shared them with his mother yet.

"Just look at her. Helene is beautiful, and her mother tells me she is also pious."

He nodded at his mother but didn't smile. It was clear that she had already started preparations. And it was clear that it was time for him to acquiesce. He would marry. He would do his duty. But he would not pretend he thought it would solve Habsburg's problems. He would not pretend it would make him—make *them*—safe. He would forever feel the knife in his neck, hear the crowd cheering at the execution. The unrest was a living thing, a snake readying to strike.

And that wasn't even considering the danger of a looming war between Russia and France, both leaders now sending gifts and subtle threats in expectation of Franz's support.

His mother frowned, mistaking his silence for hesitation. "Franz, I did not crush a revolution so that you could be picky about brides. And with war heating up at our borders, we don't have the luxury of fighting over your marriage. Bavaria—that's a grounded and honest choice for an alliance. And anyway, it is already decided. You will meet her at your birthday party at our summer villa in Bad Ischl. There we can announce the engagement."

Sophie paused, tilted her head, and reached across the table to squeeze Franz's hand, hers warm and soft against his. However powerful she was, she was still his mother. Her squeeze meant to let him know that she genuinely thought this was best—not just for the empire, but for him as emperor.

"The people need to dream again," she continued, removing her hand.

Guilt burrowed its way into Franz's unsettled heart. His mother wasn't a fool. She knew what the country needed. She'd put him on the throne and kept him there—alive. Franz loved his mother, respected her. And he would give her this: a bride, a wedding, an heir. It would bring his mother peace—and secure the empire's future.

Franz's rooms were moody and dimly lit when he returned to them in the twilight. He unlaced his shoes and pressed his toes into the thick, red Persian rug, letting out a sigh of relief as he did so. He stripped off his jacket, catching a glimpse of himself in the tall mirror—suspenders dark against his white shirt, his brown eyes deep in shadow. He ran a hand along his face, feeling the tackiness of skin against fingertips, the sharpness of the edges of his mustache, the fatigue coursing through his veins.

From the corner, a familiar voice whispered in the dark, "Majesty."

Franz paused, caught between the desire to be alone and the *desire* sparked by the voice itself. The voice was playful, sensual. His mistress knew Franz well enough to know that today of all days he needed her, needed to feel her skin on his.

Louise stepped out of the shadow, her familiar curves hidden under a shaggy, white bearskin. Another gift from Russia. Another reminder that Habsburg was wanted at war.

Franz shook the thought away.

His shoulders loosened as he watched the bearskin approach, a pale, shapely, naked leg appearing and then disappearing as Louise made her way toward him, tantalizing and slow.

"Is this your secret fantasy?" she teased. "Your Majesty the bear, and me the helpless squirrel?"

She was in front of him now, her scent all cinnamon and fiery urgency.

"And what if it is?" He traced a finger lightly across the soft bearskin, imagining her neck and shoulders underneath.

She removed the bear head like a hood, her face coming into view in the low lamplight—hair dark as raven wings, cheekbones high, eyes faintly smudged with makeup almost as if he'd already ravaged her. His body responded with a flush of heat.

"I say, whatever turns you on." She traced his lips with a bear claw. "Nothing shocks me."

It was true, and it was still titillating even after a year of these clandestine meetings.

"We don't have much time," Franz said, starting to remove his suspenders and stepping away from the mirror. He was expected at an evening event and had only come in for a few moments of peace.

But Louise turned away, sidling up to the portrait of Helene that had been delivered to Franz's rooms. Teasing, she locked eyes with him. "I heard you are to be engaged."

Franz didn't answer. He didn't want to talk about obligation brides when what he really wanted was in the room with him right now.

"She looks very obedient. Do you like her?" Louise traced a finger along the edge of the wooden frame.

Franz stepped to the edge of the rug and lowered himself into a cushioned chair, watching her movements—measured, sensual, as if the very air on her skin gave her pleasure. She was the kind of person you couldn't help but watch.

Louise raised an eyebrow at him. Someone who didn't know her might think she was jealous. But Franz knew she was only mocking his intended. Louise knew she was the sexier, wilder, more desirable one. The court's little secret: disobedient, unobtainable.

There was a time when he thought he might love her. But eventually he realized that *wanting* wasn't love. When he told her his dreams—how he wanted to improve the empire, improve the lives of the people—she asked him why he'd bother. When he wanted to hold her hand, she slid that hand down his trousers. Not that he was complaining. But this was a meeting of bodies, desires—not minds and hearts. They both knew it.

"Come here." Franz's voice was deep and low, echoing in the quiet room. "Now."

Her bare feet moved silently across the thick rug. And then she was a few feet away and dropped the bearskin, letting it slide down over her arms, breasts, waist, and hips. She was all soft curves and sharp knowing eyes, and Franz's body tightened with desire.

Louise leaned across the chair, her hands on the armrests, and kissed him. Long, slow, deep. The way she liked it. When she pulled back, her eyes gleamed with mischief.

"What's wrong with her, I wonder? Does she have a mustache?" Then, after a pause: "Come, my emperor. What do I have to say to make you laugh, just once?"

Franz stood from his chair and pulled her, naked, against him, her nipples hard against his chest through the thin fabric of his shirt. He kissed her neck, her skin sweet under his lips, his tongue. He needed to lose himself in her.

When he moved to her mouth, she was ready, pliant, opening herself to him. She kissed him long and slow and nipped at his lip with her teeth—a reminder that she wasn't all soft edges. His body ached for her, his clothes so restrictive now. But he wouldn't take her yet. He knew how to please her, loved the sounds she made whenever he did.

He laid her down on the bearskin.

"Will I lose you?" she whispered. But the question wasn't a worry; it was a command.

"Every emperor has an empress," he answered, keeping her gaze. "That's how it is. It won't change." Then he kissed his way across neck, shoulder blades, and breasts, moving lower until she stopped asking questions and started trying to catch her breath.

EIGHT

HELENE'S APPEARANCE WAS CAREFULLY CONSTRUCTED: her blouse white silk covered by a pale pink jacket that complemented her skin tone. Her skirt, hand embroidered, curved gently outward, as did the puffed ends of her sleeves. Her hat sat atop fashionable braids, a deep purple ribbon drawing the eye up to it. She felt pretty, vibrant, a jumble of excitement and nerves that she couldn't quite tease out from each other. If the emperor arrived at the villa before them, she'd be ready to greet him, perfectly poised.

To all the world, Sisi was also the picture of true nobility. Her hair perfectly styled with elaborate braids circling her ears, eyebrows plucked. She was wearing a white blouse, a large black-and-white bow at her neckline, and a striped jacket to match. Ankles crossed as she sat facing Helene in the gently rocking carriage.

But Helene could see what their mother couldn't; Sisi had kept pieces of herself in the places Mother hadn't thought to look. A braid of Puck's clipped under her hair, a spot of mud just above the ankle from when Sisi had stepped into the garden before they departed. Helene's heart was hopeful that this signaled a kind of compromise. Sisi could keep her quirks, just as long as the world never saw them. Especially Mother, who was asleep, chin pressed against her sunshine-yellow coat, hat tilting precariously against the window.

The carriage made a reassuring crunch across the gravel road as Helene stared down at a small portrait of Franz—her soon-to-be betrothed—sent with Sophie's latest letter. She traced a nervous finger along his face. What would it look like in person? Less stony, surely. Warmer when he looked at her. Unless he didn't like her.

Oh God, what if he didn't like her?

Helene shouldn't think like that, of course. Mother had told her too many times to count: it didn't matter if they liked each other. It only mattered that they were both suited for their roles.

Helene knew it was true. But she also wanted him to like her. To see her and immediately understand that they were meant to be. She wanted it more than anything.

When Helene looked up again, Sisi was watching her closely, eyes sly with mischief, pencil poised above her diary. Poems, Helene knew. Poems upon poems upon poems. Sisi must have written a thousand of them by now. She used to read them all to Helene, even sometimes the scandalous ones. Helene remembered the lines:

See how she hurries to her lover in the moonlight . . .
We exchanged hot kisses, sultry, like a full moon night,
We think nothing of the approaching morning . . .

That one had filled Helene with an unnamed longing she hadn't even known existed. It was before Franz, before the letter that had changed everything—and when she'd tried to imagine herself with a lover in the moonlight, his face was all shadow, undefined. Now she imagined the face in the little portrait, Helene hurrying toward him, him thinking nothing of the approaching morning.

Guilt fluttered across her happy thoughts. Sisi was playing with fire, she reminded herself. Helene wasn't supposed to encourage her.

"You know it's because of your poems that Mother wants to send you to the asylum." She kept her voice low to keep from waking Mother.

"Well, if that little picture starts talking to you, let me know. I'll take you into the madhouse with me," Sisi joked back, all lightness.

Helene rolled her eyes, amused despite herself. And then, an olive branch. "I'm happy you're coming with me."

Sisi quirked a half smile and a raised eyebrow in the direction of their sleeping mother. "She wants to keep an eye on me, that's all."

Helene shook her head. "I wanted you here."

Sisi's eyebrows rose in surprise.

"I talked to Mother about it, and she agreed."

"What did she say?"

Helene pursed her lips. "That the emperor's three brothers will also be there and . . . well, something about how a piece of sausage sometimes falls off the plate and into the dog's mouth."

"And was I the sausage or the dog?" Sisi raised an eyebrow.

Helene affected an exaggerated shrug. "No telling."

Sisi laughed, and Helene's heart went light as a feather. It was the first time in so long that they'd joked like this. They'd been in the same house, as always, but Sisi had felt so far away—never showing up for lessons, always disappearing into the mountains. Did Sisi miss Helene as much as Helene missed her? Did she understand how much Helene wanted her to step up, to behave as a lady of the court would, so that Helene didn't have to face it all alone?

"Sisi, I'm worried about you." Helene caught her sister's gaze and held it. "I'm worried that you'll get lost."

Sisi paused, surprise nudging her eyebrows upward, then waved a hand dismissively. "You don't have to be. You know me—thick-skinned."

"No, you aren't."

They both paused a moment, then Helene extended her arm, reaching for the diary. Another olive branch. "Show me."

Elisabeth let her take it, and Helene read out loud:

Swallow, lend me your wings
Take me to a faraway land
When I float
Free
With you
Up there in the eternal blue firmament
Then I will praise the God of freedom.

It was good. Though they were always good. That wasn't the problem. Helene handed the journal back. "Don't let Mother see you with this."

She said it lightly but hoped Sisi understood her full meaning.

Her sister stared back, deadpan in a way that usually meant a jest was coming. But Helene was relieved at the next words. Not a jest: a promise.

"I'll behave. I'll be invisible. You have my word."

Helene let out a long breath, relief warming across her skin. But before the relief could fully sink in, Sisi winked suggestively, turned to the window, and spit extravagantly out of the carriage.

Helene felt her mouth drop open as Sisi put on her serious face again. "From now on."

NINE

B Y THE TIME THEY ARRIVED AT THE KAISERVILLA IN BAD Ischl, Mother was awake, and the carriage felt like it had shrunk by half. Elisabeth couldn't wait to be out of it.

Helene must have felt the same. She was grinning ear to ear when they stepped from the coach, her eyes sparkling with excitement as her gaze swept the elegant villa.

Elisabeth took it all in too: the rustling green trees and iron lampposts artfully placed around the drive, the warm pink stone of the building's exterior. In the center of the drive, children and giant fish had been carefully carved into a stone fountain, water cascading joyfully over them as they laughed and played. Elisabeth had half a mind to join them.

But before she could give in to the temptation, Helene took her hand and led her from the drive, past cheerful blue shutters, and into the Kaiservilla.

"Now," Mother said as they stepped out of the hot summer afternoon and into the cool of the marble entry, "the emperor is not here for idle chatter. So don't ask him any personal questions. He is not interested in feelings. No womanish opinions or comments."

Elisabeth's heart twisted for her sister as Helene released her hand and stepped up to walk obediently beside Mother. What a contradiction it was: bringing Helene here to get to know the emperor and telling her to keep her thoughts to herself. Elisabeth hoped it wasn't true that the emperor wasn't interested in feelings. Asked to give up that part of herself, Elisabeth would disappear entirely. She didn't think her sister was so different.

Less than an hour after arriving, the sisters were in the sauna, scrubbing the carriage ride off their skin. As Elisabeth ran a comb through Néné's honeycomb hair, her sister fidgeted. Helene must be terribly nervous. Elisabeth was glad they were able to bathe just the two of them. She would take all the womanish opinions Helene wasn't allowed to share with her future husband. *Spill your secrets, Néné. Remember how we used to be*, she thought.

"Careful, Sisi!" Helene pulled away as the comb caught on a knot.

"Sorry." Elisabeth kissed Néné's head in apology. "At least you'll have a lady-in-waiting to do it for you soon."

Helene gave a gentle laugh and the silence stretched comfortably around them. Elisabeth melted into it. She and Helene could still be close in these quiet moments, no expectations or engagements to drive them apart.

"What if I can't stand him, Sisi?" Helene asked then, her voice the barest whisper.

Elisabeth harbored the same fear, but she wouldn't allow Helene to worry about it. Helene was hopeful, and hope was precious.

"Well, I did hear he's hairy all over, like a wild boar. And he likes it when ladies ruffle his fur. So, there's your strategy to get him in a good mood." Elisabeth's face was deadpan when Helene turned to look at her.

A heartbeat, two, and then Helene let out a laugh, poked Elisabeth with her elbow, and made a noise that Elisabeth knew meant *you're not as witty as you think you are.*

Elisabeth stuck out her tongue a little, winked.

Helene made a face back—the old Néné peeking out through the fancy facade. It reminded Elisabeth of when they were little, sitting in the garden plucking will-o'-the-wisps and blowing out their wishes. Each warned the other that if all the little seed parachutes didn't blow away, the wish wouldn't come true. Elisabeth's favorite memory of that time was when Néné once stuffed a will-o'-the-wisp into her mouth to hide the evidence of a wish unfulfilled.

That version of Helene was here now. She'd said it was *her idea* to bring Elisabeth to Bad Ischl. It made Elisabeth want to cry. But what if Helene really couldn't stand the emperor? Néné deserved more than a joking response to her question. Elisabeth reached a hand out and held her sister's, answering earnestly this time. "I'm sure he's a good man."

"But what if he doesn't like me? What if he thinks I'm boring?"

Now that—*that* was impossible. Of course he would love her. She was Helene. And no matter how much her sister had changed these past months, Elisabeth could see no other option but for anyone who met her to love Helene instantly and fully.

Elisabeth answered without hesitation. "You will be a wonderful empress. You're always elegant without having to fake it. You always know what is right and what is wrong. What should be said and what should not."

Helene smiled. "Unlike you."

Yes, unlike her. And if Elisabeth were softer around the edges, able to keep her thoughts to herself and her feet planted on the ground, she knew her life might have been easier for it.

"Come here." Helene turned to face her and pulled her in, leaning their foreheads together, a movement Elisabeth would find forever comforting. However on edge she felt about everything—Mother's threat of the asylum, Helene leaving her forever—Helene was still the person she loved most in the world.

"I'm going to miss you," she whispered.

But she knew that wasn't quite right. Elisabeth already *did* miss Helene, and she wasn't even gone.

TEN

O H, THE SCANDAL THEY'D BE AT THE EMPEROR'S birthday! Elisabeth held back a laugh.

It was early the next morning, and her mother was sifting frantically through their trunks. Undergarments accounted for. Sleepwear, check. Black mourning dresses? Here and perfectly presentable. But their other things, the beautiful dresses her mother had painstakingly chosen for her daughters' first meeting with the emperor: nowhere to be found.

"It can't be!" Mother shrieked at an impressive decibel. "It simply isn't possible!"

Helene looked ill, watching Mother dig through the trunk as if her best gown might suddenly appear. She twisted the ends of her hair, her brows pulled silently, distressingly together.

Elisabeth sat on her bed, the swirls of its embroidered white lace cover pressing into her bare legs. She leaned over the footboard and listened to her mother's panic spiral.

"There was another trunk." Mother paused her frantic search to address the maid, now frightened and cowering in the corner of the room.

"Your Highness, these were the only trunks on the carriage." The maid's voice was hesitant. "Perhaps the others will arrive later."

"This can't be happening," Helene interjected, her own voice laced with disbelief.

Mother dropped heavily into a chair at the foot of Helene's bed.

"Why did we pack mourning clothes anyhow?" Elisabeth couldn't stifle her curiosity.

"Uncle Georg died. We're stopping by on the way home," Mother answered.

Elisabeth's eyebrows drew together in confusion. "Who is Uncle Georg?"

"That doesn't matter right now, Sisi!" Mother shook her head like it was obvious that Elisabeth shouldn't care about the poor, dead uncle she'd never heard of.

"So . . . all we have are yesterday's dirty clothes?" Helene was on the edge of tears.

Elisabeth tried to sound comforting. "What you wear won't matter, Néné."

"Of course it matters!" Helene's voice was uncharacteristically sharp. "He is the Emperor of Austria, and it's his birthday."

Elisabeth quieted in surrender.

Mother fanned herself, speaking to the shaky maid. "Be so kind as to bring me a glass of sherry."

Elisabeth picked up her own mourning dress from where Mother had tossed it beside her on the bed. She'd always regretted that it was reserved for funerals. It was a pretty thing, not

too itchy or stifling like so many things her mother stuffed her
into.

Trying again to be helpful, she spoke up. "I read that in London and Paris, all the artists wear nothing but black."

Apparently, no one else in the room found the information
comforting because Mother narrowed her eyes. Beside her, Helene tightened her fist around her own dress and looked up
sharply. "You don't understand!" A pause, then, "Go, leave us
alone."

Elisabeth blinked fast, hurt. She was just trying to help, and
now Helene was banishing her. Could she never say the right
thing? Well, fine. Let them fret and cry over a thing they could
do nothing about. If a man's love was as fragile as two missing
dresses, his love wasn't worth having at all. If they couldn't see
that, they were the ones who didn't understand.

Elisabeth rose from the bed and slipped into yesterday's
dress. If she was banished, she might as well explore.

It was early, the sky still orange and pink with sunrise. Preparations for the emperor's birthday party were well underway, and
as Elisabeth wandered into a dining room, servants busied
themselves around her. A redheaded girl dusted the grand piano
in a corner. Two older women were sweeping on either side of
the room. And the smells of fresh bread and mixed spices drifted
in from a nearby kitchen, making Elisabeth's mouth water.

As she stepped farther into the room, a young man caught his
foot on the edge of a cream-colored Persian rug and stumbled,
scattering fruit from a three-tiered silver display across the
floor. He bowed as she rushed forward and stooped to help him

collect the oranges, lemons, and peaches, gently putting them back in place.

From the next room, a clipped scream sounded, and Elisabeth looked up from the floor and saw a bird had swooped in through the open door. Before she could react, there was an audible smack as it collided with the window on the far side of the room. It dropped to the floor, and Elisabeth's heart fell with it.

Birds were some of Elisabeth's favorite animals. Swift sparrow hawks. Elegant gulls. Cheeky songbirds. She felt a kinship with them, those freedom-seeking feathered things forever singing a song. This one had only wanted to escape.

Elisabeth moved toward the feathery bundle, lifting it gently from the tile where it now lay stunned. It was a tiny thing, brown-backed, white-bellied, with a collection of black-and-white feathers pointing straight up like a cowlick on its head. A crested tit, she thought, if her memory was correct. But the poor thing was injured, fluttering its wings in confusion, staggering like her mother after a few shots of schnapps. Then he went still.

Elisabeth took the bird, stunned but alive, out to the gardens, walking down paths bright with flowers and under trees swaying gently in the summer breeze. Behind her, the cheerful pink of the villa peeked through the leaves like the promise of a good day. Under her gown, she was secretly barefoot, reveling in the feel of cold, soft grass between her toes.

A horse whinnied to her left, and the sound shook her from her reverie. She had thought she was alone. But she could now see a man standing at a small stone fountain ahead, back turned, gently attending to his creamy, long-lashed mare.

Elisabeth watched curiously as he ran a hand along the horse's neck, threading his fingers through mane, untangling and straightening it. He was tall—so tall—in his black riding breeches and polished riding boots. There was something endearing about the affectionate way he touched his horse. Something familiar about those broad shoulders, the blond hair. She wondered who he was.

And then he turned, and she knew—the strong jaw and dark eyes identical to the portrait her sister kept tucked away in her skirts.

Franz. The emperor.

He hadn't seen her yet—only had eyes for his horse. He adjusted the saddle, then stepped forward and looked into his horse's eyes, smiling as if they shared a secret. He whispered something in its ear, and it twitched both ears back at him. There was something familiar in the gesture, an intimacy. Elisabeth was almost embarrassed to be watching. Like she'd stumbled on him undressing.

Oh God, what was wrong with her? Why would she ever think about *her sister's intended* undressing? A blush spread across her face and chest. She shook her head and tried to banish the impropriety from her mind. But then Franz looked her way— and all she could think was how much she didn't want him knowing she'd been staring. She panicked, darting behind a tree and closing her eyes like a child, willing him to go away.

But no. She could hear hooves approaching. She took a steadying breath and opened her eyes.

"Good morning." His voice was deeper than she'd thought it would be. "Why are you hiding?"

"I'm not hiding," she lied, stepping out from behind the tree.

"You're Helene's sister," he said.

She realized she'd forgotten to bow, so she remedied the situation with a small curtesy, the bird still cupped in her hands like an offering.

"Your Majesty."

"Do you always secretly watch people?"

Elisabeth's heart lodged in her throat. Her mother would hate this.

"No, Your Majesty." She avoided his eyes, staring down at where her bare toes peeked out from beneath her skirt.

When she chanced a glance back up at him, he raised both eyebrows. "May I ask why you aren't wearing shoes?"

She pulled her foot back under her skirts. The real question was: Why did everyone else insist on wearing shoes when it was so much more fun to feel the earth, all soft grass and silky dirt, against your bare skin? "I like to go barefoot."

"And why is there a bird in your hands?" He cocked his head.

Elisabeth cupped her hands protectively around the little feathery bundle. "Why do *you* have so many questions this early in the morning?"

Immediately, she bit her tongue. Why wasn't she able to hold a nonconfrontational conversation with a man? And with the emperor himself, no less? Had she gone and done the very thing her mother was afraid of—ruined Helene's prospects with a few sharp, unnecessary words? Her mother was right: she really must be mad.

But no. After a pause, the emperor *laughed*. Just the barest amount, a smile and then a soft exhale. She got the sense that the laugh surprised even him, like she'd unlocked a door that had been jammed shut, the key long forgotten.

"The bird was trapped in the palace. It couldn't get out."

And there it was again, the slightest laugh, the crinkling around the eyes, which were deep and brown and threaded through with gold. "I know the feeling."

She smiled in return. He was funny. Earnest too. And now that she was really looking at his face: handsome. The strong jaw, dark eyebrows, hair with just the slightest curl. Broad shoulders and soulful eyes. She realized she was staring.

She searched for something to say, and his horse appeared at the edge of her vision. "It's a beautiful morning for riding."

He nodded. "It helps me think clearly."

"I know the feeling."

And now, an unguarded smile. Elisabeth couldn't help but notice how it softened his face, made him seem approachable. Her idea of an emperor had been all power and severity. But this man was amused by her, sweet with his horse, and smiling at her like a regular person. Like he could be anyone, and she could talk to him, and they could be—

Friends.

After a long pause and a thoughtful look, he said, "If you would excuse me."

He inclined his head and turned back to his horse, leading it away past the fountain and into the trees. As she watched him go, something pulled at her to follow.

In her palms, the little bird regained its senses, fluttering delicate wings.

She opened her hands and let it take flight.

ELEVEN

FRANZ COULDN'T REMEMBER THE LAST TIME HE'D laughed like that. His face still tingled with the memory of it. The laugh had sounded small, but the relief of it was full body—an untightening, unwinding. His shoulders, so tense only a few minutes ago, had loosened. His agitated mind: now calm.

He glanced over his shoulder at the girl as he mounted his horse, her dark hair somehow a dozen shades of brown, gold, and auburn in a patch of sunlight breaking through the trees. She was watching the bird fly away: it free, she its rescuer.

He hadn't asked her name. He knew who she was, of course. Helene's younger sister. But if his mother had ever mentioned her name, he hadn't been paying attention. He could kick himself now. This was a pretty girl rescuing a bird, caring more about that bird's tiny disaster than about preparing for an official meeting with his family. Someone whose name he *wanted* to know, not one he was forced to memorize.

He liked her, he realized. Liked her more than anyone he'd met at court in years.

His horse made a small, impatient noise and Franz reached down to pat her on the neck. "All right, I won't keep you from the hills."

He turned and urged her out of the gardens, through a slice of forest, and into the rolling green fields that surrounded the villa. The landscape was draped in the last bits of fog that the rising sun had yet to burn away. He could feel his mare relax beneath him. She loved getting away from the palace, and he should really take her out more. He wondered if Helene's sister would like to ride out later in the day. Perhaps he could invite her.

The thought almost made him laugh again, but this time the feeling was bitter. Oh, how his mother's face would pinch together if she knew he wanted to go riding with a woman who wasn't Helene. Maxi might be free to know as many women as he pleased; Franz certainly was not. Every dalliance or even friendship he'd carried on until now had been secret in a way Maxi's never were. The only person who knew about Franz's current mistress was Maxi.

Maxi who had, apparently, wanted Louise for himself. When he found out she was sneaking into Franz's rooms at night, he punched Franz in the jaw. As if Maxi didn't have enough women in rotation. As if he wasn't already making them all look foolish with his rakish reputation.

Then again, the boys had been in competition ever since they were young. The punch might have been about more than just Louise. It might have been about every time Maxi had lost a battle. By being denied an ambassador position he'd felt should be his. By being denied Louise's affections. Maxi seemed to have no memory for the battles he'd won: the time he charmed Franz's first love—Isabella—away, the time Mother took him to Italy but left Franz behind with the tutors. Let alone the many times Franz was scolded over nothing while Maxi got away with everything.

Franz rubbed at his jaw now, remembering the blow.

The sound of another horse approached from behind and Franz turned, his first fleeting thought that he'd somehow manifested Helene's sister with the power of his mind.

But no. Maxi was the one he'd summoned with his thoughts. Riding out on a honey-colored mare, looking like he'd just rolled out of bed, all cowlick and rumpled shirt and a smile that said he'd left more than one woman tangled up in sweat-damp sheets behind him.

"Brother." Maxi quirked a smile and pulled his horse to a stop beside Franz.

"Brother," Franz replied, unenthusiastic, noting—as usual—that Maxi never used his title. A slight meant to cut.

"The stable master told me you rode out." Maxi tilted his head toward the river. "So, are we just going to stand here or are we going for a ride?"

"What do you want, Maxi?"

"Only to ride with my eldest brother."

"Nothing more?"

"Well, I wouldn't turn down some good French wine and a girl with heart-shaped lips and a heaving bosom."

Franz gave Maxi a long look.

After a beat, Maxi continued, "Ah, I see. You weren't serious. Then let's ride, shall we?"

Franz urged his horse on, and Maxi followed.

"So, how was the execution? Delightfully gruesome, I assume?"

Franz's heart leapt into his throat. He had only just stopped replaying the scene in his head. The girl and her bird had driven it from him like springtime breaking up the ice. But now Franz's body tightened again, ready to run. The faces of dead men flashed behind his eyes.

"I don't want to talk about it."

Maxi raised an inquisitive eyebrow but for once decided to honor his brother's request. "All right, no dead men. How about living women? I saw your future bride standing at her window this morning. Do you want to know what she looks like?"

Franz let out a long breath. "I've seen the portraits."

"Ah, but portraits can be embellished."

"If you're trying to tell me she isn't beautiful, I don't care."

"I suppose you wouldn't, dutiful emperor that you are. But she's more beautiful than dead revolutionaries, so she'll be the prettiest thing you see this week."

There it was again. Maxi could never let things go, always waiting to stab him unexpectedly. As if the conversation were a fencing match and not a discussion.

Franz didn't answer, so Maxi continued. "I suppose this means you won't need your mistress anymore. I presume you're just going to toss her to the side, like you always accuse me of doing. Then your high horse won't be quite so high."

Franz pulled his mare to a stop. "Leave."

Maxi stopped beside him, quirking a smile.

"I said go. I've had enough."

Maxi smirked then, happy to have gotten under Franz's skin—as usual. He tipped an invisible hat and turned his horse around toward the villa. "As you wish, *Your Majesty*."

As Maxi took off, Franz tried to unclench his jaw. His brother had stolen his peace—again. He had a real gift for it.

Franz wondered, foolishly, if the girl was still in the garden. Would he find her there again if he turned his horse around? Rescuing another bird, hiding behind another tree? Making Franz laugh and wanting nothing from him? If that girl had wanted anything from Franz, it was for him *not* to notice her. That was a first for any person at court.

Franz's heart relaxed with the thought. There was something charming about her, something not yet tainted by an ever-darkening world.

He realized that he was suddenly looking forward to meeting his intended's family in a few hours. Seeing the girl again. Discovering whether he could laugh like that a second time.

TWELVE

HELENE'S HEART WAS A RAINSTORM OF DOUBT, AND she was afraid she might drown. Nothing had gone right since they discovered the trunks were missing. She was in a mourning dress. Imagine! Meeting the emperor—the most powerful man in the empire, the most powerful, perhaps, in the world—in a mourning dress. It was laced too tight. It was too dark. The neckline was too high. Helene knew she looked like a corpse, pale as death and twice as quiet.

And it was made even worse because of where she and Mother were sitting: on plush golden chairs in the most beautiful room Helene had seen in her life. Elaborate crystal chandeliers hung from a ceiling intricately painted in pink and white. The walls around them were a hundred shades of blue and gray that brought out the purple in the marble columns and their gold-drenched tops. And the vases—oh, the vases! Painted with such detail, so many subtle shades of color, Helene could stare at them all day. It was all stunning. Breathtaking, even. And Helene knew that the room's lightness only made her look more austere.

This wasn't at all how she'd imagined meeting Franz. She'd pictured it so many times. In her daydreams, she was wearing a white dress with embroidered daisies, fresh flowers laced through her hair, their green stalks and pink petals drawing out the whites and golds of her clothes. The blue puff sleeves of her jacket brought out the blue in her eyes. Oh, how Franz would have gasped when he saw her. It may have been unseemly, but he wouldn't have been able to help it.

She had always been planning to marry Franz out of duty, but this was Helene's secret: she imagined he'd love her at first sight, too.

But now.

Would he even like her? Without that gasp-worthy entrance, how would she find the courage to be charming? She'd imagined herself making him laugh, too, but she'd never felt less funny in her life. Oh God, what if she fainted when he walked in? The chances felt high.

Not to mention that Sisi was nowhere to be found, the third chair, supposed to be hers, empty.

"Helene," her mother said sternly, fanning herself in the stiflingly hot room, "you look pale. Pinch your cheeks, child. You don't want your aunt to see you in this state."

The comment brought another worry jangling across Helene's nerves: her aunt. Franz's mother. The real power behind the throne. Even if Franz found Helene charming, it was Sophie she really needed to impress. Mother had made that clear. Sophie was the one who'd arranged all of this. What if she thought Helene was unsuitable? Pale and nauseated and nervous. The thought was terrifying.

Helene wished Sisi were there to comfort her. Though, come to think of it, her words would probably be wildly unhelpful. As always. Helene could imagine what Sisi would say: *It doesn't matter if the archduchess doesn't like you; it's not her you're marrying anyway.* And Helene would want to rage because what Sisi didn't ever seem to understand was that by becoming empress, Helene was marrying it all: the position, the man, the family, the empire.

Sisi never understood the gravity of things. Not one moment in her life. It was because their father had spoiled her, Helene knew. Because he'd taken her on ridiculous adventures around the countryside, hiked through mountains, dined with villagers. As if they weren't noble.

Sisi loved it. Loved every new adventure, every new person. And the people she met always loved her in return. She never had to work for their love, never had to worry that someone might *not* love her.

The only person who didn't love Sisi was Mother. But Helene wasn't sure Mother loved anyone. There were only people Mother approved of and people she did not. The latter list was particularly long.

The room was as quiet as a grave. Fitting for the dresses they were wearing. Helene bit at the inside of her cheek, wishing they didn't have to wait so long for the emperor, wishing even more that Sisi had arrived early with them. It was going to ruin everything if she burst in—probably barefoot and muddy and damp—halfway through introductions.

Helene needed Sisi here. To support her. In shoes. Why couldn't her sister do this one thing for her? Just show up and behave normally for *one day*.

THIRTEEN

ELISABETH WAS RUNNING LATE, AND MOTHER WOULD BE furious. Her heart constricted around the truth of it. She'd spent too long in the gardens, tucking herself against the trunk of a friendly tree and composing poetry in her head. Today's poems took the shape of accidental meetings, shy smiles, tall men. The lines replayed in her head as she finished dressing and rushed down the corridor:

> *Her red lips glowed love-hot and life-warm.*
> *I could see—so clearly—the slender form of his body*
> *In the light.*
> *But the details, deep in shadow,*
> *Were impossible to decipher.*

Elisabeth was proud of these lines—but now she was late. She'd promised not to make trouble on this trip, promised to behave. And she'd be blamed if she didn't make it back in time to cross her ankles and smile politely at her future brother-in-law.

Her heart sped up at the thought. Franz. Who'd laughed like she was charm itself. She wondered what he'd be like on this second meeting, surrounded by all the pomp and circumstance that the palace—and her mother—provided. She wondered how she'd feel when she saw him again, then chided herself for even wondering. It was Helene's feelings that mattered. She was the one he was going to marry.

The sound of footsteps caught Elisabeth by surprise. She was almost to the sitting room where they were supposed to meet the imperial family, but someone was coming around the corner from the opposite direction. On impulse, embarrassed by her lateness, she scrambled to the nearest window, folding herself inside a deep purple curtain.

The footsteps stopped nearby, and shame tingled hot across Elisabeth's face. Why had she hidden? She needed to get to the sitting room immediately, but if she emerged from the curtain now, whoever was out there would know she'd been hiding. She'd look like a real fool. A madwoman, even.

From outside the curtain, a feminine voice spoke in Italian. Elisabeth was glad for her lessons. She knew just enough to understand. "Imagine when I tell everyone back in Venice that I celebrated the emperor's birthday with him! They'll die of shock!"

Curious, Elisabeth peeked around the curtain. The speaker was an olive-skinned woman who looked only a little older than Helene, her dark eyes bright with excitement, smile all-encompassing, Next to her, a short man with tousled blond hair and dramatic sideburns looked on with nonchalant disinterest, his navy coat unbuttoned with the kind of casualness that was usually on purpose in Elisabeth's experience. She couldn't decide if it was appealing or dangerous.

The man yawned and started to turn to face her hiding place. Elisabeth ducked back behind the curtain, heart fluttering. Was her introduction to every person here going to be her hiding and being found out? This time with no bird to blame her behavior on.

The footsteps continued and Elisabeth chanced another glance around the curtain. The couple was standing at the bottom of a nearby staircase, waiting. And Elisabeth's breath hitched in her chest when she saw who they were waiting for.

Archduchess Sophie: dark eyed, dark haired, snow white, with a heart-shaped birthmark at the corner of one perfect eyebrow, just like the portraits Elisabeth had seen. Her dress was the kind that would make Mother swoon: an airy yellow blouse with steel-blue, hand-embroidered flowers at the ends of the sleeves and collar.

Sophie's reputation was blade sharp and steel strong, and everything about her appearance suggested the same: her spine straight, her expression shrewd, not a hair out of place. She was the wicked queen of fairy tales, the siren that lured men happily to the drowning deep. She was power itself, a beauty made of stone and ice and walls you wouldn't dare try to scale.

Behind her, two boys descended the staircase, presumably her sons: one in his early twenties, stuffed uncomfortably into a uniform already dark with sweat, the other still a boy, maybe nine years old and a little ridiculous in his miniature uniform. He hugged a pretty doll with bright-green eyes and a dress made up of hundreds of hand-tied bows. If Elisabeth was guessing correctly, based on portraits she'd seen and her mother's descriptions, the older boy must be Ludwig and the little man Luziwuzi. Which meant the rakish character was Maxi.

Sophie reached the bottom of the stairs and smiled. "Maximilian, what a nice surprise. You made it after all."

He reached for her hand, kissed it.

"Welcome, my beautiful boy." The look on Maxi's face flashed raw, vulnerable. A contrast to his rakish grin just moments ago.

Elisabeth felt a familiar pang, a realization that she shouldn't be witnessing something so personal. She ducked back behind the curtain and pressed her hands to her hot, embarrassed cheeks.

"And who is this?" Sophie's voice echoed in the hall.

"The enchanting Francesca, Baroness of . . . something."

Elisabeth smiled. He was funny, Maxi. Maybe they all were. Maybe she'd misjudged the imperial family, thinking they were more like the dukes she'd met. But the dukes had everything to prove, where the royal family did not. It made sense that they'd be more capable of jest.

"I thought the Italians hated us at the moment." Another joke, this time from Sophie.

"The baroness came along on a whim. I couldn't send word," said Maxi, as Elisabeth peeked around the curtain once again.

"Oh, darling, I don't mind. What you do is not important." Sophie's tone was indulgent, but the look on Maxi's face suggested that the words were a blow. Elisabeth knew what it was to not matter to your own mother. She felt for him.

"Wherever is Franz?" Sophie asked, glancing around. To Sophie, perhaps this was an innocent question. But to Maxi, it was clearly a dismissal, another way of saying that what he did wasn't important. That his mother's mind was with her other child.

Maxi's voice was bitter and quiet when he answered. "He's probably suffocating under his mistress's skirts."

Surprise flickered through Elisabeth. Was Maxi the type of person to say something shocking just to get a rise out of his mother? Or was Franz actually with another woman? Her heart twisted. Helene was going to end up like their mother, pretending her husband wasn't entertaining other women right under her nose.

Elisabeth's surprise reflected on Sophie's face before disapproval took over the older woman's features. "Darling, Franz would never jeopardize this union. Be careful of the accusations you make."

"Mother, don't pretend he doesn't have secrets. We all do, you included."

"Your Royal Highness, your guests are waiting in the salon," announced a servant.

Elisabeth peeked out from behind her curtain and watched the group turn down the grand hall. She knew there was another way to get to the salon. She still had time to reach it—but only if she ran.

Elisabeth was flushed and breathless, barely having made it into her seat before a servant pulled the double doors open and stepped inside. "Her Imperial Highness, the Archduchess. And Their Imperial Highnesses, the Archdukes of Austria."

Helene flashed her a look of pure panic, her cheeks blotchy with nerves, but all too quickly Archduchess Sophie was in the room, and everyone's eyes were on her. Here was a woman who took up space in a way that Elisabeth had only seen men do before. Everyone in the room stood in respect.

They all curtsied.

"Ludovika, my beloved sister," Sophie said, reaching for Mother and kissing her on both cheeks.

"You must excuse us." Mother ducked her head apologetically. "There was some trouble with the dresses."

Sophie paused, taking in their mourning clothes, and then gave Mother a curious look. Elisabeth couldn't tell if it was disappointment or indulgence.

Sophie stepped toward Helene, about to speak, when a servant announced, "His Majesty, the Emperor."

The room stilled. Elisabeth's breath caught in her chest. A strand of hair escaped her braids and tickled at the back of her neck as she glanced over at Helene, who looked on the verge of collapse.

Franz strode into the room, eyes bright. He'd traded his riding breeches and cloud-white shirt for a blue-checkered jacket and a teal necktie that brought out the shades of blond and brown in his hair. He looked so light, so alive, even though his face was much more serious than it had been in the garden.

He glanced from one woman to another, his eyes landing on Elisabeth and—

Lingering.

Or perhaps she only imagined it.

"Ladies," he said.

"Your Majesty," her mother said with a bow.

"Your Majesty." Helene's voice was an excited whisper.

"Your Majesty." Elisabeth's was a private joke.

Franz's eyes caught on hers again, and the silence stretched between them. It tightened across her skin.

Sophie was the one to cut the thread of quiet. "So, this is she. Let him look at you, Helene. Doesn't she look just like her portrait?"

Helene bowed her head, curtsied, then stood still to let them take her in.

Then Sophie's eyes moved to Elisabeth. "And this is?"

"Sisi," Mother answered before Elisabeth could.

"Elisabeth," she corrected, before realizing that her correction might be seen as another rebellion. Her heart sank.

Elisabeth looked past Sophie and saw both Franz and Maxi staring at her. Their heads were tilted, identical—even if what she'd seen of their personalities was not.

Before she could apologize, Franz asked, "How is the bird?"

Elisabeth smiled, then immediately lowered her eyes and let her smile drop. Because she shouldn't be smiling. No one knew about the bird, the garden, the surprise meeting. Their laughter. And—if she was honest—she didn't want them to know, didn't want them to break the magic of that memory. It was as fragile and perfect as a snowflake.

Now it melted in the heat of her family's gazes.

FOURTEEN

E LISABETH WAS SAVED FROM EXPLANATION BY A SERVANT'S interruption: lunch was about to be served. They moved to two tables set intricately for the meal. On the other side of the room, under a carved Habsburg eagle and against a backdrop of watery ethereal blue, two violinists began to play. The music danced around the room, cheerful.

"What was that about a bird?" Helene's whisper was urgent as she passed Elisabeth on her way to the table.

"It was nothing. Please don't worry about it."

"It's *something* if the emperor is asking about it."

Elisabeth shook her head.

"Helene, dear, come sit here," Sophie commanded. "Next to Franz."

Helene closed her mouth, nodded slightly at her sister, and went. Elisabeth let out a quiet sigh of relief and followed Sophie's next direction to sit at the other table, next to little Luzi and his elaborate doll, positioned in its own chair beside him. Her heart lightened. Luzi was the least likely of the diners to ask her for bird explanations at the table. Except perhaps for the Baroness Francesca, seated across from Elisabeth and very clearly not following the conversation in German. Maxi was at the table too, but Elisabeth hoped he'd ignore the bird in favor of his date.

Lunch was a rich tafelspitz beef boiled in spiced broth and served with minced apples and horseradish. Elisabeth attacked it with gusto; if her mouth was full, she could hardly embarrass Helene. Could hardly think about how just across the room, Helene was speaking in hushed tones with Franz. Him: leaning in to point out something about the art adorning the walls. Her: smiling.

Was this what falling in love looked like?

Across the table, Maxi was speaking animatedly. "The tsar wants our help. To destroy the sultan and divide up the Ottoman Empire"—he leaned toward Luzi—"but it's a bad idea."

"Why?" Luzi asked.

"The British and French won't allow it. There would be an unnecessary war."

"Is Habsburg unbeatable?" Luzi was so earnest. Just like Spatz. Elisabeth suddenly missed her so much it almost hurt.

"No one is invincible, Luzi. Not even Habsburg," Maxi answered.

The idea of war sat uneasy on Elisabeth's skin. Would Franz join the tsar? What would that mean for Habsburg? What would it mean for Helene as future empress? There had been that attempt on Franz's life. Might there be another?

Elisabeth glanced at Luzi, who was carefully tightening his doll's loose bow. She frowned. He should be allowed to just be a child, without all this talk of war. She picked up the feathered yellow fan she'd been given and, once Luzi had finished his task, she caught his eye and made a silly face through the feathers. He grinned, relaxing into himself, letting his tight little frame ease.

"Is he always like this?" she whispered conspiratorially, pointing her eyes briefly toward Maxi.

Luzi's smile widened. Like Spatz, he loved being in confidence with an adult.

"Your hair, Helene: it's so beautifully braided." Sophie's voice traveled from the other table. "Don't you agree Franz?"

"Very pretty." His voice was kind.

"I do it myself," Helene answered, demure as always.

"Helene has never been difficult a day in her life." Mother's volume was twice anyone else's, as usual.

The words, a lie, also as usual.

How her mother had raged that day at the river. Helene wasn't her perfect angel then. That day, Helene had been her *most difficult* child. Not to mention the day Helene had found a nest of baby garden snakes and brought them into the nursery to play with. Or the time their father took them into town and had the two of them perform a song and dance in the market square for coins. Or when Helene went through her thieving phase, stealing hot pies off kitchen windowsills for her and Elisabeth to gorge themselves on under the sleepy willow tree by the river.

Elisabeth hoped that Néné still existed somewhere inside. That she had only been driven into hiding by their mother. A fate Elisabeth would never allow for herself.

Elisabeth glanced toward her sister, hoping to telegraph her support. Instead, her eyes found Franz. Sitting quietly, as Helene spoke to Sophie. Staring—

At Elisabeth.

Her skin prickled. The room narrowed. Her gaze traced his elegant eyebrows, strong chin, lips hovering somewhere between an expression curious and serious. What was he thinking? What did he see when he looked at her?

"And you?" Maxi shattered the moment, and Elisabeth jumped in her seat, turning toward him. "Which sister are you? The boring one or the naughty one?"

Elisabeth raised an eyebrow at the rogue, touching her face lightly with the soft yellow feathers of the fan. It wasn't the kind of question you asked at a formal lunch, but he clearly wasn't the kind of person for formal lunches. And if she was being honest, neither was she.

"What do you think?" Elisabeth threw the question back.

His eyes sparkled now with recognition. "I thought as much."

She set the fan down, smiling despite herself.

"And your sister"—he glanced at the other table, as conspiratorial as she'd been with Luzi moments ago—"is she the right one for my brother?"

Elisabeth held Maxi's gaze. "Seems like something we should let His Majesty decide. And my sister, of course."

"Ah, but you see, I have to sign off on all potential brides."

Elisabeth laughed, shook her head. "Sounds like an important task."

"It is." Maxi leaned back in his chair, smirking. "I think you're the one to marry, though."

Elisabeth's heart leapt to her throat. Had Maxi seen her looking at Franz? Had Franz said something to him? He couldn't have. They'd only spoken the once, only about a bird, only about her hiding in a garden—

"I beg your pardon?"

"Well, you'll never become fat. I can deduce it from your wrists."

Elisabeth couldn't decide if the answer was a relief or an annoyance. He hadn't seen her staring at her sister's intended. But fixating on her wrists, considering how her appearance might change over the years . . . Was that what mattered in a wife—that she not get fat? Never mind if she was kind or smart or cared about people or loved her husband. What a thing to care about.

Elisabeth removed her hands from the table.

Maxi continued, oblivious. "With her"—he pointed at Francesca with his fork, who startled beside him at the sudden action—"it's different. I need to make sure I get away before it's too late."

Elisabeth stared. It was one thing to be cheeky, another to be cruel.

"Don't worry," Maxi said, misinterpreting her expression, "she can't understand us."

He smiled at Francesca, who was glancing quickly between the two of them.

"You look beautiful," he said in Italian.

"Grazie," she replied, happy.

Maxi leaned over and pretended to bite her neck suggestively. She giggled, leaned back. Elisabeth turned her head away, reminded unpleasantly of her father. Such rakish behavior didn't require a witness.

The attendants started serving the cake. Beside Elisabeth, Luzi adjusted his doll's elaborate hat and forked a small piece of cake toward her pretty, rose-petal mouth. Elisabeth smiled, glad to turn her attention away from Maxi.

But he didn't allow it. "Luziwuzi, you're making me lose my appetite," Maxi said. "Maybe you could caress your doll in your room."

Elisabeth's head snapped up. Now, this was too far. She straightened her back and met his eyes. "How funny. I was about to request the same of *you.*"

She must have spoken louder than she intended because the entire room went quiet. She bit her tongue. Mother would *not* interpret this as behaving. She wondered, with a grim sort of humor, if the carriage would be sent for immediately to take her to the asylum. Or would Mother wait until they were back home? It was difficult to say.

But Maxi was staring at her with an expression of—not disgust or affront, as she expected. It was—

Admiration.

Delight, even.

Like at any moment, he might burst out laughing.

Elisabeth chanced a glance at Franz and what she saw in his face was similar: not affront but surprise. And there was mirth there, too, she thought. At the corners of his mouth, the edges of his eyes, the quirk of his eyebrow.

From beside him, Helene shot her an embarrassed glance. Elisabeth shook her head ever so slightly, hoping her sister would take it as an apology. She refused to meet her mother's eyes.

Elisabeth leaned toward Maxi. "Please forgive me. I didn't mean it like that."

He laughed, his face bright as he shook his head in wonder at her.

Relief warmed across her skin. She was glad he thought it funny. Even gladder that the kind of outburst that had always earned her disapproving stares from Mother was now . . . What? A reason to be charmed by her.

She glanced toward Helene again and saw Mother and Sophie exchange a look. All right. So, not *everyone* was charmed.

Mother turned to Sophie. "How about a little walk? So the young people can get to know each other better—without interruptions." Elisabeth felt the dagger aimed in her direction.

"A stroll in the afternoon sun—a wonderful idea." Sophie stood, and everyone else followed suit.

Next to Sophie, Helene smiled shyly at Franz. Slowly, Franz's eyes found Helene's, and he smiled too.

Elisabeth pressed her fingernails into her palm.

Enough, Elisabeth.

Let your sister fall in love.

FIFTEEN

FRANZ LEANED OVER THE GREEN-AND-WHITE SWIRLED basin and splashed water on his face. He'd spent the meal trying to focus on Helene, matching her smile for smile, nod for nod—but Elisabeth had tugged at the edges of his attention the whole time. Waving her little yellow fan against her face, whispering to Luzi, putting Maxi in his place.

Putting Maxi in his place. His smile had been real then, and it pulled at the corners of his mouth again now. How could he focus on Helene when all of that was happening at the next table over?

He dabbed the water off his face with a cloth, staring into the mirror in front of him. His mother would hate how he was thinking, how intrigued he was by Helene's sister.

He thought back to a conversation they had a year ago. Before the assassination attempt, before Helene's name had crossed Mother's lips. After months of meet and greets with duchesses and princesses he felt nothing for, Franz had asked, foolishly, why he couldn't pick his own bride.

"The most important thing is finding the right girl for the position," his mother had said. "Falling in love is not the point . . . As long as she's likable, that's better than many of us have had in our marriages."

She had been speaking of her own marriage, he knew. Franz's father adored his mother. She was life and breath to him. He was a sunflower, she the sun. But Franz knew his mother didn't feel the same. He'd heard her say once that she loved his father as if he were a child who needed looking after. Perhaps that's why his father no longer lived with them; Sophie had tired of raising yet another boy.

And now Franz was supposed to be Helene's sun. And what would Mother say if he told her that he might not be the sun at all, but rather a sunflower, turned toward—

A knock sounded at the door: a servant checking on him.

"Coming," he called, straightening.

He wondered what his mother would say now if he told her it was the other sister burning bright as a sun, and another conversation came back to him, tying his stomach in a knot.

"Now, her family is a little wild. I'll give you that," Mother had said of Helene on the carriage ride here.

"In what way?"

"Well, to start with, the father fraternizes with peasants. Remember that joke he made in his book about us censoring him? Ridiculous. And then there's the younger girl, Sisi. My sister says that she's always disappearing into the mountains, neglecting her lessons."

He'd been mildly amused then. But now—*now*—the comment pained him. A promise that his mother did not and would not approve of Elisabeth.

"But we won't worry about Helene's relations," she'd added. "They can't be helped. Just spend time with Helene. You will like her—and you will learn to love her. Don't forget your duty. Every empire needs an empress."

When she'd said them, the words had been only words. He'd readied himself to marry Helene, to serve Habsburg. But now, something was changing. Some*one* had changed things. And his mother's words were bonds, growing tighter.

SIXTEEN

THE THINGS MOTHER WAS WRONG ABOUT COULD FILL the Kaiservilla, seep into every nook and cranny and steal the air from each of its elegant, ethereal, gold-trimmed rooms. She was wrong that Franz only wanted Helene to be pretty and polite. She was wrong that if Helene just followed the rules, everything would work out. And she was wrong that a walk would fix what was becoming abundantly clear: Franz wasn't interested.

Helene had been happier back when she didn't follow the rules. Happier when she hid frogs under her skirts and laid under the stars with Elisabeth. Happier, even, when Mother would hit her for stealing freshly cooked pies, and Helene would respond by hiding a single earring from Mother's favorite pair—and watching in satisfaction while she spun out over the loss.

She wished she was back home. Anywhere but here, trying so hard to reach across the space to this man she was supposed to marry—and finding no one reaching back. She was trying so hard that she could barely breathe, and still nothing had gone right since they arrived. Not the dresses, not the introductions, not the lunch with Sisi embarrassing them all.

Now they were walking through the gardens—perhaps the most magical gardens Helene had ever seen in her life. The grounds were threaded through with a playful stream, bursting with flowers in every shade, from bright magenta to cloud white, and shaded occasionally by clusters of trees. They strolled slowly past horse-head fountains and along walkways of perfectly inset stones. The air smelled of rose and honeysuckle. It should have been perfect. But all Helene could notice was the sun beating down like a hammer through her parasol, the bugs sticking to her sweating skin, the man beside her looking distant.

She wanted to cry.

"I have a present for you," she tried, taking Franz's hand as he helped her down some narrow mossy steps. "For your birthday."

She pulled it from her waistband, wrapped in delicate paper and—Helene was horrified to discover—damp with her sweat. She thought she might faint from the embarrassment.

Franz looked surprised, murmuring his thanks as he reached for the package and took it carefully without touching her hand at all. As if she were poison.

Of course, they weren't *supposed* to touch—except when he was helping her down the stairs or kissing her hand in greeting. Still, Helene wanted him to. If he touched her, perhaps she would feel something. Perhaps the tightness across her skin would snap back like a rubber band, releasing her from this terrible tension.

Instead, Franz pulled back, polite, unwrapping her gift. It was a handkerchief she'd embroidered. The flowers had made her happy at the time, so green and purple and blue and bright, popping against the cream of the cloth. She'd sewn an F at the bottom, in the same style as the ribbon tying the flowers together.

"Did you make this yourself?" he asked.

"Yes, Your Majesty."

"Thank you." He gave her a slight smile.

Franz tucked the handkerchief into his front jacket pocket and resumed walking. Helene followed in silence. Did he actually like the gift? She hadn't expected raptures—of course not. But she wished she could read more on his face. It was a kind face, if indecipherable. She thought she could love that face if only they could break through this silence.

Perhaps Sisi had been right all along. Helene had thought she was doing the right thing—growing up, taking her responsibilities seriously, keeping her opinions to herself. She'd sided with Mother, and at first it seemed she'd been right. Her reward: a promise of empire and engagement.

But now the promise looked flimsy compared to the life she'd given up. Coming here was supposed to make her larger, more important, more loved; instead, she was smaller. How could Franz fall in love with her? She barely liked herself. She'd filed off her sharp edges and all that was left were nerves.

"Have you been here before?" Franz asked, finally.

Helene panicked. Did he mean the palace or the gardens or somewhere else entirely? All she could think to say was no, hating that she didn't have a better contribution.

"Well, do you like it here?" he tried again.

Helene decided he was talking about the gardens.

"Yes, it is very beautiful." She searched for something more substantial to say but found only the tightness in her gut, her throat. Mother had told her not to talk too much, but Helene couldn't help but feel like she was disappointing Franz.

"I'm glad." He was all politeness, smiling a little at her.

The heat of the day sat heavy on her skin as they walked on in silence. Sweat dripped cold down the small of her back, gathered in her armpits, beaded across her forehead. She tried to swipe at the beads surreptitiously before they released into her eyes.

Seeing the movement, Franz reached across the space. Helene's heart stopped. Would he touch her now?

But no. In his hands: the handkerchief she'd so studiously made for him. For a moment, she wondered if he was returning it, and her chest tightened in embarrassment. They hadn't even had their spark yet, that moment promised in Sisi's poetry, that recognition of soul to soul. And he was already seeing her sweat-drenched, already having to offer her the insult—or kindness—of a handkerchief.

She took it and dabbed at her forehead, simultaneously relieved and embarrassed. She didn't know whether to tuck the cloth away or return it to Franz, so she just folded it discreetly into her hand.

A little ways behind them, Helene could see Mother looking satisfied. The offer of the handkerchief must have looked especially gallant from afar. And perhaps it was. Perhaps the doubts were simply Helene's worries getting in the way. She couldn't expect love to spark like a wildfire at first sight, could she? No, love would grow with time. An offered handkerchief wasn't an insult; it was a seed. Polite conversation was another. They'd keep tending their garden and it would grow.

It had to grow.

The thought made her bolder, and she reached out with two fingers to gently touch Franz's arm. "Thank you for walking with me."

SEVENTEEN

I F SPATZ WERE WITH THEM, SHE WOULD ACCUSE THE PARK of harboring fairy magic.

Elisabeth could picture it: the way her eyes would light up, the way they'd both peek under bushes and into the hollows of trees, searching for the telltale flutter of fairy wings. They'd trace their fingers along the trunks of trees and press their faces shamelessly into the bark. They'd breathe in the green smell of the moss-covered rocks, the cool air cast off by the streams. Elisabeth wished she could show her sister this place; she'd love it inordinately.

This park was the perfect place to fall in love—all poetry and possibility. And that's precisely what Helene was doing across the way. Elisabeth couldn't hear their conversation, but she could see her sister speaking to Franz, Helene handing him the handkerchief she'd spent so many hours on. Elisabeth's heart ached. Oh how she longed to fall in love like that.

Behind her on the path, Mother and Sophie were deep in conversation.

"Don't worry, Sister. Franz will ask Helene for her hand."
Sophie's voice was warm and confident.

"Because all the men in this family do what you say?" It was a
joke, but Mother was bad at them.

Elisabeth glanced behind her as Sophie touched her sister's
arm. "Because he knows it is the right thing to do."

Oh, how Elisabeth wished she could so easily know the right
things to do.

"Ah, and thank you for leaving the vagabond at home," Sophie said.

Elisabeth's defensiveness rose like a tide. Certainly, her father was an odd man and unfaithful husband, but he didn't
deserve such a label. Elisabeth knew the court hadn't been
impressed with her father's book, especially the jokes about cen-
sorship from the crown. But Sophie shouldn't be so humorless—
not with a son like Maxi, who Elisabeth imagined would find
her father's jokes riotously funny.

"Oh, Sister, please! The last thing my husband wants to do is
put his trousers on to travel," Mother joked back.

"He really should move in with my Karl at Auhof." Both
women laughed.

"Margarete," Sophie commanded, then, letting the topic
drop and turning to a servant following silently in their wake.
"Would you prepare some music for tonight?"

"Something lively, Your Imperial Highness?"

"Quite the contrary. I'd like something *tender*." Sophie's voice
was satisfied, and it only took a glance toward Helene to see why.
She'd reached out to touch Franz's arm, and he was smiling at her.

The smile made Elisabeth sad in a way she couldn't quite explain. Like she'd lost something. A favorite ring dropped in a

lake. A favorite poem erased by a careless spill of ink. Helene's hand only lingered a moment, but Elisabeth's gaze was stuck on them now. She sped up to get away from Sophie's and her mother's hopes, wondering how great a slight they'd think it if she disappeared into the brush.

Behind Elisabeth, a man's voice joined the conversation, pulling her attention away from Helene and Franz, now disappearing into a line of trees.

Maxi caught up to her.

"You were rather rude this afternoon." There was no reproach in his words. Only amusement.

"I do apologize again."

"You don't have to. You were honest with me. No one is ever honest with me."

Maxi sounded so sincere that Elisabeth tore her gaze away from the trees where she'd been waiting for Franz to reappear, wishing she could hear what he was saying to her sister.

"I liked it," Maxi finished.

She turned and smiled at him, studying his face. There was something charming about it. She could see why he had a reputation as both beloved and a danger.

"Once you get to know me, you'll see I'm not a bad person," he said as they descended a stone staircase overgrown with moss and wreathed in vines.

"I believe that." And she did. He'd certainly been cruel to Francesca at lunch, but people weren't defined by their worst moments.

"I'm the black sheep of the family, just like you."

She raised an eyebrow.

"We should stick together." He stepped off the path and plucked a bright yellow flower, flourishing it at Elisabeth with a serious expression, standing too close and smelling comfortingly of cedar and cinnamon. He held the flower before her, expectant.

Francesca was only a couple yards behind them, and Elisabeth turned and waved to her to catch up. Out of the corner of her eye, she could see Helene and Franz reemerging from the trees up ahead.

"Baroness, the archduke was just looking for you. Look what he picked for you." Elisabeth spoke the last part in halting Italian.

Francesca tilted her head back, raised her eyebrows suggestively until Maxi, backed into a corner, handed her the flower. Elisabeth registered something akin to disappointment in his face as he did so.

"Grazie," Francesca murmured sweetly—and then smacked him with her walking stick. Not understanding German wasn't the same as not understanding body language. Elisabeth smiled to herself. If Elisabeth's Italian were better, she imagined she and Francesca could be friends.

In the distance, Helene laughed—the sound burying Elisabeth in emotion. Joy because she loved to hear Helene laugh. But also a sinking, drowning knowledge that Franz was the one who had inspired that laugh and—worse—Elisabeth wished she were the one laughing.

FRANZ OWED IT TO HIS MOTHER TO TRY HARDER.

He had been quiet at lunch, polite but uninterested. Now, as he and Helene wove through oak groves scented with springtime flowers, he tried. As they meandered past manicured hedges, their leaves sharp edged, he tried. And as they passed over little wooden footbridges, their feet beating out an even rhythm on the oak, he tried again. He asked questions, thanked Helene for the gift, took her hand to help her down the stone steps, took it again to help her up onto the circular stone terrace where they'd paused their walk.

His mother wasn't wrong about her: she was pretty, elegant. She floated more than walked, seemed embarrassed to be sweating, ducked her head when he asked her a question. She was what an empress should be.

But Franz was tired. It took so much effort to talk to Helene. And the way she looked at him . . . that look told him he was failing her by feeling nothing. She was all hope and nerves, bright eyes and shaking hands—the things he *should* be feeling, he supposed. Instead, duty tightened around his neck like a noose.

His mother had told him in no uncertain terms that love at first sight didn't exist. But what if it did? What if love at first sight was secret laughter in a garden? An unexpected smile over cake? What if love was *easy*, if it just happened without so much damn work?

Franz's jaw ached from the fight raging in his head. Why couldn't he just be content with his lot?

The rest of the party soon joined them on the terrace. Mother and Ludovika, heads bowed in conversation. A collection of servants carrying food and drink. And Maxi with his Italian mistress, who—Franz suddenly realized—looked *strikingly* like Isabella.

Franz took a cold drink from a servant and handed it to Helene. Out of the corner of his eye, he could see his mother's face, approving. He supposed this was the answer: he could keep doing the right things, even if they felt like the wrong ones.

Sophie raised a toast. "To our emperor, my son, Franz Joseph, and his new year of life. To the beginning of a new chapter."

She meant a new chapter with Helene. But Franz knew she wasn't only talking about marriage and heirs. She was also reminding him to think about the bigger picture, the next chapter of Habsburg. Sophie thought he should choose a side in the conflict between Russia and France; she didn't like that he'd pushed back against war altogether. She'd told him that the advisors thought him weak, wavering. But he believed his advisors treated war too casually.

Was it weak to understand how serious war was? They didn't know what it was like to feel the knife slice through your neck, to say goodbye to your life, sure that it was over. The Russians may be ready to lose thousands of soldiers like that; Franz was not.

He recalled one of his favorite Longfellow verses:

The heights by great men reached and kept
Were not attained by sudden flight,
But they, while their companions slept,
Were toiling upward in the night.

He'd approach such a weighty decision slowly. No sudden alliances, no thoughtless attacks, no snap decisions. Franz wanted Habsburg to reach its greatest heights. An expanded road system, perhaps. Railways. An end to the unrest that had tried to kill him. War wouldn't accomplish any of that.

His mother's voice brought him back to the moment. "And to you, dear Helene . . . How lovely of you to have come. I hope that we will be able to make a big announcement soon."

A bird twittered in the tree above him, another answering it, the sounds friendly, relaxed. Franz's eyes caught Elisabeth's across the terrace. He wondered if he would ever be alone with her again. Wondered if he might get one more moment, one more laugh, with her before that door locked forever.

NINETEEN

E LISABETH WAS SO TIRED OF THE BIRD. WELL, NOT THE
bird itself. But the questions the poor little creature had
unwittingly forced into her life.

They were in a corridor painted coral pink with golden leaves
arching toward the ceiling. Mother walked on the left side, Helene on the right, Elisabeth a half step behind. Both glanced
over their shoulders at her as they moved toward their rooms,
questions in their eyes.

"I promise, it was nothing. I was in the garden this morning
. . . and he saw me."

"You spoke?" Helene's voice pitched upward in alarm.

"No."

"This is your last warning, Sisi," Mother said, less panic and
more bite as she pointed her little black fan at Elisabeth's chest.

They both turned away from her and picked up speed, and
Elisabeth fell another half step back. She felt bad about lying
to them, of course, but the truth would only invite more
scrutiny. They'd already tainted her memory of the morning

with a hard knot of guilt; she didn't want them to destroy it entirely, turn it into another reason Helene's future was going to be ruined.

Mother turned to Helene. "We need to figure out what you're going to wear for the emperor's birthday tomorrow."

Elisabeth let out a long, quiet breath and stopped walking. The last thing she wanted was to be roped into another panic about clothes or, worse, hairstyles. Her own hair was pleasantly escaping from its braids in a way that made her feel like a wild thing—a fox or falcon or fairy spirit.

"He barely wanted to know anything about me," Helene said quietly. "He barely asked any questions."

Elisabeth's heart fluttered. She'd thought they'd looked engaged a few times, talking in low voices. But . . . had it not gone well? Was Franz's heart not in it?

Mother waved a hand dismissively. "All he needs to know is that you're pretty and polite. If he wants to learn something else, he can go to the library."

Helene went quiet, and Elisabeth hoped that Mother's foolish perspective was comforting to her. Even if it was terrible.

As her mother and sister turned a corner and began walking down another hallway, Elisabeth turned to a simple, whitewashed window and leaned on the sill. The gauzy white curtains billowed out around her in the light breeze, and she closed her eyes. She focused on the feel of the smooth wood against her palm, the fever-hot sun on her skin, the subtle rise and fall of her chest. She pictured the morning again. It'd been a string of serendipitous moments—with a man whom she couldn't help but want to talk to again.

Mother's voice echoed distantly down the hall. "This awful heat! How could anyone fall in love like this?"

It's easy, Mother, Elisabeth thought. It's easy and impossible all at once.

TWENTY

Franz hadn't been alone with his thoughts for more than five minutes, hand cooling on the marble railing, birdsong calling to him through the open window, when Maxi found him in the stairwell.

"So, you're going to marry the Bavarian sheep?" Maxi was tactless as ever.

"Not a good idea?"

"It is. She's perfect for you. Not my taste, of course. Too . . ." He waved a hand in front of him, trying to find and pluck the right word from the air.

"Virtuous?" Franz suggested, needling.

"Predictable."

Maxi meant it as an insult, but Franz didn't rise to the fight. Instead, he reached over to touch his brother lightly on the back, inviting confidence. "Tell me more about your trip."

Maxi raised an eyebrow. "Well, everything with your troops is fine. And the empire . . ." Something sparked in Maxi as he spoke, an aliveness Franz hadn't seen from his brother in some time. Maxi turned and walked up the stairs backward in order to face Franz as he spoke. "Our empire is so exciting. The people are colorful and diverse."

"I'm glad."

"But strangely, they do have one thing in common." Maxi's voice was mock seriousness. He stopped on the landing, eye-to-eye with Franz. "They don't like *you*."

Franz paused, anger and a sense of danger grating across his skin. This wasn't news. Franz *knew* they didn't like him. He'd felt it in the jeers of the crowd at the execution. One danger gone, a thousand more still waiting, knives at the ready around dark corners.

When Franz said nothing, Maxi took up his thoughts again. "I'm joking, Franz."

He wasn't.

"But seriously, I'm worried. We are *not* popular. Well, *you*, that is."

Franz's heart beat harder, his throat tight.

"The common opinion is that Mother gives the orders and you'll shit your pants if the French or Prussians come. But don't worry; I always told them you haven't shat your pants in years."

"Thank you, Maximilian. That's enough." Franz was finished with Maxi's childish humor. Finished hearing rumors and opinions and threats he already knew, especially from someone who should be his ally.

Maxi didn't back down. "They say you have no vision."

That one hurt. Franz had so much vision he ached with it, so many things he'd love to do. A railroad to connect the empire.

Roads and canals, too. Business would thrive under his rule. He was sure that he'd achieve his aims. If only they would let him live long enough to share his plans with everyone.

Maxi lowered his eyes. "But what do I know? I'm only the Habsburg mascot." He started to walk away, throwing his last words back over his shoulder like they didn't matter. "Let me know if you need another barn christened."

Only weeks ago, their mother had asked Franz to bring Maxi back to court. *He's floundering*, she'd said, wanting to rein him in. She was right, Franz had since realized. But for Franz it wasn't just about Maxi needing purpose. It was about the *danger* of his purposelessness. The easy way his brother made enemies. The easy way those enemies might support a rebellion. Maxi might be more of a liability away from court than in it, where Franz could keep an eye on him. Franz had decided to keep the danger close.

He bridged the gap between them with one sentence. "I want you to return to Vienna with me."

Maxi turned, studying Franz's face for the joke.

"As my advisor," Franz finished.

Maxi was speechless: a first.

"I need someone at court I can trust." Never mind that Franz didn't *fully* trust his brother. Didn't trust his impulsiveness, the cold-hearted way he reveled in hurting others. Didn't trust the smile he was giving Franz now, closed and amused.

"I'll think it over," Maxi replied with a triumphant smirk. As if the offer hadn't been everything he'd ever wanted.

As Maxi started up the next level of stairs, Franz turned into a hall. He didn't even know where he was going. Just somewhere he could let his frustrations fizzle out without an audience.

TWENTY-ONE

I T WAS SCORCHING HOT IN THE VILLA. EVEN HOTTER IN the heavy black dress. Still hotter when Elisabeth thought about joining her agitated sister and mother in their rooms. So instead, she slipped away to a quiet, empty room where she lay on the cool wood floor alone.

Here—in the silence and out of the heat—Elisabeth could breathe.

There was no one in this part of the palace. Not a single footstep, not one hushed conversation within hearing distance. Only the sound of birdsong through the open window, its melody moving through the room like a waltz.

The day had been so full, so overwhelming, that Elisabeth now craved the serenity of a field of wildflowers, a rocky mountain path, somewhere she could gather her thoughts. Trapped in the villa, she settled for stretching out on the floor, tracing her hands along its grooves.

"Are you unwell?"

Her breath hitched at the interruption, and she turned her head.

Franz stood above her, his face unreadable. Elisabeth sat up, cheeks warming with embarrassment yet again. Why was he always finding her at her most ridiculous moments?

"No. I . . . I feel fine."

"Then what are you doing?" There was only curiosity in his voice, no judgement.

"It's hot and the floor is nice and cool. Soothing."

For a beat, Franz didn't move. Then, to her surprise, the emperor slowly lowered himself to sit beside her. This close, she could see where his hair curled behind his ear, how perfectly straight his mustache was, the slight dimple in his chin. They were friendly details, the kind of details a person could stare at all day.

He lay back, mimicking her earlier position on the floor, and folded his hands over his stomach, his arm mere inches from hers. Elisabeth did the same, both of them now looking up at the fanciful ceiling. The color was a powdery blue, and against it, intricately detailed dragons frolicked as if flying across real sky. Tails curved in loop-de-loops, narrowing to arrow points at their ends. Wings spread in every direction, some small and birdlike, others reptilian, curving outward like claws.

"You're right," Franz said. "It *is* nice and cool." His voice was pleasant, gentle. Intimate but not demanding. It was how she'd always wanted to talk to a man.

She glanced over and found he was already looking at her. Really looking at her—their faces such a short space apart, their shoulders even closer. She could see the curve of his lips so well from here, could have counted his eyelashes if she'd wanted to.

Her heart skipped and sped up, her skin heating even against the cool floor.

"I heard what you said to my brother at lunch."

Elisabeth sat up. "I'm sorry. Sometimes I can't help it."

"Can't help what?" There was mirth at the corner of Franz's mouth, as he sat up beside her, a laugh in his eyes. Her heart fluttered. He wasn't angry.

"Saying exactly what I think." Well, not *exactly* what she thought. If she said exactly what she thought, she'd say something about his eyes—how they were kind and strong and deep all at once. She'd tell him the way he laughed in the garden made her feel like she knew him already. She'd admit that he seemed like a hero from a poem, the kind of man she might ask to—

Kiss her.

It was a dangerous thought. An unexpected one. Startling. Thrilling.

"Maybe you can teach me," Franz said. "I could use a lesson in saying what I think."

Elisabeth laughed. She couldn't believe she'd thought he'd be as arrogant as the dukes. Instead, he was humble, knowing his limitations, wanting to learn.

Franz held her eyes for a moment. "You've got something there, in your hair."

He reached across the space between them, now stunningly small. She could smell him, then: all cloves and cardamom and something earthy, like a spring rain. Goose bumps flickered to life across her exposed arms. She hoped he didn't hear her gasp, feel the jolt of electricity across her skin. She hadn't known her skin, her heart, every inch of her could feel so fully realized. Before she'd been a shadow; the touch made her *real*. Even the guilt of Helene only two hallways away couldn't break through the storm that was the brush of fingers across skin.

Carefully, gently, Franz lifted a strand of Elisabeth's hair to reveal Puck's braid. Her reminder of wildness, friendship, love. The mountains. Adventures. Wind in her face, the earth speeding past.

"It's not mine," she said after a long pause. "I only braided it in."

"Then whose is it?" His voice was tender.

"Puck. So that I don't forget the way he was."

A pause.

"A man?" Was that pain in his voice?

"A horse." She smiled, just a little, wrapped up in the breathlessness of the moment and the sadness at its edges.

Franz returned the smile, the corner of his mouth twitching in a way that was starting to feel familiar, like a secret shared between them, the kind of secret she'd always wanted to have.

TWENTY-TWO

A HORSE. NOT A MAN, BUT A HORSE. FRANZ FELT GIDDY. He'd dared touch her neck; he'd seen the way her lips had parted. He hadn't dared touch *those*. But one day...

His mother would hate it; he forced her from his thoughts.

"Don't say I've lost my mind," Elisabeth said. "I hear it far too often."

His heart raced at that. Franz knew what it was to feel like you were losing your mind. Elisabeth clearly knew what it was to be accused of the same. Was she the person he could confide in? Is that what his heart was doing, recognizing safety?

She tilted her head, the braided hair falling gently over her shoulder, along the perfect curve of her neck. There was a small mole there, a precious thing. He suddenly wanted to kiss it.

He shook himself a little. No getting carried away. He'd start with a small secret, tentative. Not a test of her, but a test of himself. Could he tell her his truths?

"I punched Maxi once, knocked out a tooth. I kept it, too. Is that insane?" It was a truth, but not *the* truth. Not the one he wanted to tell her. He held his breath, awaiting her reaction.

And then there it was: a smile. Brilliant and dazzling.

"Now, that is *completely* crazy." Her voice was cheeky in the best way.

They both laughed, the sound blending with birdsong through the window. Then Elisabeth was the one reaching across the gap between them. He wondered if she could see the way the air froze in his lungs.

But it wasn't *him* she was reaching for. It was the ever-present scar peeking above his collar. Alarm spiked through him, and his hand came up automatically, grabbing hers and moving it quickly away.

"Does it still hurt?" Now her voice was tender, and his heart reached toward it.

He'd never wanted anyone to touch the scar, or to even remind him of it. But now—with *her*—he wished he hadn't stopped her, wished he'd let her trace her fingers along his neck, inside his collar. That part of himself, that constant reminder of violence—he suddenly wanted it to be touched. To feel tenderness. Pleasure. The heat of life, not death.

But he shouldn't be feeling any of this. If he stayed, he'd kiss her. And then he'd be no better than Maxi, stealing kisses from a woman he wasn't intended for.

"No, it doesn't hurt." Franz let out a breath, reached toward the scar, and then stood. Elisabeth followed him to her feet.

"Thank you for . . ." He searched for the the right way to finish the sentence and, not finding it, bowed slightly. "This was very . . . interesting." He hated how stiff he sounded, how he had so much to say and yet had said so little.

As he turned to leave, he could feel her standing there, light and energy, fire and wildness, watching him go.

TWENTY-THREE

I T SEEMED HELENE'S DAY WAS TO REVOLVE AROUND THE
dining room. First, their long lunch, and now back after
their walk for coffee and cake with Mother, Sophie, and
Sisi—who'd only remembered to attend after Mother sent servants to retrieve her from whatever corner of the palace she'd
been hiding in. Helene tried one of the cakes and was surprised
at the sunny burst of bright lemon on her tongue. She was equally
surprised by how much better it made her feel. Perhaps she'd
only been panicking before because of the heat and how little
she'd eaten. She'd been too nervous to touch a thing at lunch.

Now her body relaxed into itself. Sophie was smiling fondly
at her across the lace-clothed table. Mother looked unusually
calm, occasionally leaning over to pat her sister's hand, the two
of them closer away from the formalities of a group setting.

Even Sisi was behaving—sitting quietly, ankles crossed, sipping coffee—and that pleased Helene too.

After some pleasantries, Sophie got straight to the point, her
eyes on Helene. "How was your time with Franz?"

"It was very pleasant, Your Highness."

"And what do you think of him?"

"He's honorable and kind, Highness."

"That he is." Pride lit up in Sophie's eyes. "The most obedient of my boys."

Helene supposed the person Sophie was comparing him to was Maxi—the other half of Sisi's lunchtime disturbance, her sister's coconspirator. Or antagonist. Helene couldn't decide which. Helene had noticed how he and Sisi walked together in the gardens, bodies close together and clearly comfortable in each other's presence. She'd hoped Sisi might fall in love this weekend, but something about Maxi worried at the edges of her heart. He was impulsive, like Sisi. And what Sisi needed was someone to rein her in, not encourage her wildness.

"What does the emperor think of Helene?" Sisi broke in, and Helene's breath caught in her chest. She wasn't sure if she wanted to know the answer to that question.

Sophie raised an eyebrow at Sisi—it *was* an impertinent question—then waved a hand dismissively. "You know men. They rarely speak of their feelings, unless they're one of those poetic types, which Franz certainly is not."

Helene's heart sighed in disappointment. It would have made everything easier if Franz had told his mother of a spark, an interest.

"Is the courtship going as you expected?" Sophie asked, turning back to Helene.

Helene hesitated. Should she be agreeable or follow Sisi's lead with brazen honesty? She settled somewhere in the middle. "I'll confess, Your Highness, I'm as uncertain as you are of his feelings."

Sophie reached over to squeeze Helene's hand. "Don't fret, dear Helene. The boy will do what he's told; he always does. And besides, love grows over time."

"Yes, and fretting leads to wrinkles," Mother chimed in, unhelpfully.

"And everyone knows wrinkles are the worst curse in existence," Sisi whispered, barely audible.

Mother must not have heard—thank God—because she only turned toward her sister as Sophie continued speaking. "And Helene, you are being too modest. You're a beautiful, graceful girl, as polite and well-mannered as your mother has always said. Franz has no reason not to fall in love with you."

The words were the comfort Helene needed. She settled into them like a favorite chair, letting her heart lift a little at the thought that love was just around the corner.

Coffee and cake were over, and Helene found herself deliciously, unexpectedly alone in the room she shared with Sisi, facing a vanity mirror with scalloped edges. She freed her hair from its braids, watching it fall in loose waves around her face, the tension easing across her scalp. The low lantern light of evening was flattering on her skin, softening her hair, her eyes.

How light everything seemed in this moment. How much easier it was to look at her face and feel *peace* after some time alone with her thoughts. She'd been tied up in knots over nothing. She'd let herself get so caught up in Sisi's romantic ideas— love at first sight, passion like a tide pulling a person out—that she'd ignored her own convictions.

Whether Franz had fallen for her at first sight or not didn't matter. Helene was the one who'd ultimately gotten it right: love was a tree you planted and nurtured and patiently waited on. Duty was the tide. What you owed the world, what you owed your family—those were the forces that swept you away.

She knew her next conversation with Franz would be better. She would be calmer. And they'd find their way to each other across the silences. She could picture it now: she'd be sitting in the tearoom, ankles crossed beneath pink lace and white over-skirt now that the missing trunk had finally arrived. Embroidered vines would hug her tiny waist, a silver vine circling her throat as a necklace.

Franz would join her there, his eyes kind as always. Unlike reality, in Helene's mind they could be alone. No one staring at them across a tree-lined path, no one interrupting their conversation. Helene hadn't realized before just how much that had been part of the pressure. Not Franz, but Sophie, Mother. Wanting so badly for the women who'd chosen her to be proud.

Helene turned from the vanity and lay on the soft, cloudlike bed, closed her eyes. She imagined herself reaching for Franz, placing her hand on top of his as he sat down on a couch beside her. "Is something wrong, Your Majesty?" Her heart would flutter with the thrill, the boldness of asking such a vulnerable, direct question.

"Have your head and heart ever been at war?" the Franz in her mind would ask.

She would laugh a little, soft and natural. "Every day."

He'd raise an eyebrow. "And what do you do about it?"

She'd pause. What did she do? When Sisi had fallen into the

river, Helene had chosen to grow up. She'd chosen her head over her heart. And that was what she was choosing again—now—here at Bad Ischl, wasn't it? Choosing to do the right thing no matter how she felt or how long it took her to feel.

"I suppose I err on the side of logic, Your Highness."

"Please call me Franz." Oh, how she would feel when he told her to abandon the formalities. "And tell me, why logic?" She thrilled at the idea of his asking her opinion, seeking her counsel.

"The heart's an unreliable keeper." That's what she'd say to him.

He would nod, thoughtful. "Thank you, sweet Helene. I needed that."

Helene opened her eyes and slipped back into reality, staring at the gauzy white of the inner curtain on the window, the raindrop-like crystals of a small chandelier hanging from the ceiling. She smiled to herself. *This* was what their courtship was meant to feel like. Easy conversation in a sun-kissed room between two people committed to doing the right thing—and finding love in the process. This was what it would feel like from now on.

Still alone in her room, Helene let her mind wander to something else: the other intimacy that would eventually come. Franz—even more handsome than his portrait—would do more than simply court her. She pictured his lips, traced a finger along her own. She'd never been kissed, but she could imagine it: skin against soft skin, the way the feeling would carry from lips to heart, electric.

She traced a hand along the contours of her face, down the sensitive skin of her neck and across collarbone, to breast only thinly shrouded in nightgown. What would it feel like for his hand to follow this path? Her nipples grew taut, a thrilling, terrifying urgency tickling from her abdomen, lower.

Her body shivered involuntarily. It wouldn't be long before Franz touched her like this, before she would know where that knot of nerves and longings, daydreams and promises, could lead.

TWENTY-FOUR

A S THE AFTERNOON COOLED TO EVENING, ELISABETH slipped barefoot into the gardens, the sun-warmed stone rough beneath her feet, the leaves a richer, deeper green now that the sun was nearly set. Honeysuckle perfumed the air. The soft pink of the oncoming sunset made the surrounding garden seem to glow.

She pressed a hand lightly against the shrub to her right, ruffling its perfectly manicured leaves as she walked, breathing deep. Finally, *finally*, she could think. The tensions of the day ran off her skin like water.

The ladies' coffee had confirmed what Elisabeth had heard before: that Sophie was the real power behind the throne, that Franz would do as he was told. Her heart bumped against those thoughts, bruising slightly. They were the same thoughts she'd felt so viscerally across her own skin the first time she saw Sophie in the hallway—her boys moving around her like they were blades of grass and she a strong wind. The archduchess was the chess master, everyone else a piece.

But, she told herself, *that's fine*. Right, even. Franz was a perfect gentleman, and he was for Helene. Here, in the cool, quiet garden, it seemed so much more possible to let her feelings go. Open her hands and let that *something* between her and Franz dart away like the little bird regaining its senses. She hoped the feelings would land on Helene's heart instead.

Elisabeth turned along the path, circling out of view of the villa and into view of the little stream they'd crossed earlier. She stooped beside the bank, trailing her fingers through the cold, clear water, and—

"Good evening."

She froze. It *couldn't be*. She'd just released him from her mind, told her feelings to fly away. But here Franz was, as if those feelings had turned directly around and flown back to perch on her shoulder.

"It's you," she answered foolishly, standing to face him.

"It's me," he agreed, holding an inviting hand toward the path. "Would you like to walk with me?"

She knew the right answer, and she betrayed it. "Certainly, Your Majesty."

"So, what brings you back to the garden?" He looked at her intently as they walked, her bare feet pressing into soft moss and rough stone, his shoes clipping lightly against the path.

"I'm not used to being surrounded by people all day. Sometimes I prefer the company of trees. And you?"

"I needed to think. There are too many people back at the villa—some of them taking up enough space for two, or ten."

Elisabeth smiled. She imagined her mother was one of them. Maxi probably counted too. And perhaps the expectations of the court were taking up whatever air remained.

"You prefer the quiet then?" he asked after a long beat.

"Sometimes."

"Am I talking too much even now?"

He sounded nervous and Elisabeth put out a hand, resting it gently on his arm before she knew what she was doing. "Not at all. I like when people speak their minds."

The heat of him through his sleeve warmed her own skin. She could feel a flush creeping across her cheeks. She removed her hand.

"And if I spoke my mind now?"

Her heart flipped, then flipped again. "Please do."

"Sometimes I wish I could go—leave—just travel the world like my brother does. No decisions. No worries. Just freedom. Nobody counting on me. Nobody's lives ruined because I made the wrong choice that day."

Elisabeth's eyebrows flickered upward in surprise. She hadn't really thought about how heavy it must feel to be emperor. Making choices that either fed your people or didn't, freed them or held them hostage.

"Would you give it up if you could?"

He shook his head without hesitation. "No. I want to be a good emperor. I want to change things. I just wish I could have both. Be emperor most of the time and have an hour each day to be—me."

Elisabeth's heart wrapped protectively around him. She wished that for him too. Wished she could be the one to give him those hours, let him forget responsibility for a short time.

What would it feel like for them to forget together? For Elisabeth to kiss that jaw at the hollow where it met neck, to trace a finger up it, jawline to ear. To press him against the dark outline of a tree and tilt her face to his. The thoughts came unbidden, and if Elisabeth's face hadn't already been pink, she was sure it would be now. She'd just let go of this. Why was her heart betraying her again?

"If I could give you wings, I would," she said.

"'We have not wings, we cannot soar; but we have feet to scale and climb,'" Franz recited, almost to himself.

Elisabeth's mouth dropped open, unable to contain her surprise. "You've read Longfellow?"

Had the emperor just quoted her favorite poet to her? It didn't feel real. It was like he'd reached straight into her soul and seen what lived there. Poems and wings, nature and longing, truth wrapped in rhymes.

"I read him when I need to feel like the world makes sense."

She was speechless.

"Is that foolish?" He stopped at a small wrought iron bench, motioned for her to sit with him.

"No, it's perfect," she whispered, then realized that might be too honest. "It's everything I would hope an emperor would be."

He made a small, surprised noise. "I never thought of poetry being an asset to the empire. I've always just read it for myself."

"What is an asset to the empire, if not poetry?"

Franz paused a long time. "Strength."

"Poetry is strength."

He smiled, his mouth twitching upward, the faint light of a nearby garden lamp mirrored in his eyes. "Earlier, you promised me a lesson in speaking my mind. So, tell me now: If you stand up for yourself, go against someone, how do you know you're right?"

"You don't." She shrugged.

"But if you're the emperor, you *must*."

"But if you're a human, you can't."

"You seem certain."

"I'm not certain about most things. I just refuse to let anyone make me into something I'm not. And if I don't speak my mind, people will make me into whatever they want me to be."

"So, you're saying damn the consequences because no one else gets to define who you are?"

Elisabeth laughed. Hearing it said so simply made her heart light. It was the first time in so long she'd heard herself echoed back with such clarity. The first time that someone had really *seen* Elisabeth in months. Her heart thrilled at it.

"You've already made a good start," she pointed out. "You said *damn*."

He laughed again, and that thrilled her too.

TWENTY-FIVE

I F ONLY IT WERE ELISABETH'S PORTRAIT SITTING IN Franz's room instead of Helene's. How easy it would be if duty and longing were on the same path. How much simpler his life would be if there weren't a war in his heart as well as at his borders.

He'd stumbled upon her by accident again, and his heart couldn't stop feeling that accident and fate weren't so far apart. Would it be so bad if he chose her instead of Helene? If he ruined Mother's plans? The only consequences he could think of for letting his heart have this one thing it truly wanted were—

Joy.

Laughter.

It had been so long since someone had reminded him so fully of who he was, how he wasn't just emperor but also *Franz*. The same Franz who used to read poetry by candlelight, staying up late thinking about all the ways he could change his world. Before worry and danger and an endless list of duties and an attempt on his life had crowded all that out. Before he'd realized the depth of consequences to his own foolishness, how much stepping off the path of obligation cost.

Who could he be now if he gave in and let his heart love Elisabeth? Who would he be if he didn't?

As he strolled toward the villa's back entrance, Maxi appeared at his elbow, cigarette in hand. "Nighttime stroll in the garden, Brother? That's not like you."

Irritation bunched in Franz's shoulders. It was actually *just* like him, but Maxi wouldn't know. Maxi had barely been around in the last year as the pressures of Habsburg piled up and Franz sought out quiet corners of manicured gardens as a solace.

Franz pressed his lips together. He was tempted to ask what Maxi was doing out here, but the answer was probably something illicit. And if Franz didn't give in to the temptation to ask, maybe Maxi would go away.

Instead, his brother skipped a half step ahead and turned to walk backward, facing Franz again. "Perhaps we should talk about something other than your garden habits. How about Helene's sister? I bet she's as passionate in love as she is about putting a man in his place."

Franz kept his mouth shut, his jaw tensing, lightness evaporating in an instant. Had Maxi seen them together? He didn't think for one second that Maxi would let it pass if he had. He'd find a way to hurt Franz with the knowledge, either by leveraging the secret to get what he wanted or by screaming it from the rooftops, ruining everyone's plans in a sentence or two.

But no, Franz realized. This was about Maxi—not Franz. Maxi had liked it when Elisabeth told him off at lunch.

"Your bride may be virtuous as they say. But it's the sister I want to get alone." Maxi grinned, and Franz's jaw locked tighter.

It wasn't that he hadn't pictured it himself, of course: what it would feel like to kiss the smirk at the corner of her mouth, run a finger up the curve of her neck, press his lips to her collarbone. But the thought of *Maxi* picturing the same thing made him sick.

"Leave her alone, Maxi."

He threw up his hands. "Brother, I would, but I think her mother brought her here specifically so that I *wouldn't*."

"You can't scandalize the sister of the woman Mother has chosen as empress."

"Who said anything about scandal? Maybe I'll marry her. Make an honest man of myself."

Franz clenched his fists at his sides. "Don't play, Maxi."

"What do you care, anyway?" Maxi eyed him, pulling in his brows.

"I care because you make fools of us all. You're a Habsburg; you need to follow the rules."

"Like you follow the rules? Have you forgotten about Louise?"

Franz bit his tongue. Having one discreet affair was different than having one hundred not-so-discreet affairs, and Maxi knew it.

When Franz didn't answer, Maxi continued. "You get everything you want—damn the rules—and you know it. Habsburg. Louise. Mother's attention. Father stepped down from the throne for you, for God's sake. The rules bend themselves around you, and you don't even see it. So don't tell me to follow rules that won't bend for me unless I break them."

Franz wanted to laugh. Maxi thought the rules bent for Franz? Maxi was the one the rules were always bending for, the one Mother indulged even when he made them all look like

fools with his sharp comments and cavalier affairs. Even when
he cost them goodwill from countless noble families whose support they needed. Franz kept his voice steady as he returned to
the real issue at hand. "If you won't leave Elisabeth alone for the
sake of your family, do it because you agreed to be my advisor.
That's the position you wanted; now you have it. And more
power at court comes with more responsibility, Maxi."

It was only half of the truth. Maxi couldn't have Elisabeth,
not because he was Franz's advisor but because he was a *danger*.
Elisabeth was all poetry and wildness and hope. A person who
saw the world in terms of its possibilities. And she deserved better. She deserved someone who loved her. She deserved—

Someone like Franz.

The truth knocked at his heart, and he tried to ignore it.

TWENTY-SIX

HELENE WAS ALREADY IN BED WHEN SISI CAME IN. Helene's hair was down, nightclothes freeing her from the tight laces of the daytime, and the windows were thrown open to try and coax in a small breeze. She was lying back, hair fanning out around her, staring up at the decorative ceiling. Was the art above her a dragon, a tree, or a woman in gold? Perhaps it was all three, depending which way you turned your head.

"I think he looks much better than in his picture," Helene said as Sisi joined her in bed, Helene's head on the pillow, Sisi's at her sister's feet. "Don't you think so?"

Sisi didn't answer.

Helene reached out to tap her sister's leg. "What's wrong? Are you listening?"

"Yes, of course." Sisi sat up and crawled to the top of the bed, spooning her body around Helene, who relaxed into the comfort, the familiarity of it.

"I can hardly wait for tomorrow." Helene cast her mind back to her earlier daydream, how real it had felt, how right. The proposal would change things, she'd decided. It would remove the awkwardness of their meetings, nudge him toward opening up to her. Her heart stretched toward the hope of it like a sleepy, contented cat.

"I think I can love him, Sisi." She tested the words, the idea, out loud. "How lucky is that, really?"

Another long silence and Helene's heart faltered a little. Did Sisi not think so? Helene wanted so badly for her sister to agree, to say, *Yes, Helene, your hard work will pay off, you'll see*. Sisi had said Helene would make a good empress, and Helene needed to hear it again.

Sisi only pressed her face to Helene's hair, kissed her on the head. A comforting gesture, but not the excitement Helene was hoping for.

"Where did you sneak off to anyway?"

"Nowhere," Sisi replied quietly.

"Do you think I'll make a good empress?" Helene asked, wishing she didn't need the validation so very much. Wishing her hope wasn't so fragile.

"Of course I do. You were made for it." Sisi said the words, but her heart was somewhere else. Helene could tell. And it hurt.

"Better me than you, right?" She tried to bridge the gap between them, draw Sisi back into the conversation.

Sisi stiffened around her. "What do you mean by that?"

Oh no, had she said something unkind? She tried to explain. "Only what you said yourself: that you don't know the right things to say or how to behave at court."

"Like Maria Theresa, though."

Helene turned her head.

"Maria Theresa was ruler for forty years, and she wasn't proper at all," Sisi went on.

"I suppose not," Helene agreed, not sure where this was going.

"They say she rode horses through the hallways. She was a rogue."

"I know, Sisi. We've read the same books."

"It's *Elisabeth*." The word was pointed. Helene supposed she now knew that she was as forbidden from the nickname as her mother. It stung. Another wall up between them—and an unexpected one. Helene didn't know what she'd done wrong.

"I'm sorry . . . Elisabeth."

"It's nothing," her sister said, turning over to snuff out her lamp.

"Are you all right?" Helene whispered into the darkness.

"Yes, fine."

"I didn't mean to imply you wouldn't be a good empress."

"No—no—you didn't."

Helene stared out the window at the stars. What could be bothering her sister? Perhaps it was just too much, being here. It had been Helene's idea to bring her, but perhaps Elisabeth would have been happier at home.

Oh.

It *was* about the empress comment. How could Helene have been so thoughtless? Talking about becoming empress was the same as talking about *leaving* Elisabeth. Helene hadn't told Elisabeth that she was hoping to bring her to Vienna. Elisabeth didn't know her sister's plans. The thought was chastisement and relief all at once. Elisabeth must be grieving, and Helene talking so hopefully, so happily about her new life was a shot aimed at that grief. Elisabeth would miss her; Elisabeth still loved her.

Helene didn't speak again. She'd let Elisabeth feel whatever she needed to feel, and tomorrow—perhaps—they could talk about Vienna. Then maybe they'd both feel better.

TWENTY-SEVEN

H ELENE WAS ASLEEP, BUT ELISABETH WAS DREAMING wide-awake. Sitting beside the window, inking out poetry by moonlight.

> *Do you still think of the night in the shining hall?*
> *It's been a long time . . .*
> *Since two souls*
> *Met as one.*
> *. . . I gave the soul its light, friend,*
> *Who was more than a friend,*
> *Yes, more than a friend.*

A soft knock sounded on the door—a surprise this late. She paused, quill poised above journal, so wrapped up in the words, the images, the emotions, that it took a second gentle knock for her to realize that the door required her attention. Elisabeth slipped from the windowsill and padded across the room, opening the door just enough to see who was behind it.

The servant at the door bowed. "Your Royal Highness, if you would please follow me."

"Me?" Surprise fluttered in Elisabeth's stomach like a little sparrow. "Why?"

Intrigue and danger sparked across her skin. Was she allowed to follow the servant? Wouldn't she get in trouble for leaving her room in the middle of the night? But, then again, was she allowed to say no? Could it be Mother or Sophie calling for her, some emergency she couldn't picture? And if not that, where exactly was he taking her? What adventure awaited?

She glanced back at Helene, still fast asleep, and made her choice. Allowed or not, no one would even know she was gone. She would follow the young man and see where fate led her.

Elisabeth slowly opened the door, careful to not let it creak, and followed the servant into the dark hall. Her bare feet pressed against the smooth wood floors, the halls so quiet that she could hear her skirt swishing against itself. She never asked where they were going, relishing the mystery of it all. But when the servant led her into a wing of the villa exclusively reserved for the imperial family, her pulse beat faster, curiosity sparking into hope.

Another turn, another archway, and then the servant ushered her through a set of white doors etched with golden vines and green leaves. An elegant room opened up before her, with deep-red-and-yellow wallpaper, tall, white-trimmed doors leading to a balcony overlooking the fountain she liked so much, and—

Franz.

He was looking out the window, face tilted toward the stars, his back to her. She'd studied the width of those shoulders, the slight curl of that blond hair, enough to recognize him instantly, even from this angle. He was dressed casually, like the first time she'd seen him: white shirt with the collar raised, suspenders pressing into his strong back, and black trousers accentuating his height.

"Her Royal Highness, the Duchess." The servant bowed to Franz as he turned. "And the Champagne, Your Majesty."

A shiver swept through Elisabeth like the tide kissing the shore. Champagne. Franz. It was like something from a dream, the kind of night that inspired poetry and art. And yet—it was also a danger. The kind of night she could be sent to the asylum for, the kind of night that could ruin Helene's future.

"To your health," the servant continued. "I bid you good night." And then he backed out of the room, disappearing from sight.

The clock struck midnight, singing out in the distance.

Elisabeth held herself in a nervous hug, her thoughts spilling out before she could stop them. "So, you send for me in the middle of the night to drink Champagne with you?"

She was pleased to find her voice was steady, even as her heart crashed like a wave. He'd summoned her in the middle of the night. It meant *something*, though she wasn't quite sure what.

"It's my birthday," he said, as if that explained it.

"I wish you a happy birthday, Your Majesty."

"Did I wake you?" he asked, stepping closer, surrounding her with his usual scent of spring rain and cloves.

"No. I'm often awake at night."

"That doesn't surprise me."

"And why not?"

"I can't imagine you sleeping more than a few minutes a day. You'd miss out on too much. And the world would miss out on you."

Some of the tightness in her body loosened. It was true that she drank life in like she was a desert and it was rain. If she could help it, she wouldn't sleep. Wouldn't miss a star winking into life. Wouldn't miss a sunrise.

"I'm surprised you're not asleep, though," she said. "I imagine running an empire requires rest."

There was something raw in his expression, and he paused—deciding something—then said, "I don't sleep much either . . . because of the nightmares."

"Nightmares?"

"About . . ." Franz left his sentence unfinished, but the hand he brought up to his neck, to the scar peeking out from his collar, made it clear what he meant.

"Do you want to tell me about it?"

"You'll think I'm insane."

"Well, then we'll be quite the pair since I too am, apparently, insane."

His shoulders relaxed. He motioned to the settee, and they sat, inches apart. And, as if he couldn't bear to hold them back any longer, all the things he must have been suppressing for months—nightmares, terror—poured out. He spoke of sweat and screaming, darkness swallowing his vision, of a body detached from its mind. And Elisabeth's heart wrapped itself protectively around him—this man who was so many things at once: a strong emperor, a secret poetry lover, a vulnerable heart.

"And now. Are you here with me now?" she asked.

"Very much so."

The silence, and the intimacy it held, left her breathless. Her eyes caught on his and she couldn't look away. But then, unbidden, Helene's peaceful sleeping face flashed into her mind, guilt hot on its heels, and Elisabeth came back to her senses. *You aren't supposed to be doing this.* She stood suddenly, and Franz followed. "I must get back before she realizes I'm gone. I shouldn't have come."

Elisabeth started to turn, but Franz's voice caught on her heart and held her in place. "Stay." It was request framed as command. "Please." So much longing for such a small word. So many things unsaid in between the letters.

She turned back to him. He at least deserved the truth. "I promised not to mess anything up this weekend."

"It's too late for that," he whispered.

He was so close to her now, eyes caught on hers. One step closer, and she could reach across the space and—

Touch his face.

Trace his lips.

Feel the strength of muscled shoulders under her hands.

She'd never been so aware of her own breathing: every breath that passed across her sensitive lips, every rise and fall of her chest.

But the joy, the thrill of it, flickered into cold, dark guilt. What about her sister? What about the promise she'd made? Elisabeth's legs were ready to turn, to run back to the room. But her heart held her firmly in place.

"I have to go, Your Majesty."

"Can we dispense with the formalities, Elisabeth?"

Her name in his mouth was a holy thing, a true thing.

He handed her the Champagne flute she'd abandoned when she'd started to leave. "That is your name, isn't it?"

She took it, pressed uncertain fingers to the stem. "Yes, I just haven't heard it in a while."

She sipped the Champagne. They said it was like drinking stars, and she could see why. The sip was a hundred stars shooting through the heavens, and so was the moment—the look in the eyes of the man across from her. She set down her flute, and he followed her lead.

"You reminded me of something today," he said. "You reminded me of what I was like before I became emperor."

"And what were you like?"

"Alive," he said, smiling fully now. His face held nothing back.

Oh, how Elisabeth's heart longed to join in, to hold nothing back. But Helene tugged at her still, and Elisabeth shook her head ever so slightly as Franz stepped toward her. "No. No, we can't. You're going to marry my sister. That's what they've arranged."

Still, Elisabeth didn't go. Didn't run. Didn't leave. Couldn't quite betray her sister and couldn't quite betray her heart.

His eyes searched hers. "But I want you."

The words were simple. An impossible truth.

He continued, "I've been told what to do my whole life."

Oh, how Elisabeth knew that feeling. Being pinched into a smaller shape, stuffed into a smaller box. Do this, don't do that. It was impossible to bear. And here was the emperor telling her that he, too, felt the weight of it, the way it made a person smaller.

His next words were another echo of her own heart. "I can't take it anymore."

And that was it. Neither could she. They were the same, a perfect match.

"I've felt dead inside for months. But with you, I suddenly want to celebrate my birthday."

"But you don't know me." In one way, it was true. But in another, it wasn't. They'd had so little time and yet he *did* know her. Knew her in a way that didn't seem possible.

He rose to the challenge. "You tell the truth when no one else will. And you see things differently than other people."

Her heart warmed and softened. It was what she'd been longing for someone to say. That her honesty, her truths, were something to be loved, not something to be banished. That her poet's sensibility was charm, not oddity.

"I need someone like you."

Elisabeth drank the words in. Someone like *her*. No *keep your womanish opinions to yourself, Sisi*. No *don't go barefoot, Sisi*. No *do what I want not what you want, Sisi*. She wanted to cry, and she wanted to laugh. She'd found her great love—she knew it then. She was falling, flying, over the edge of some invisible line, knowing someone would be hurt at the end, but unable to help herself all the same.

"You aren't what I expected," she whispered. "On the outside, you stand there like a soldier, but you're completely different inside."

"Weaker, you mean?" His smile faltered.

"Stronger, I mean."

He searched her eyes. Her heart paused, waiting, as he lifted a hand to run it—soft, so perfectly, achingly, soft—down her cheek. Her eyes closed without her permission as she melted into the touch. It was everything poetry promised it would be—fire and ice, tears and songs. Wild joy and tender heartache.

And then he was kissing her, his hands on her face, fingers tracing the edges of her jawline. His lips were soft, warm. She pressed in hard, opening her mouth to his, and his hands moved up, tangling in the ringlets of her hair.

Her heart sang and flew, itself a bird. She was falling; she was soaring. She was a windstorm, a wave, swept up, fallen, lost.

But no.

No.

Helene. She was betraying Helene.

Elisabeth stopped, pulled backward, tried to keep from crying. One more look at his face—surprise and desire and confusion—and she couldn't do this.

"Happy birthday . . . Franz," she whispered.

Then she turned and left, her face crumpling into despair.

TWENTY-EIGHT

THE KISS WAS EVERYTHING. THE NIGHT WAS EVERY-thing. *She* was everything.

She'd seen him—really seen him—and had thought him *strong*. He'd told her his truth, and she'd reached for him instead of retreating.

He hadn't felt this way—ever.

But then she had pulled away. And he knew why: not because of him but *them*. Her family. His family. The tangled mess of obligations set up by someone else.

She had been so beautiful just then: lips red with kissing, cheeks and neck blushing pink, eyes sparkling, a lock of hair escaping her braid. He wanted to tuck it back in, trail his fingers through her hair.

"You're going to marry my sister," she'd said. But couldn't she see that it didn't matter anymore? Nothing mattered except this moment—when they'd seen each other so clearly.

But still she had left, turning through the ivy-twined doors. He had reached for her, but she'd slipped through his fingers.

Now he watched her go, braid swinging at her back, the soles of her bare feet peeking out from under a deep-blue skirt. Of course she would be barefoot, as close to the earth as she could get.

He slipped back into the room and took his own shoes off, pressing feet to warm wood, closing his eyes, as if feeling the same thing she felt would keep him close to her. And then, on impulse, he lay down on the floor, tracing it with his fingers, transporting himself back to the afternoon. It was like being a boy again, giving in to whims, feeling everything around him so acutely. The orange of the sconce light. The smoothness of the wood. The smell of lemon lingering in the air.

It was like he'd been dead, and she'd brought him back to life. He'd been gray, and she'd brought things back to color.

But her leaving—

Was she going to ignore this thing that hung in the air between them, this thread connecting them across space? If she felt even half of what he did, she couldn't possibly.

Could she?

TWENTY-NINE

FRANZ WENT TO SLEEP REPLAYING THE KISS IN HIS HEAD, and he woke up in a nightmare. The knife was in his neck, and he was on the ground, screaming—except no screams came out. His heart was throwing itself against his rib cage, its last act an attempt at escape. His body grew cold, shivers shuddering through him, each sending a new spasm of pain radiating out from his neck.

No, no, *no*. He couldn't leave. He didn't want to go. The darkness gripped him, ice taking hold of his limbs. Tears burned down his cheeks; screams tore through his body even as they couldn't escape his mouth.

He was awake and not awake, knowing it wasn't real, that he wasn't *there* anymore, yet unable to shake the feeling that his body still was. He opened his eyes, saw silver curtains along the edge of a canopy bed frame, ceiling painted in navy night and silver stars. But he could still feel the cold, sharp, breath-stealing knife in his neck, the way his lips went numb, his throat went small.

You aren't there, Franz. You are here. You are safe.

The weight on his chest was unbearable—the invisible weight of a life nearly lost. So physical, so painful in the moment. He clenched and unclenched his fists, relieved that he could move again, digging fingernails into palms just to feel alive. Real. Here—still here.

His cheeks were a wreckage. He must have bit them in his sleep again. While screaming or trying to run away. His jaw ached. He rolled from back to stomach and pressed his face into the pillow, muffling a frustrated, terrified shout. He'd been so happy last night and now—

Franz was forced straight back into hell again.

He punched a fist into the mattress. It had been months. Months and months. When would it stop?

He'd felt so seen when he'd told Elisabeth about the nightmares, but now doubt poured down in drenching, drowning waves. Nightmares didn't sound so bad until you were in them. Until you woke up screaming in a cold sweat, the inside of your cheeks torn raw. Or until you woke up next to the person having them. What had he been thinking? He couldn't ask Elisabeth to live like this.

Franz breathed deep into the pillow, pressing his sweat-soaked forehead into the soft cotton, breathing in the lavender oil the servants scented the sheets with, waiting for his heart to stop punching wildly at his chest from the inside.

It was his birthday, he realized, and made an ironic noise— part laugh, part sob—into the pillow. The day he was supposed to announce his engagement to Helene. Last night he'd been so sure that those plans—that duty—didn't matter.

But this . . .

This was a reminder that it did. That there were things happening in Habsburg that were bigger—more important—than this strange, magical thing between Elisabeth and him. There was a reason his heart wasn't his to give; empires rose and fell on the choice of an empress, the raising of an heir. The darkness at his door wasn't a thing to be fought with poetry and lingering gazes. The empire was danger and violence and unrest that ended with a knife in your neck. A war bearing down like a nightmare, ready to snatch you up without your consent.

The thing that existed between him and Elisabeth would be crushed by it. *She* would be crushed by it. She had been the one who was right last night. Right to remind him he was marrying Helene, right to run away, right to stop him from going further than a kiss.

The nightmare was the world he lived in. The kiss was the dream.

Franz was suddenly certain he couldn't have both.

THIRTY

I F ONLY ELISABETH HAD MET FRANZ *BEFORE*. BEFORE THE dukes and the counts. Before the letter had come with Helene's name on it instead of Elisabeth's. Before arrangements and expectations and threats of asylums bound together to build an impenetrable wall.

Back in her bed that night, with Helene still fast asleep beside her, Elisabeth had traced a finger along a page in her diary wet with tears:

Too late we met
On life's sharp path
It had already carried us too far—
The unstoppable wheel of time.
Too late,
Your fathoms-deep eyes
Drew me in like magnets.

She'd fallen asleep on her stomach, her diary still turned to that page, her face pressed against it. A poem that was more than a poem, for a friend who was more than a friend.

Now it was a new day. *The* new day. The day Franz was supposed to announce his engagement to Helene. It was the end of something that had only just begun, possibility cut off at the legs. Elisabeth wished the dresses hadn't arrived yesterday; mourning clothes would have been more fitting.

She hoped none of her feelings were visible on her face as she stood in the velvet-trimmed dressing room and watched them fit Helene's gown. It was stunning: bright pink slipping off ivory shoulders, billowing out at the sleeves and the waist. Helene was a flower, a garden, the brightest thing in the room. Franz would propose to her, and she would grow brighter still.

Elisabeth wished it could be different, and then hated herself for the wish. Wanted to shove it in her mouth like Néné's unfinished will-o'-the-wisp. She was supposed to be here supporting her sister. Instead, she was wishing her pain. Still secretly wishing that Franz would say no. No to his mother. No to the arrangements. Yes to an impossible thing: a life with Elisabeth. The very thing Elisabeth had said no to just hours before.

The seamstress stepped back from where she'd been tidying Helene's hem, and Helene twirled, skirt sweeping outward, swirling in the half dozen mirrors arranged around them.

"Beautiful." Mother's face was alight with a rare, unbridled smile. "Helene, you've grown so slender. It's very becoming."

Helene smiled and cast her eyes downward, then looked up at Elisabeth. "What do you think?"

The hope in her eyes, the spark, sank into Elisabeth like a knife, guilt lodging in her stomach, her chest, her throat. Her beautiful, hopeful sister wanted reassurance, and only hours before, Elisabeth had been kissing Helene's intended. Not only kissing him: *wanting* him. Which would mean disappointing Helene. No, *disappointing* was too kind a word. It would *crush* her. The words stuck in Elisabeth's throat, and she tried to smile back at her beaming sister.

"You look perfect, Néné." Elisabeth turned to the seamstress. "Could we do a fitting for my dress, too?"

If she couldn't have the thing her heart wanted most, at least she could look her best while she watched the dream slip through her fingers. After the announcement, they were leaving—and then Elisabeth would find a way not to come back for Helene's wedding. Or at least find a way to forget Franz in the months to come. Forget the way her heart had thrown itself against her chest, the feeling of being undone in front of another person, perfectly yourself and perfectly seen.

She knew she was lying to herself, knew she could never forget. But what she could do was stand tall as she watched the inevitable unfold.

Mother's eyebrows rose in approval, Helene's in surprise. The seamstress motioned for Elisabeth to step into the mirrored center of the room.

For the first time in her life, Elisabeth let her mother's attendants fix her dress without complaint. Staring into the mirror, she thought she looked like a dream: all steel-blue curves and poppy lips. She'd never admit to her mother that she might have a point about the power and pleasure of dresses and hairstyles. But she was willing to admit to herself that she now saw why Helene bore the indignities of hairpins and rosewater facial serums and hair scrubbed through with raw eggs.

Elisabeth raised her arms, turned this way and that, twirled on command. "What do you think?"

"Spatz would say you were a wood nymph," Helene said as the seamstress finished tidying up the cinched waist of Elisabeth's steel-blue skirt.

Or a siren, Elisabeth thought, wryly, guiltily. Siren. Temptress. Her traitor heart calling out across the waves to her sister's intended.

THIRTY-ONE

HELENE'S DRESS WAS COOL AND FEATHERLIGHT against her skin. She twirled and a shimmering, sparkling quality danced around her with the motion. In this dress, with her slender figure, gold-blond hair, and teardrop earrings lightly dancing against her jawline, Helene was the most beautiful she'd ever seen herself. And this dress, this beauty, was the next seed she was planting toward eventual love. Perhaps it would even be the breakthrough: the moment when Franz started to fall for her.

Helene hated to take the dress off, but after the fitting, the hairdressers insisted both women strip down to their undergarments so as not to wrinkle their gowns. Now the two sisters sat in simple white linens, leaning back, as servants fluttered around their heads, brushing, braiding, twisting, perfecting every strand.

It was a surprise that Elisabeth had asked to participate, that she could actually be still long enough for an elaborate French twist. It gave Helene hope—that Elisabeth was coming around, embracing her role as the future empress's sister. And even if the sudden change of heart was because Elisabeth was attaching herself to unpredictable Maxi—which Helene had wondered about a few times—Helene's hopes were bigger than her concern.

Helene felt a rush of affection for her sister, held out a hand, and squeezed Elisabeth's, resting on the arm of the chair beside her. They hadn't talked about Vienna yet, but Helene was looking forward to that moment. She was sure that as empress she'd be able to invite Elisabeth to be one of her ladies-in-waiting. And perhaps that was the answer to everything; if being here had made Elisabeth want to be patient with the hairdressers, being at court might help her embrace responsibility in a larger way. Being surrounded by glamour and manners would be easier than reading about them in books and practicing etiquette in an empty manor room. And then Mother couldn't send Elisabeth away because Helene could keep her out of trouble.

Helene just needed to ask Mother and Sophie about it first. Then she could bring it up with her sister. It would be perfect.

Mother left the room to collect a forgotten ribbon from the trunks and Helene turned to Elisabeth, joking, "You should ask to have your hair done more often. It's the first time in a year that the three of us have been together and Mother hasn't asked for a sherry."

"Or claimed she was going to bleed to death," Elisabeth said, returning the jest. "But maybe we're letting her have too much peace. Since I'm feeling well-behaved today, you should do something to irritate her ulcer. Wink at a stable boy or something."

Helene giggled, let herself joke freely in a way she hadn't in a while. "Maybe I'll flash my ankles at dinner."

God, it felt good to joke with Elisabeth. The tensions of the past months shrank and shrank again, turning to nothing. Helene's heart warmed with the idea of having her sister with her in Vienna. They could do this every day: dress fittings and little jokes. It was the perfect life she could almost taste.

THIRTY-TWO

WHEN MOTHER CAME TO ROUSE FRANZ, SHE FOUND him already awake—half dressed, standing at the window, staring across fog-draped grounds. His body was still weighed down by the nightmare, his mind even heavier. It had been foolish to think that something as fragile and perfect as what he felt for Elisabeth could survive the ravages of reality.

"Such an early riser these days," Mother said, joining him beside the window.

"I had a nightmare." It was a simple sentence, but the confession sent a spike of adrenaline through him.

She dismissed the statement with a wave of her hand. "Today is your engagement, darling. Let's not dwell on a dream."

She didn't understand how the nightmare was still in the room with him, the dread, the loss still raw across his skin. And if he was going to give up the one person he thought might understand, he needed someone else to see him. Really see him.

He tried again. "It wasn't just a dream, Mother. It was the assassination—"

Sophie cut him off, her tone shifting so quickly from light to sharp. "We've talked about this. Those men are dead, and I don't want to dwell on what they did to us. You're stronger than this, Franz."

The words were a dismissal and a blow. He hadn't even confessed the full truth—the agony—of the nightmares, the memories, and already she thought him weak. He could feel his heart walling itself off.

When he didn't speak, his mother said, "If you think this kind of weakness will play on people's sympathies, trust me, dear, it won't."

Another gut punch. Not only did she think him weak, she thought him an attention-seeker. An especially ironic accusation since her other son was Vienna's most notorious attention-seeker, scandals piling up in his wake, and she'd always seemed to love him for it. Maxi often said Franz was Mother's favorite, but it was moments like these that convinced Franz the opposite was true. Mother gave Maxi the freedom to be whatever he was—performer, rogue, unreliable, cruel—while Franz was allowed no such thing.

He wished Elisabeth were here. Longed for those fleeting moments when he'd felt so seen by her. Just minutes ago, he'd been certain she was right to run away, to tell him no. He'd decided to marry her sister, to stop believing in the magic of the thing between them.

But now—

If he really let her go, was he letting go of his only chance to be seen? The last thread connecting him to the truth of himself?

"Come now, it's time." Mother beckoned Franz to follow her from the room.

She was right. It was time—and Franz still didn't know what he was going to do.

A table was set with elaborate cakes piled with flowers and fruits. There were pyramids of cream puffs and bowls of pink candies. The ceilings were high, the chandelier glittering, the room full of well-dressed well-wishers, and Franz—standing at the front of it all, facing the guests—had never felt so alone.

Well, except for the day he'd almost died.

What are you going to do, Franz? his heart asked. The answer was a trap: betray empire and family, or betray himself.

He wished he could ask Elisabeth what to do—and the irony made him want to laugh with despair. She was the one he wanted advice from, and she was the last one he could ask. They were in the same room, and yet they might as well be worlds apart. And hadn't she made her feelings clear when she left? Wasn't her leaving the answer in itself? Wasn't it that simple?

Except, it wasn't. Because of the kiss. Because she had *seen* him, and Franz had seen her too.

The doors opened and a parade of servants filed in. "For he's a jolly good fellow," they crowed, their voices echoing off the ceiling.

Across from him, the weekend's guests stood smiling, each holding a Champagne flute, ready to toast to his birthday, his health. Franz tried to catch Elisabeth's eyes, to find an answer in them. Which meant more: the kiss or her departure?

She avoided his eyes. If Franz hadn't been in a room full of dignitaries, he might have wept with frustration.

Helene stood next to Elisabeth, bright-eyed and smiling in a fashionable pink dress. Her hair was prettily knotted behind her slender neck. Her smiles were another weight across his shoulders. It wasn't her fault there hadn't been an immediate spark, the recognition of like to like. And now he was letting her down no matter what happened. He'd marry her while loving her sister or he'd turn her hopes to ash alongside his mother's.

The song ended. The servants filed out. Sophie nodded slightly at Franz.

It was time.

Elisabeth's gaze flickered up and caught on Franz's for just a moment. A single heartbeat. One beat of a sparrow's wings. And Franz knew.

He knew what he was going to do.

THIRTY-THREE

ELISABETH WAS FALLING APART, UNRAVELING FROM THE inside out. She felt strangely cold in the stiflingly hot ballroom, naked even in her seafoam jacket and modest dress, skirt billowing wide. The large comb holding back her braids was like an anchor weighing her down. How ironic it was to look like an angel and be trapped in hell. Waiting for the death knell on your dreams, waiting to have to pretend to be happy about it.

Franz was on his feet facing them all, and when Elisabeth finally looked at him—really looked at him—tears lodged in her throat. Tall and broad shouldered, that strong jaw, those kind eyes, the lips she'd felt the contours of. He looked—

Like *home*.

If only he weren't the emperor. If only he hadn't been intended for Helene. If only Elisabeth had stayed instead of running away last night. If only she'd felt she could.

He'd said he wanted her, and she had told him no. No when her heart was screaming yes. She'd chosen her sister's happiness, and it was the right thing to do—she knew it was right. And yet . . . how could the right thing feel so wrong? She felt the wrongness in her chest, her gut, the deepest parts of herself. She had asked him—no, told him—to break her heart, but now all she wanted was to take it back.

Franz raised his glass. "Thank you. Thank you all for being here."

Elisabeth stared hard at the tile floor, willing her heart to stop beating in her ears.

"I have something to announce," Franz continued, every word dragging them closer to the end.

If Elisabeth could only cover her ears, hide under the table like Spatz might. Helene reached for her hand, and Elisabeth hoped her sister couldn't tell how clammy it was. It was taking every ounce of her strength to maintain a calm exterior.

"I want to ask a young lady for her hand." Franz's voice jangled, nervous, and it grated against Elisabeth's skin—fingernails on chalkboards, the uneasy shudder of a fork hitting a tooth.

She closed her eyes. This was it.

"The Duchess of Bavaria."

Elisabeth's heart prepared itself for the blow.

"Elisabeth."

A beat. A collective intake of breath across the room. Her thoughts ran into a wall and stopped. She opened her eyes.

Had he said . . . ?

"Elisabeth."

He was looking at her, the corners of his eyes smile creased and questioning, his glass raised.

Elisabeth turned to Helene, and they both stared. Helene's face was white with shock. Elisabeth couldn't tell what her own expression was. Wonder? Relief? Guilt? Helene let go of Elisabeth's hand.

"No." Their mother was the first to gasp out a response.

"Congratulazioni!" Francesca beamed, not understanding the turn things had taken.

Out of the corner of Elisabeth's eye, she could see Maxi, anger slipping past his normal mask of indifference. Sophie's face was pure shock. Mother's eyes bulged.

It was Mother's face that told her it was real. Elisabeth hadn't heard wrong.

Franz was proposing to her. Not Helene. *Elisabeth*.

Her whole body lightened.

I want you. That's what he'd said the night before. And somehow Elisabeth's leaving hadn't ruined it, hadn't stopped him. It was a promise, unbreakable. He was the person she'd met in the quiet moments, her vulnerable moments, also unbreakable.

She'd thought this would be the end. But this was no ending.

This was a beginning.

They locked eyes, and she pictured what this would mean. Them together—him pressing his lips to the tender skin behind her ear, her kissing that jawline—lying side by side, fully exposed. Knowing each other in every way that word could mean.

Beside her, she heard the hitch in her sister's breath, the coming storm of tears.

Elisabeth stood frozen in the truth of it. The beauty and the disaster.

THIRTY-FOUR

FUTURE EMPRESS? ELISABETH? HELENE'S BODY CON-
tracted with the horror of it. She'd been planting seeds
and struggling through walks and finding her way back to
anticipation and contentment. She'd been fighting so hard for
this, working so tirelessly. And all the while her sister had been
stealing her future.

The cruelty of it was breathtaking. She hadn't known Sisi was
capable of it.

And now she—Helene—was standing in the most glorious
room, everything dazzling with six-tier cakes and handmade
sugar flowers, lights like fireflies dappling in from the sunshine
through gauzy curtains. And she had thought she was the most
beautiful thing in that room: all draped pink silk and dangling
pearl earrings and hope. *Hope*. She'd fought so hard for it. Fought
for it and still lost it in one fell swoop.

The room swam in her vision, and she knew she couldn't stay.
She couldn't bear the shame, standing there in elegant silks,

rejected. Her legs moved before her mind even knew she was leaving. She rushed past Franz without looking at him.

In the hall, she choked on her tears and started to run up the stairs.

"Helene, wait!" It was Sisi. Sister. Betrayer. Wielder of the knife that was sticking out of Helene's back.

"Please, Helene! I didn't know he was going to do that!"

Sisi's hand caught Helene's elbow, and Helene whirled, shame transforming into anger in the space of a single breath. "Don't touch me!"

Helene shook her head, took her sister in. For once, Sisi's hair was in place, her clothes unwrinkled. Her feet, in shoes, black with little heels. Helene could see them peeking out of the drapes of the deep-blue skirt. So simple. So much less beautiful than Helene's. How had this happened?

"You have to say no," Helene demanded.

Sisi only stared at her, her expression hurt. As if *she* should be the one hurt.

"Please," Helene whispered, though in her mind it was a scream. "Please."

Her anger melted into despair.

Sisi's face trembled, tears building in her eyes to match Helene's own.

Helene forged on. "Say *no*, Sisi, and everything can be fixed. It's not too late."

"It is too late, Néné."

Helene wanted to smack her. How dare she use her nickname at a time like this. How dare she remind her of the love between them. Sisi was the one who'd broken it—smashed it to pieces on the polished marble floor, ground it to dust under their heels.

"I've never felt anything like this." Sisi's voice was so tender it hurt. Salt rubbed in an open wound.

Helene's mouth dropped open, the incredulousness bitter on her tongue, hurt burning back to anger. "Did you sneak into his bed so he would choose you? Is that where you've been disappearing to?"

The blow landed—Sisi's face going white with shock—and Helene wanted to laugh. *Good. Feel one tiny portion of the shame I do.*

"Of course not." Sisi reached for her hand.

Helene pulled it away. "Then what? Why should he want *you*?"

Guilt needled at her heart, but she shoved it away. Sisi was childish and unruly. She'd refused every opportunity to be trained for a life like this. She didn't deserve it. Helene did. Helene had earned it.

The thoughts built up until Helene could no longer hold them back. "I meant what I said before. You will *never* be a good empress. You're going to ruin him."

It suddenly made horrible sense why Sisi had been so offended when Helene joked she wasn't cut out for the throne. It hadn't been theoretical to her.

And it hadn't been because Helene was leaving.

Helene's face folded in on itself again, tears cutting down her cheeks. She'd thought her sister would miss her! She'd thought she loved her. Instead, she'd been plotting against her the whole time. The hurt swallowed Helene whole. It hurt so much more than losing Franz. She'd lost her sister somewhere along the way, and there was no getting her back now. Helene's heart was a cliff, and she was hurtling off it.

Sisi followed Helene up the last steps and pulled her into the nearest room, messy with shed clothes, empty wineglasses, a mussed canopy bed. The cheerful yellow wallpaper mocked Helene; the cream carpet laughed at her.

"What are you doing?" Helene's voice was cutting. She didn't try to soften it.

"Explaining myself—somewhere other than a hallway where anyone might hear us."

Helene crossed her arms. "Then explain."

"We kept meeting by accident. In the garden when I was rescuing a bird. Once when I was just trying to stay cool from the heat. I didn't mean for this to happen."

Another wave of shame knocked Helene's heart over. Helene had been working so hard for love, and it had come to Sisi *by accident*. So easily. What a fool Helene had been the whole time. It was just like their childhood: Sisi so easily loved, Helene so invisible.

"He called me to his rooms last night."

Helene's head jerked up in surprise and horror.

"But I left, Helene! I left. I chose you. You have to believe me."

Sisi took Helene's ice-cold hands in her warm ones, but Helene pulled them back. She turned her head away from her sister, focused on the corner of a window thrown wide, the sun staring unbearably down.

"I never wanted to be empress. I only wanted—him."

The tenderness in Sisi's voice ended the conversation for Helene. She stormed past her sister, throwing the door open. Her voice was cold. "Don't follow me. Don't speak to me. Don't ever come near me again."

THIRTY-FIVE

T HE BALLROOM WAS EMPTY EXCEPT FOR FRANZ, Sophie, and Ludovika.

"Everyone out," Sophie had said simply, and their guests had all retreated. That was her power. The power Franz had challenged.

Challenged when Elisabeth's eyes flickered up to his and the nightmare and the doubts had simply fled. If anyone was going to wake with him in the throes of a nightmare, he wanted it to be her. If anyone was going to face the danger brewing in Habsburg at his side, he wanted it to be her.

He still wasn't sure if something as fragile and perfect as what was between them could survive this world. But he was ready to try.

His mother spoke quietly, firmly. "This woman will become the empress of the second-largest empire on earth. You've had fun with your little game, but now the joke is over."

Franz steadied his nerves, his voice. "It's not a joke, Mother."

Sophie's face was incredulous, her fists tight at her sides. "Franz, I thought long and hard about which woman is right for Habsburg. Remember that we are fulfilling a divine duty."

Franz took a deep breath. This was the real test. Him and Mother face-to-face. The guilt crashed against him in waves. She'd saved his life, and he was repaying her with trouble, with a choice that toppled her strategic plans.

"Helene is so well prepared, Your Majesty." Ludovika bowed as she spoke, stepped toward him. "She will be no trouble to you."

As if trouble was the problem here. As if he'd made this decision because he felt Helene was troublesome.

"Sisi is still so . . ." Ludovika was still speaking, and Franz turned to face her, eyes hard, daring her to say something negative about the woman he loved. She paused, choosing her last word with care: ". . . young."

He turned his attention back to his own mother and answered, pressing every bit of his will into the words and leaning into the strength, the certainty, that now stretched warm and definitive through his body—sparked into life by *her*. The girl with wild hair, bare feet, and a poem-draped heart.

"It's Elisabeth or no one."

Sophie's hands clenched. Franz knew she was angrier than she was letting on.

"I'll speak with her," she finally said, turning toward the door. Franz followed.

When they reached Elisabeth's room, a servant announced them, and Elisabeth rose from where she'd been sitting on the floor, skirt pooled around her like water. Franz's anxious heart calmed at the sight of her. He had to hold himself back from wrapping his arms around her and pressing her warmth, her brightness, to his chest.

Ludovika stepped to her first and Elisabeth straightened, anxiety flitting across her features in a way that made Franz want to protect her. "Tell your aunt this is all a big misunderstanding, Sisi. Tell her. Right now."

Sophie raised a hand. "Enough, Sister. I want to hear from Elisabeth herself." She stepped forward, searching Elisabeth's face. "Do you want to be Habsburg's empress?"

There was a long pause. Too long, in fact, and Franz's heart crept into his throat. After all this, he just needed her to say yes. *Say yes, Elisabeth.*

"Yes, I do."

Franz hadn't realized he'd been holding his breath, but now it came out in a rush. Elisabeth caught his eyes, and he held her gaze, held it like the precious thing it was. He could feel a smile overtaking his face.

She hadn't had time to say yes before, and it was stunning how that one word unknotted every knot in his soul, every uncertainty. That yes could move mountains, could face the darkness lapping at the gates of Habsburg. To think—he'd almost let a nightmare steal that certainty from him.

Sophie pursed her lips, her face severe. "And you know what it means to be empress? You know that you are committing not only to a marriage but also an empire?"

Elisabeth held his mother's gaze and nodded. "Yes."

"And you are willing to do the work it will take to make you a suitable ruler?"

"Yes."

His mother didn't ask any more questions, just stared at Sisi, but Franz knew that didn't mean she supported his choice. She was the type to bide her time. "The world," she'd once told him, "won't bend for you if you shout at it and cry. But it will bend if you wait long enough to find its weaknesses."

For now, his mother stepped aside and told her sister they should give the couple a moment alone. Without speaking, the older women turned and left the room.

Alone. Finally alone. And this time not in secret. Franz moved toward Elisabeth, reaching out his hand and running a thumb along her hairline, tracing the heart of her face, wondering at it. She was his. He was hers. They'd made it happen.

She closed her eyes at his touch, leaning into it. His thumb wandered to her lips, pressing lightly on the bottom one, watching them part. Franz leaned in, kissed her bottom lip gently. She smiled, and he kissed each corner of the smile, each happy crease at the corners of her eyes. And then they were lip to lip, and she was taking the kiss deeper, drinking him in. Franz ran his hands softly up the curve of the back of her neck, fingers pressing into her hair. Then he traced back down—from delicate shoulder to the gentle slope of her back, hips curving outward. He pulled her toward him, her fingers tracing his jawline. Then her arms wrapped around his neck, and she pressed her whole body to his. His rose up to meet it.

She was the one to pull away first, breathless, pressing hands to flushed cheeks. The happiness in her face shivered into something else: unease.

"What is it?" he asked.

Elisabeth shook her head, closed her eyes. "She will never forgive me."

Franz knew she meant Helene. He'd seen Helene's face, heard their raised voices in the hall. He pulled Elisabeth back into his arms, this time resting his chin on her head.

"Do you regret it?" His heart waited.

She wrapped her arms tighter around his torso. "No. I regret how hurt she is. But I could never regret *you*."

Franz smiled. He'd never felt so expansive, so powerful, so fully himself. The most incredible woman he'd ever met had fallen in love with him. For him, not his power. It took his breath away. She had so much to lose, and still she didn't regret it. Didn't regret him.

"What happens now?" she asked.

"Now you go home. And in a few months, we'll be married in Vienna."

Married. It was the first time he'd said the word aloud, and instead of feeling like a cage, it was wildness and freedom. Elisabeth wasn't another person he had to please; she was a person he *wanted* to please.

She pulled back, blinked at him in surprise. "A few *months*?"

He nodded.

A familiar spark lit in her eyes, teasing. "And what if I want to marry someone else by then?"

He touched those perfect lips again. "Lucky man, whoever he is."

She laughed then, fully, relaxing into herself. It was a laugh that released the lingering tensions of the moment, a laugh that banished thoughts of anyone else from the room.

She went up on her toes again and kissed him. He could think of nothing else but the featherlight softness of her skin, the groove of her collarbone under his fingers, his hands tangling in the laces of her dress, pulling. Her hands rose up to match his urgency, fumbling with the first button of his uniform, the second, the third. And then—

A knock. They both jumped.

A servant entered. "Your Royal Majesty, your mother sent me with a message."

Franz blinked at him.

"She said I'm not to leave you alone with the young lady anymore."

He knew Sophie would never allow them to be alone for more than a few minutes, but still the disappointment was as cold as ice.

He straightened his jacket, tucked a rogue hair behind Elisabeth's ear, and stepped back. "I'll see you soon."

She nodded, and he could feel her watching as he followed the servant out of the room.

In the hall, Maxi leaned against the wall, hands in pockets, head tilted. "I see you've gotten exactly what you want. Again. Even if you had to embrace scandal to do it. Bravo, brother. Never thought I'd live to see that."

Maxi's voice was amused, but his face was tight. It was the same look he'd worn when he found out about Louise. Jealousy—and pain. Franz wondered for a moment if it might be genuine. But no. He knew Maxi too well. His brother was, as always, just irritated that Franz had gotten what he wanted. Any win of Franz's was a loss of Maxi's.

Any other day, Maxi might have gotten to him, but today no biting words could touch Franz. He was too happy. Too relieved. That joy was armor against all things Maxi.

Franz smiled at his brother, mimicking Maxi's habit of tipping an invisible hat as he passed by and tucking away the knowledge that the fallout was coming. Another reason to keep Maxi in his sights.

THIRTY-SIX

A SINGLE DAY WAS ALL THEY HAD TO CELEBRATE, TO feel the weight lift off their shoulders, to brush fingers in the hall, fold themselves into curtains to steal a minute, two, of kissing, exploring.

Each momentary look, each touch, was an electric shock. A breathless flight from one world to the next. Elisabeth's whole body tingled with those touches, her skin alive with the heat of his. She'd never felt so aware of her own body: the curve of her breasts, the way fabric brushed against them as she moved. The sensitivity of an inner wrist, an inner thigh. A wanting that reached all the way inside her.

She pulled Franz behind a heavy curtain, and he kissed along her throat, the neckline of her dress, lips brushing bare skin that had never been touched before.

"Empress," he whispered.

"Not yet." She kissed her reply into his neck.

"If I rule the empire and you rule me, you already are."

She laughed, but the word scraped against her. It was the word, the title, that Helene had wanted. Helene who was now refusing to speak to her, look at her. How was it possible to be so perfectly happy and so unbearably sad all at once?

"I think I've lost my sister," she confessed, running a finger along his collar.

"She'll come around. She just needs time."

He didn't know Helene, though. Not really. He'd only met the polite, obedient version of her. Elisabeth knew all of her versions, including the one who could hold a grudge. It worried Elisabeth even through the thrill of each stolen moment with Franz.

She buried her face in his neck, breathed him in. The warmth, the steadiness of him nudged away the scraping fear, cleared her head. Perhaps he was right. Helene couldn't stay angry with her forever. They'd loved each other for too long, been allies almost since the day Elisabeth was born. These last few months wouldn't define their relationship; Elisabeth wouldn't let them. She couldn't expect Helene to tuck the hurt away just yet. It was too fresh. But give it a few days, a week, a month, and they'd find their way back to each other. Elisabeth would keep reaching toward her until Helene felt like reaching back.

The curtain suddenly swung away to reveal a pinch-faced Esterházy with a hand on one hip, her other fist clenched around the curtain. Her expression fell when she saw Franz, and her hand dropped from her hip as she curtsied. "My apologies, Your Majesty. The duchess's family is waiting for her."

Elisabeth supposed the woman must have thought she was hiding back there alone. She wondered what had given her away: A rogue toe poking out from the curtain? A too-loud whisper?

Elisabeth pulled back reluctantly. It would be months until they saw each other again. She almost laughed at how she'd longed for those months only hours ago, thinking they'd be a time for forgetting. Now they'd be a time of unbearable waiting. And Elisabeth had never been good at waiting.

Her whole body felt the loss of his as they stepped out from behind the curtain, stepped apart. He held on to the edges of her fingers even as she started to walk away.

When Elisabeth made it to Mother's rooms, Helene was standing by the window, resolutely staring across the grounds.

Mother flapped toward her, all anxious energy. "Sisi, the carriages are waiting. It's time."

Elisabeth sighed, her skin still aching for Franz's.

"We have to get going. Are you ready?" Her mother waved impatiently at her. "You, an empress. I never imagined."

Mother's voice was equal parts disappointment and wonder. She'd lost an opportunity for one daughter, gained the same for the other. Elisabeth knew it wasn't her ideal outcome, but it still made Mother important in the ways she always wanted.

"We have a lot of work ahead of us," she said. "Helene would have been prepared, but you . . ."

Helene flinched. Elisabeth started to reach toward her, to squeeze her hand, but Helene closed herself off, hugging her torso, and left the room.

Mother continued, "We'll have to start immediately. Tomorrow."

Elisabeth didn't answer. Instead, she followed her mother and sister out of the room, down the marble staircase, and into the high-ceilinged hall. She stopped at the bottom of the staircase, where a map of Habsburg stretched across the floor nearly wall to wall—intimidating, enormous, powerful. More than half of Europe. Soon to become her responsibility. Her duty. She shivered, the weight of it all starting to sink in.

She stepped back, watching her skirts swish across the map, her land. The weight of the duty she'd chosen was a fearsome thing. But there was excitement at its edges. Because with duty came the power to *change* things. The power to address injustice. The poverty she'd read about in books. The reasons the people had wanted Franz dead. Responsibility wasn't only a bridle on her adventures; it was a map to the future. A map to a better Habsburg.

She'd always thought she'd have to choose between obligation and her heart. But in the end, the choice hadn't been duty *or* love. It had been both or none. She'd chosen both, and she'd choose the same again.

"Sisi, are you listening to me?" Mother stood, hand on hip.

Elisabeth straightened, held her gaze. The complete dismissal of her preferred name scraped against her yet again. It was time for that to end. "Call me Elisabeth."

Mother didn't answer. She simply left the room, crossing from cool marble onto humid drive.

Elisabeth tore herself away from the map. She was delaying on purpose, pushing back against the journey. Hours upon hours stuffed into such a small space with Mother and Helene. Mother unbearable in her ambition, Helene unbearable in her pain. She wished she could stay there. Or go directly to Vienna. She wanted to climb back behind the curtain with Franz, to unbutton the fourth button on his uniform, the fifth, press a bare hand to bare chest and feel the heart beating there. She imagined her own would take up the same rhythm.

"Sisi!" Mother's voice echoed through the halls.

She'd dallied too long. She sighed and forced herself to leave the hall. But from behind her, through an open doorway, an unfamiliar voice reached out and hooked Elisabeth's attention. "Don't worry, Your Imperial Majesty, even the wildest grass bends."

Elisabeth stopped, strained to hear.

And then Sophie's voice—recognizable in its confidence, its sharpness—replied, "I'm not worried. Anything that doesn't bend will break."

Elisabeth went cold, the words sinking in, hard and dangerous. They were talking about her, she was sure of it. She was the wild grass, unbending. Elisabeth had hoped Sophie was on her side. But now her heart beat faster with the ominous words.

Elisabeth walked to the carriage, nerves fraying at the edges of her happiness. From an upper window, golden hair flashed in the sun—Franz. His eyes caught on hers.

Be careful, Franz. Take care of the heart I'm leaving behind with you.

She hoped they were strong enough to survive whatever was going to come next.

1854

PART II

THIRTY-SEVEN

HELENE WANTED TO BREAK SOMETHING. FRANZ HAD sent Sisi forty-four letters.

Forty-four.

Helene had received *one* letter before her supposed engagement—and only from Sophie. She laughed at her own foolishness. A man who'd been excited to meet her would have sent his own letters. A man ready for love would have sent forty-four of them.

Sometimes Helene tired of being angry. But then another letter would arrive, and her anger would spark anew. Each missive was a reminder of just how much she'd failed, of how her hard work had ended in disaster. Of how *easy* it had been for Sisi to get the thing Helene had spent months working and worrying and bending herself over backward for.

Helene had worked for love, and still it gave her the cold shoulder.

The only thing that made her feel better—if only for a few moments—was seeing Sisi's expression when Helene refused to pass the butter, answer a question, or go for a walk. The only power she had left was to hurt, and she couldn't stop using it.

Now Helene was standing in the hallway outside Sisi's door, preparing to steal the latest letter. To torture herself with it while Sisi sat through French conjugation downstairs.

Helene gently pushed the door open, cursing the familiar creak for betraying her intentions to the whole house. She stepped into Sisi's room and, as usual, it was like a storm had come through: the window was wide-open, spilling a scattering of leaves and feathers onto the sill and floor. Clothes in a dozen shades of black and white and eggplant lay in heaps on the rug. And the bed was a war zone—unmade and scattered with books, journals, poems, and the very thing Helene was looking for: the letters.

Not only Franz's letters but also a half-crafted reply of Sisi's. Helene could so rarely torment herself with those. They were sent off too quickly.

She lifted the paper from the bed, moving two other letters carelessly as she did. She always left things out of place whenever she took a letter, taking a pained sort of satisfaction in the knowledge that her whirlwind sister didn't keep track of where she'd placed things. If someone had gone through Helene's things, she'd know right away. Not a corner of a book was askew. That was supposed to be the kind of person an empress was—tidy, attentive, detailed.

Helene read the half-written letter, squeezing the paper hard between her fingers, pausing on the phrase "who could not love a man like you?" Her jaw tightened. She thought about ripping the letter up, throwing it away. Burying it in a grave with her own dreams. She knew Sisi wouldn't even notice. She would just think she'd mislaid the paper. Would never blame Helene. Or ask her. Sisi would simply rewrite it—like she had the last time Helene tore one up.

Helene lifted another crisp piece of paper. This one was from Franz—one Helene had already read. It was the first he'd signed with "your tailor." A private joke. A response to something Sisi had once written after struggling with a particularly challenging French lesson: "If only you were a tailor and not the emperor! I only wanted you, never all this!"

Helene hated how many of their letters she knew by heart. She hated that she thought about what she would have told him in her own letters: about her childhood as a rogue, stealing baked goods and spying on Father. Or about how she foraged the garden for toads, the satisfaction she felt when she saved one from the well they always fell into.

Downstairs, a heavy door closed, and Helene knew her time was almost up. She lifted one last letter—this one not from Franz, but Maxi.

His were the most interesting. He had surprisingly good penmanship. There was something elegant in the sprawl of it, the flourishes. Helene wondered if he'd practiced often on notes to ladies of the court. It would certainly match his reputation.

His letters were always about travel and horseback riding. Sisi had always wished to go to Greece, and Maxi's most recent letter had answered that wish with a promise: "Then to Greece we shall go. And to Hungary and Spain and France and Geneva as well."

Maxi's letters weren't romantic like Franz's, but Helene could read between the flourishes. The emperor's brother was in love with her sister, too. His dedication to writing Elisabeth and his promises of travel and adventure made it clear. The way he held back from flirting too shamelessly also made it clear; his respect for her sister belied his reputation entirely.

It was another cut in Helene's heart, another way in which Sisi was always beloved without trying, another arrow Helene tucked away in her own arsenal.

Helene slipped from Sisi's room before anyone caught her. Not that they would. No one—not even Mother—seemed to bother with her these days. She was the ghost child, the failure, the bomb ready to explode. Sisi tried to defuse her, but everyone else just stayed out of the blast radius.

The thought came with a wave of shame. Of course they all avoided her; Helene would have avoided herself if she could.

Helene had never disliked herself before, but now she did. All the time. Before, she'd been afraid that maybe she was too boring. Too nervous. But she had never *hated* herself. Not like now. Now she was a roiling boil of fury and shame, and if she looked too hard at her own heart, she'd be sick at what it had become.

Something was broken inside her, and she didn't know how to fix it.

THIRTY-EIGHT

ELISABETH WASN'T RIDING ANYWHERE SPECIFIC, BUT SHE found herself in the Bavarian hills again, cresting ridges, easing down hills to mirror-bright lakes. She wondered, not for the first time, at the lush greenness of her home. The audacity of it to have so many shades: deep evergreen, rich forest green, the frosty green of silver firs.

She slowed her horse and slipped from its back, pressing bare feet to dusty ridge, breathing in the wet-earth smell of the place. It was so rare that she could be alone these days, and she reveled in the feeling, the freedom, the space. No French conjugation. No table settings to memorize. Only her and the birds and—

Thoughts of him.

She was full of them, overflowing.

Elisabeth led her horse to a little grove, tied her at the edge, and slipped between the trunks, picturing Franz weaving his way toward her.

She closed her eyes and imagined his lips. What would it be like to kiss them again, this time without guilt tugging at the back of her mind, promises pushing her away? To feel his arms around her waist, his hands tangled in her hair? And then, perhaps, for his hand to find the laces of her dress, pulling them gently out and away, the cloth loosening, sliding free?

Pressing her back to rough tree bark and tilting her throat up toward the sun mottling through the leaves, she let her mind wander, unfettered, unguarded. Every day, she doled out memories of him to herself like chocolates: rare, sweet, savored slowly. The kiss behind the curtains. The way he'd held her when their mothers had left, pressed to his chest like she was a part of him. The thrill of lying on the floor next to him, staring into his eyes, almost touching. The vulnerable tremor in his voice as he shared his secrets.

Now, in the quiet space between the trees, she traced the shape of new memories she wanted to make. Her fingers slowly unfastening the buttons on his uniform, sliding over his broad shoulders, pushing off his jacket, his shirt. She pictured the skin of her chest against the skin of his. She would kiss along his jawline. He would kiss along her collarbone, then lower. Lower still—

She licked her lips, reveled in the images. She could almost feel his hands on her skin, coaxing goose bumps over neck, arms, stomach, breasts. He was a tinderbox, she a match. She reached her hand up into her skirts, pressed it to her upper thigh. She let her fingers explore the softness of her skin, slipping inside her, imagining her hand was not her own.

"I love you." She tested the words aloud: even more delicious than on paper.

Her whole body trembled as she pressed into herself, recalling a poem he'd written for her in one of his letters as she urged her body on toward a crescendo:

Sparrow, fly to me,
Fly to me,
Quickly—
I need you like a gull needs
The salt-drenched air under his wings.

She rode the wave of the poem, the rhythm of her fingers, and felt it all crash over her, pressing her body against rough bark, releasing her soul into the ether.

"Franz." She whispered it, then said it louder—no one around for miles to hear.

Soon, they would be together. Soon, the long silences and longer lessons of her stifling house would be behind her. And it would be his fingers tracing the curve of her breast, the tender skin of her inner thigh, the climax between her legs.

She felt drunk with the possibility of it, stretched out with the longing.

She only had to wait two more days.

THIRTY-NINE

LOVE WASN'T A WORD FRANZ HAD SAID TO ANY OTHER woman.

He'd had affairs, of course. Any young man did. He'd felt the urgency of want, the breathlessness of secret rendezvous. But this was something new. She was something new.

In his letters, he'd started writing the word. And now it was on the tip of his tongue, ready for letters to become conversations, laughter, whispers in the candlelight.

He was in his room writing another letter, the last he'd send before she was here. It might not even get to her in time, but he could picture the smile on her face if it did, if it sneaked up the day before she left.

She'd sent him another poem, and he reread it now:

> *You are my sun,*
> *O noble Achilles!*
> *O thrust your spear into my heart,*
> *Release me from a world that is*

Without you
So desolate, so empty
So vainly keeping me distant.

Franz pressed a hand to his scar, feeling the edges of it, the way his skin stretched tight there. The moment Elisabeth first traced her finger along it—perhaps that was the moment he'd fallen, the moment there was no turning back. He'd been fully clothed and yet more naked than he'd ever been with another person. She'd traced soul before body and every part of him had lit up with want. It was more intimate, more erotic, than sex.

He pictured her then: dark-blue dress against tanned skin, a constellation of freckles kissed along her arms by the sun, the curve of a breast rising and falling with her breath, the alluring curve of a smile always hinted at. And those eyes—so deep you could hold your breath forever and never reach their end.

He imagined what he'd do if she was here now. How he'd unlace each bow on her dress, revealing her skin inch by inch, kissing each new revelation into his memory. He'd trace each perfect curve of her, let his hands linger where waist met hip. He'd kiss her navel, the curve of her stomach.

She would arch her back then, sweetness disappearing into want—bold, changed, a fierce night creature come to claim his soul. He'd give it to her with open hands.

Over and over in her letters, she had called him strong, called him her dreamer. His heart swelled with it, how much she saw through him and loved what she saw. She'd also encouraged him to stand by his heart. It wasn't something anyone else had ever told him to do. They all had their opinions. They all wanted to offer him guidance. But she was the first to say that his own heart was strong enough, right enough, smart enough to find the way.

Not for the first time, Franz wished Habsburg had a railroad. He'd always wanted to build one, but his separation from Elisabeth had made him realize just how urgent it was, just how many problems a railway could solve. He'd spent countless hours irritated that he couldn't get to her. A railroad would solve that pain for every other man. Not to mention that it would encourage business, trade, and connect people to faraway family. More important: it would connect cities to more food, more opportunity. The elegance of the solution took his breath away.

A knock sounded on the door, making him jump. And then his mother swooped into the room, stoic and impressive as always.

"Mother." Franz stood and motioned for her to sit on the nearby couch.

As he lowered himself into a chair across from her, she started without preamble. "I must ask you once more to reconsider your choice. It's not too late; you still have two days."

When he didn't answer, she continued. "I must remind you that Elisabeth is"—Sophie searched for a word, waving her fingers through air—"unpredictable. Court requires politeness and gentility. Neither word describes the younger duchess."

She was right, of course: Elisabeth was many things, but Franz would not describe her as demure, polite. But who was to say that those were the only things that could work at court? Just because unpredictable people had been kept out didn't mean they couldn't survive there—even thrive.

Sophie and Franz had had this conversation more than once since returning to Vienna. But each time his mother reiterated her objections, Franz found them easier to dismiss. The more Elisabeth's letters piled up, the less his guilt or fear could break through the bond they'd built.

Franz's voice was comfortable when he answered. "That's ironic given how thrilled you were when I invited Maxi to the capital. He's the very definition of unpredictable."

Sophie shook her head slightly. "But he's a man, darling. There are more ways to be a man at court than to be a woman."

Franz hadn't thought about it quite like that before, but she was right. The women at court fell into a few well-defined categories. He'd never realized that maybe they *had to*. The thought chafed at him.

"You're saying we haven't given women the chance to be anything else at court. So why not start now?"

Sophie redirected the conversation. "Franz, you have always been a sensible man. Even as a child, you were the smartest, the most self-controlled of your brothers. You always made the hard choices, the good choices. And you've grown into the exact man you needed to be to rule this empire."

She paused. "Please, darling, see reason. There's still time to call this off. To be sensible. Is the girl beautiful? Yes, of course. She's charming and draws all eyes in the room. But those are not the qualities you need in an empress."

Franz closed his eyes slowly, opened them again. It was a shame that Mother did not approve, did not want Elisabeth for a daughter-in-law. But he was a new man now, one who let his heart and mind guide him together, not separately. He would not cut one part of himself off from another.

"Mother, you're going to have to accept this." He stood from his chair and motioned for Sophie to leave. "The empress will be here soon."

T HE CARRIAGES STOPPED ON A TREE-LINED LANE, FOREST
stretching around them like a rich green blanket. The
slightest hint of autumn colors had come early, turning
the edges of the forest lightly gold. Elisabeth could feel the
brightness in her very soul, pulling her toward Vienna.

She'd told the carriages to stop so that she could relieve herself, but really she just wanted to walk into the woods for a moment, breathe in the earthy, leafy smell, and escape. Exiting the
carriage had been a relief, like a deep breath after being
underwater.

The carriage with Helene and Mother in it felt as small as a
matchbox—full of disappointed hopes and razor blade silences. Spatz was also there but was wisely keeping silent. And
the carriage with her father carried its own disappointments:
that his wild child was becoming someone else. She'd told him
it wasn't so, but his disbelief sat heavy in between their jokes.
His uncharacteristic seriousness prodded at her comfort. She
wished he could be her ally always, not just when it suited him.

Her feet crunched over fallen leaves and rough stones until she couldn't see the carriages anymore, couldn't hear the hushed conversation in one or her father banging around looking for a cigar in the other. She pressed her back against a pine, leaned her head back, and closed her eyes. She wished they were in Vienna already, wished that she were in this grove with Franz, a story from his childhood on his lips, his letters turned to real conversation.

Each one had made her love him even more. His most recent story was about the time he'd tried to free all the horses in the stable at Bad Ischl when he was ten years old. He'd gotten it into his head that horses deserved to run wild, and he'd managed to free a good half dozen before one of the stable hands caught on. It took a whole day for them to corral the last two obstinate mares who'd managed to get halfway up a steep mountain trail.

He said he'd never seen his mother so furious. Not because of the horses. But because there was an important delegation in town and Franz had made Habsburg look ridiculous. It was funny now, but he'd felt awful then. Hot with shame for doing the wrong thing and hotter still when Sophie chastised him for crying.

"Will you hurry up?" Papa's voice traveled through the trees, shattering the moment.

She'd almost forgotten where she was.

She smoothed a hand across her skirts and pushed away from the pine. When she emerged from the trees, Papa was leaning out the carriage window, a cigar held lazily between two fingers. He took a puff. "That was probably the last time you'll piss in the woods."

"Papa, please." She raised an eyebrow. "You mean, it was the last time you'll piss in the woods, *Your Majesty*." He had jokes; she had better ones.

He grinned. "That's my girl."

Elisabeth rejoined him in the carriage, folded herself into the seat opposite, and held out a hand for a cigar. The carriage lurched to life, on their way again. She shook her shoulders to dislodge some of the excitement.

She opened and closed her hand, palm up, in front of Father and he chortled, then placed a cigar in her palm.

"Don't tell your mother."

She gave him a look. "Since when do you have to tell me that?"

"Since you're *Your Majesty* now. I don't know how an empress behaves around her mother."

Elisabeth snorted. "I'm still me."

"Ah, but for how long?"

She furrowed her brow. The doubts and disappointments slipped back in.

"Forever," she said, holding eye contact, willing him to believe and take comfort in her resolve.

He handed her the matches. "Do me a favor."

She raised an eyebrow, inviting him to go on.

"At court, don't throw yourself at immovable problems like you usually do. Take care of yourself. Bend when you need to bend."

Elisabeth let out a long breath. She couldn't promise that. In fact, she'd made the exact opposite promise to herself every day for the last two months: she would love Franz, embrace duty, *and* stay herself. She would not forsake any one of those things.

"Don't worry, Papa. Franz knows who I am." She smiled reassuringly.

"And this"—he motioned out the window at the palace, slowly coming into sight as they emerged from the tree line—"Is this who you are?"

"Part of who I am, yes. Part of what I've chosen." She inhaled the sweet smoke, exhaled it slowly.

"Enjoy it while you can." He motioned to her cigar. "I imagine your future mother-in-law won't approve of your smoking."

"Disapproval has never stopped me before."

"Ah, but I hear she's a more formidable foe than your mother."

Formidable indeed. Elisabeth could still hear those needle-sharp words, uttered through a nearly closed door: *Anything that doesn't bend will break.* Had Sophie meant her to hear them? In any case, she was sure it meant something more than giving up smoking.

But she kept that to herself, smiling at her father. "Let me worry about that, Papa. You just worry about not getting yourself into trouble with the archduchess."

"No promises." He wiggled his eyebrows, mood lighter. Contrary to what her mother thought, travel tended to make him happier, less sharp.

Elisabeth shook her head fondly. It was like that first carriage ride with Helene, only with roles reversed: she the scolding one, Papa the one about to make mischief at court.

FORTY-ONE

HELENE'S HURT WAS A SPILLED GLASS, SOAKING through her, spreading so much farther than she'd realized. She hadn't scrubbed it out right away, and now it had set—a deep red stain on her soul. Deep and dark as the forest stretching outside the windows of the carriage as they jostled uncomfortably toward Vienna. Toward Sisi's future.

The future that should have been Helene's.

She'd thought she'd be calmer by the time they left Bavaria for the wedding, but instead her resentment had kept growing, spreading, setting. Until all she could see was the stain of it, all she could feel was the fury. She'd been told her whole life that if she behaved, good things would come to her. Now that it turned out to be a lie, she couldn't scrub the rage out.

"Is this how it will be with you now?" Mother broke through Helene's thoughts, her voice pinched with exasperation.

"How what will be?" Helene tore her eyes from the trees and leaned back against the seat to face Mother.

The look on Mother's face said *you know what*, but she explained herself anyway. "I've been staring at your unhappy fish
face for months. I've been patient, but now I've had enough.
Get over it. I did."

The words were splinters, lodging under Helene's skin. From
the one person who should be her ally! It wasn't fair. Mother
was the one who'd made her believe she was doing the right
thing, who'd dragged her through months of preparation, who'd
told her she would be rewarded for it.

"It wasn't easy for me either," Mother said, pointing a finger
at Helene. "By God, it wasn't. The preparations, the correspondence, the dowry. All without the help of any other person in
the house!"

Angry tears beaded at the corners of Helene's eyes. The failure never stopped needling. The loss never shrank.

Mother's tone went softer than usual. "It's fine, sweetheart.
Don't cry." She reached a hand across the carriage and patted
Helene's knee. "Think of it this way: you'll be there to take care
of me when I'm old. Sisi would have killed me prematurely."

Another splinter. Another hurt to add to the pile. Her
mother saw this as the end of Helene's hopes. She thought that
because one man, one emperor, didn't love Helene, no one else
ever would. Helene sat in the astonishing hurt of it.

Sometimes Helene wanted to talk to Sisi about it, to let her
joke the fury, the pain, into something smaller and more man-
ageable. She knew Sisi could do that; it was her magic power,
always had been. But every time the thought occurred, her
heart threw up a wall. *No*, it screamed. The source of the hurt
couldn't be the balm for it. And Helene would punish Sisi for

what she'd done, even if she was punishing herself at the same time.

The women rode the rest of the way to the palace in silence, Helene locking up her feelings, closing them off. Her face was stone, her heart too.

FORTY-TWO

FRANZ WAS WIDE-AWAKE AT THE BREAK OF DAWN, HIS body humming with anticipation. Today was the day, the *day, the* day. She'd arrive any minute. He tugged at his collar, nerves tangling up with the excitement in his stomach.

The need to move—to release some of the skittering anxiety under his skin—drove him out to his usual fencing spot, away from the palace, next to the wood. Now he stood in his fencing gear, facing off with Maxi—this time knowingly.

"You're awake about ten hours early." Franz settled into his fencing stance.

"You're mistaken, Brother. I haven't gone to bed yet." Maxi flourished his rapier.

Franz had invited his brother to join him—an attempt to make peace—but hadn't imagined Maxi would actually show up at this time of day. It was especially unfortunate because Franz had just received a long-delayed letter of Elisabeth's. It should have made him happy—her letters always did—but this one had been a gut punch. She'd mentioned that Maxi had been writing to her. Information Franz had not known before.

And Elisabeth might have thought that was innocent, but Franz knew his rapscallion of a brother better than that. If Maxi was writing to Elisabeth, Maxi was flirting with Elisabeth. Or trying to undermine Franz in some way. Or—even more likely—both.

Franz wished he could see the letters, parse out their exact meanings, the exact ways Maxi was planning to hurt him.

The thought made his blood boil, and he lunged toward his brother, starting the match. They fenced. Forward, back, back, forward: even through Franz's irritation, the familiar rhythm was a balm. His breathing found a pattern with his feet.

Maxi caught him with the first touch. "You're off your game today."

Franz ignored him.

"Ah, yes, I forgot. Your bride arrives today. How long do you think it'll be before you ruin her?"

Franz's stomach tightened. "In what way would I ruin her?"

A laugh filtered through Maxi's mask. "In every way. She's a butterfly and you're putting her in a jar, Franz. She'll suffocate."

"What would you know about it?"

"Everything. I'm in the same jar, half dead already." Maxi's tone was sharp, a blade's edge disguised as a joke.

"Please, you've got more freedom than anyone at court, including me." Franz went in for the kill, but Maxi blocked him. Thrust, parry. Thrust, parry.

"I've got nothing."

"That's both dramatic and untrue, Maxi." Franz frowned, blinking sweat out of his eyes under his mask. Maxi found an opening: two touches.

Maxi spoke again, his voice strained. "You can still stop this."

"You sound like Mother."

"So, you're going to wreck her for your own selfish feelings?"

Anger rose in Franz's throat, but he didn't answer. Was Maxi jealous again? It was hard to tell. Maxi had joked about marrying Elisabeth back at Bad Ischl. He'd made sly comments about her along the way. He'd flirted—shamelessly. And now Franz knew he'd been writing her letters. But then again, Maxi *always* flirted shamelessly. And he had a history of wanting what Franz wanted—just because Franz wanted it.

Frustration bunched in Franz's muscles, and he pushed harder, abandoning his form and footwork as he attacked, blocked, attacked again. The touches built up, the rapiers smacked together with a metallic shudder shaking its way up Franz's arm every time.

And then Maxi was inside his defenses again, the final touch denting the uniform at the center of Franz's chest.

"Match." Franz could hear Maxi's grin even through the mask. "I guess you don't *always* get what you want."

Franz pulled his own mask off, thrust out a hand to shake. Trying—yet again—to be the bigger man.

Never beholden to such attempts himself, Maxi swatted Franz's hand away with his rapier, turned, and marched toward the palace. Franz watched him go, wishing the fencing match had made him less unsettled instead of more.

The irritation of his match with Maxi and the news about the letters couldn't stand up to the thrill of the day. By the time

Franz returned to his rooms, his nerves were the butterfly kind. Elisabeth was on her way, drawing closer to him every second. His excitement was an almost physical thing, lifting him so high he could barely feel his feet touch the floor.

He took out the braid of Puck's hair—her precious gift, sent to him in her final letter. "To think of me until I get to you." She had sent a poem too:

> Cheerfully,
> I blow the sea air on you,
> In the center of your heart;
> Very soon then,
> Forget
> The world together with its pains.

He would forget. Today was the perfect day to do so. To forget Maxi's jabs and Mother's disapproval. To start anew.

Theo interrupted his thoughts with a cough, and Franz turned to face him. "Your Majesty, it's the countess again. Should I take care of it?"

Franz sighed. There were many countesses at court, but only one of relevance: Louise. Franz's former mistress, who—as it turned out—was actually in love with him.

He'd never meant to break her heart. And yet the wreckage lay in his hands.

"Let her in." He stowed Puck's hair in a little box in the oak writing desk, then turned as Louise walked in.

She was beautiful, as always, but this time Franz felt no desire, no draw. Nothing for her figure, cinched at the waist with a bodice like green scales. Nothing for the gold threads in her hair, accentuated by a black coat and a black hat to match. Nothing for her bright blue eyes, the delicate neck, the flutter of breath at the hollow of her throat.

If anything, he felt pity. She was a woman in mourning and looked the part, her clothes a dark cloud, her earrings shaped like battle-axes to ward off evil. The cheerfulness of his rooms—with their green-and-gold wallpaper, light wooden floors, the blue ceiling playful with baby angels—only made her look more unhappy.

"My emperor." Her voice was still hopeful, and it scraped against him. He'd called it off as soon as he'd returned to Vienna, his heart only Elisabeth's. And yet the months had done nothing to move Louise along. She wore her heartbreak like a gown.

"Countess, it's not a good time." He had nothing else to give her. He'd tried kindness. He'd tried explaining himself. And yet here she was, persistent.

"You haven't answered my letters."

"There wasn't a reason to. It's over. It's been over."

"You think you can simply discard me?"

As if it had been that easy. As if Louise had *allowed* it to be that easy.

Falling in love with Elisabeth had been easy. But Louise was used to getting what she wanted and avoiding her—with her heartsick looks and veiled threats about revealing their dalliance—*that* had been impossible.

"I made you a generous offer." He said it knowing it wasn't what she wanted. But it was how things were done. A way to say sorry, to acknowledge the depth of her regard.

She reached out and touched his hand with her gloved one. "You said you needed me."

It hadn't been a lie then. But it would be now. He wished she could understand that.

"Your Majesty." Theo interrupted and Louise pulled her hand away, lowering her gaze to the diamond-patterned floor. "The imperial bride will arrive soon."

Franz nodded, caught Louise's eye, and hoped that this time she would understand that his heart was no longer available. It was taken, consumed, fully and wholly someone else's.

"Countess, it's over." He hoped she felt the finality of it. And though he had never meant to make her cry, he could see the tears would come again as soon as she was out of sight. He hated how much it made him feel like Maxi—using people, discarding them once finished.

As she left, he turned back to the window, willing Elisabeth's carriage to appear. His soul reached for her. All he wanted was to be with her and to forget the world and its pains. The war looming over them like a toxic cloud. It was taking all of his strength to stand against it, to see something grander, less destructive for Habsburg.

He stared over the expansive grounds, touched his scar lightly. Wished he could banish the worries about war just for one day and dedicate himself to *joy* instead. To the ease of being with Elisabeth. And the delight of planning good things for Habsburg: roads and rails, commerce, business.

Franz turned back to his desk and lifted the wedding announcement from atop a pile of letters. He held it up in the light.

The photo was her—and yet not how he knew her. The rich brown hair, dark features, gently sloping hips: they were all there. But instead of the usual joke at the corner of her mouth, there was a serious slant. Instead of curls falling loose, her hair was immaculate: a perfect weave of braids, not a hair out of place. And the skirts. They were twice the normal size, a cream puff in fabric form. No longer the carefree Duchess of Bavaria, but Empress Elisabeth of Habsburg.

A knock on the door announced his mother's arrival, her sleek orange-and-black dress advertising the latest fashion at court.

Franz waved the announcement vaguely in her direction. Sophie had handled all the wedding arrangements, and he hadn't seen the wedding notice until that morning. "She doesn't look like this, Mother."

"Not yet." Sophie's tone was noncommittal, her version of waving the flag of surrender. She wouldn't go as far as to actively support his choice, but she would no longer fight him. Still, he wished for more—not just her surrender but her excitement. Her love. Elisabeth was smart, observant, empathic. She was life itself, a seed bursting into flower, a new star appearing in the sky. He wanted his mother to see it too.

He reached for his mother's hand and squeezed it. "She will make a wonderful empress, you'll see. She brought me to life; she'll do the same for Habsburg."

"I have no doubt." She released his hand, patted it, still neutral.

He would have to settle for her surrender. For now. But Elisabeth would charm his mother in time. He was sure.

FORTY-THREE

THE PALACE GATE WAS MOBBED WITH PEOPLE JOSTLING excitedly for a view of Elisabeth—their future empress. Nothing so exciting had happened in Vienna in years. Not since Luzi was born. Now, as the carriage rattled toward the gates, mothers bounced babies on their hips. Fathers swung small children onto their shoulders for a better look over the crowd. Older children darted through or clung to a forest of legs.

"Empress!" they shouted. "Elisabeth!"

Elisabeth's breath caught in her chest. This was all for her? For her arrival?

"This is insanity." She said the words with wonder, waving tentatively from the carriage window, and the crowd went wild with applause.

"Indeed, Your Majesty." Father affected a joking bow at her.

The crowd slowed the carriage's progress, and Elisabeth impulsively reached through the window toward them, shaking hands and squeezing fingers as she rode past. Their hands large and small, white and brown, soft and calloused, old and young, dirty and scrubbed clean. A symphony of people, a reflection of Vienna—her new home.

"Make way!" She heard the bodyguards shouting ahead of the carriages, as they roughly shoved people back. She frowned, wished the guards would be gentler. This crowd was happy—not dangerous.

As the crowd parted, Elisabeth's eyes were drawn beyond it. It was her first real glimpse of the palace, and her heart leapt into her throat. The enormity, the glamor—it was as awe-inspiring as the map of Habsburg on the Kaiservilla's marble floor. She'd been told the palace housed five thousand people, but she hadn't really understood what that would look like, how large it had to be to hold so many.

It was a city unto itself—an estate of multiple buildings, each of them several stories tall, their green and red rooftops sloping in every direction. An enormous rectangular fountain, all clean lines and sparkling water, beckoned them toward the grand two-story archway leading to the central building.

"This is incredible." Elisabeth pressed her face to the window.

Father's smile was surprisingly sad, still snagged on his worries. "You know, these people believe God himself chose them." He meant it as a slight and a warning not to get swept up in the luxury and self-importance of it all.

"You know I don't believe that," she answered, reassuring.

"The imperial family are just like you and me: just as sad, just as broken, just as hungry."

"Just as loving?" She tried to pull him from whatever shadowy mood had struck him.

"I'm less certain about that one."

It was clear that she wouldn't tempt him from his mood, so Elisabeth turned and focused on the architecture of the main building, even more grand as its intricacies were revealed with every progression of the carriage: reliefs of swords and crests, stone statues of people in various states of armor or undress, garlands, circles, lines. A person could spend their whole life studying those facades and never memorize their every contour.

And then the palace lost her attention entirely, because of the people arranged in front of the doorway.

Sophie. Maxi. Ludwig.

Franz.

He stood tall, strong, even more handsome than she remembered. Her heart nearly flew from her chest and went to him. God, had his eyes always been that dark, that deep? How had she forgotten the contours of his eyebrows, the delicacy of those eyelashes? She drank him in, let her mind wander back to her daydreams, her hand clutching her thigh—a stand-in for his.

It would be his hand soon. So very soon.

Her mouth went dry, her heart so loud she could hear nothing else.

Franz didn't even wait for the carriage to come to a full stop before he rushed toward her, opening the door and reaching in to take her hand. As his hand touched hers, she gasped. It was like that first touch: his fingers on her neck, placing Puck's braid so gently on her shoulder. Her whole body warmed, sizzled.

Elisabeth knew what was expected now. Her mother had drilled it into her: present herself to Sophie, curtsy, press her forehead to the archduchess's extended hand. No wild abandon. Everything according to tradition. But all of it seemed so foolish now. How could she not throw herself straight into her beloved's arms? She thought of her father's worries and smiled to herself. *Watch this, Father, and then tell me I'm lost.*

She stepped out of the carriage, wrapped a hand around the back of Franz's neck, and leaned in to kiss him. She knew she'd disappear into the joy of it, everything but him forgotten. Palace, royals, scandalized nobility—all vanished in the perfection of the moment.

But he pulled back, more restrained than she could be. In place of a kiss, he lifted her hand and pressed his lips to it—and that was enough. For now. After months of only letters, Elisabeth's skin soaked the warmth of him in like parched land in a rainstorm.

This was it. She was there, and he was there, and they were finally together. Engaged. This time Elisabeth would be the one wandering through gardens with Franz, mothers looking on in the distance. She would be the one to sit beside him at meals. The one to make him laugh.

Her happiness was perfect in that moment. Even after months of Mother's ominous proclamations about how hard it would be to be empress, even with Helene's stubborn silences.

None of that mattered.

Elisabeth had chosen her path and the boyish grin on Franz's face settled her heart. She had found her great love, and she'd fight for it if necessary.

HELENE'S HEART WAS A FORTRESS, HURT LOCKED UP inside, anger standing sentry.

She'd watched through the carriage window as Sisi flew from her own carriage and into Franz's arms. He stopped her from kissing him—a scandal—but they held hands until the last possible second, fingers still reaching for each other even as they stepped away. It made Helene feel exposed, rubbed raw. Her resentment burned brighter.

Her very bones ached with the failure of it, watching how easily love had come to them and not her. Thinking about how hard she'd tried and how little it mattered. How deep the betrayal had cut. She could feel everyone staring at her as she stepped from her own carriage. She straightened her spine, steeled her eyes. *Stare all you want*, she dared them all silently. *Your uncharitable thoughts can't break through.*

Mother emerged behind her, and Sophie embraced her warmly. "Sister, so good to see you." That made Helene angry too. Mother had Sophie; Sisi had Franz. Who would be happy to see Helene? No one. Helene had gone from hopeful to invisible in the space of a single day. She wished, not for the first time, that Mother had let her stay home.

After their greetings, Sophie—every inch as regal as Helene remembered—led her, Sisi, and their mother briskly through the palace. Sophie's necklace chimed as she walked: five golden orbs hanging from black cord. The kind of necklace Helene had hoped to own and now never would.

Papa had wandered vaguely toward a fountain with Spatz in tow, and a servant was dispatched to bring them along whenever they were ready. Now the women's footsteps echoed through the marble hallways. Life-size stone cherub statues held up large golden lamps, intricate and frozen in motion, so real that Helene felt they might reach out and touch her.

They made her want to break something.

This could have been her home. She could have belonged to the high ceilings, the lemon-cream columns, the intricate purple marble doorway, the swirling, intertwining lines of relief sculpture at the base of each column. She'd have commanded the endless halls, the wood-trimmed rooms beyond whimsically painted doors in blues and pinks and greens.

Helene barely heard the conversation ahead of her. Sophie was instructing Sisi already. Something about a glass carriage, a church, a waltz. Sisi would hate all of it: A glass carriage drawing every eye to her. A ceremony in front of hundreds of noblemen and dukes and countesses. Formal waltzes where she'd be required to—crime of all crimes—wear shoes.

Helene's heart pushed and pulled in her chest, part of it reaching toward her sister, knowing that Sisi must be overwhelmed by it all. The other part drawing back: Sisi had chosen—stolen—this life for herself. Helene was tired of being the bigger person; she kept her hand resolutely at her side, clutched her skirt to make sure it didn't betray her with a reassuring touch on Sisi's arm.

Sophie was motioning to several servants who waited silently at the top of the stairs. "Here we are. Now, please show Their Highnesses the new rose gardens."

She took Sisi by the elbow, waving Helene and Mother away. They were to follow the servants. Helene tucked away her anger. She couldn't tell which would have been worse: being denied the private tour with Sophie or being forced to take it knowing it wasn't for her.

"Néné. Wait." It was Sisi this time, her voice pleading, and oh, how Helene's feelings shifted. Where she'd resented being sent away only seconds ago, now she relished it. Relished how alone it left her sister. If Sisi needed Helene's help, she should have thought about that before ruining her life.

"It's *Helene*." She turned resolutely away and marched on, following the servants. And it wasn't until she was around the corner, down the diamond-patterned hall, that her anger dimmed. Shame—her new unshakable friend—rose up to drown it out.

Helene, is this really who you want to be? she asked herself silently.

It wasn't. It made her feel—

Out of control. A screaming, thundering avalanche. A destructive, dangerous thing that couldn't stop itself.

She kept walking, shoes tapping out a too-fast rhythm on the marble floors, hating herself more with every step.

FORTY-FIVE

E LISABETH WATCHED HELENE GO, HER WHOLE HEART A bruise. It wasn't even about Elisabeth anymore; now she was just concerned that Helene would never be the same again. That she—Elisabeth—had broken something that couldn't be mended. Helene's fury was a fire and Elisabeth worried she'd burn herself down to ash.

Where was the Helene who'd always saved her? The Helene who'd sacrificed the soles of her feet to sticks and thorns to chase Sisi down the river? The Helene who'd hidden her in a trunk when the trouser-unbuttoning count had come calling? Would she never see her again?

"She won't talk to me anymore. Not a word." Elisabeth's voice was smaller than usual.

Sophie reached across her then, taking her shoulder and gently guiding her down the ornate hall.

"We seek forgiveness from God alone, Elisabeth," she said simply. "Anything else is vanity. Not to mention a waste of time."

Elisabeth was strangely comforted, not by the words but by Sophie's tone. There was something warm in it. Something that made Elisabeth feel that perhaps she'd misread what she'd heard before they left Bad Ischl. Perhaps Sophie could be her ally.

She and Sophie were alike in some ways. Or at least Elisabeth hoped they were. Sophie was bold and original, not diminished by court but confidently ruling it. Not losing herself to duty but bending it around herself. It was what Elisabeth aspired to be; she hoped Sophie could teach her how.

Sophie led her to a set of double doors and pushed them open.

"Your rooms," she said with a flourish.

Wonder and awe rose up, nudging Elisabeth's worries about Helene to the back of her mind. The rooms were perfect. In the outer room, blue wallpaper was trimmed with a mossy green that reminded her of forest walks back home. Paintings of startled deer and birds about to take flight graced the walls, hung between brass sconces. The green-and-blue Persian rug underfoot was thick and soft, like walking over a freshly laid flower bed. A gauzy curtain lifted itself gently in the breeze, revealing a garden view, all yellowing leaves and curling green vines.

Elisabeth was surprised to find that the room was also full of women—every one of them dressed in a similar style, with blouses buttoned up the neck, corsets trimmed in at the waist, skirts billowing out and brushing the ground. They curtsied in unison.

The only one she recognized was thin-faced, long-necked Esterházy in her gray jacket and beige high-necked blouse. She was smiling, but still she managed to look unhappy.

Esterházy introduced each lady, but there were too many details to remember. They were harpists and embroiderers, linguists, readers. From Italy and Romania, Germany and France. Worry knocked at Elisabeth's heart when she learned sour, humorless Esterházy was to be her guide to the court, and the rest of these women were tasked with being at her side every minute of every day.

"And this is the Countess Leontine von Apafi of Transylvania, Your Majesty," said Esterházy, now thankfully at the end of the lineup. "She is proficient in French and outstanding at reading aloud."

Elisabeth's interest piqued. Another reader—perhaps this was a person she could be friends with. The first name she could commit to memory.

"I brought my favorite books with me," Elisabeth said excitedly. "Do you know *Werther*?"

Nervous laughter rippled through the group, and Sophie and Esterházy exchanged a knowing look. Leontine simply bowed.

Unsure why her question hadn't inspired an answer, Elisabeth reached forward to shake the girl's hand. "I'm Elisabeth."

Esterházy gasped, and Elisabeth pulled her hand back, almost involuntarily, her heart contracting. She'd done something wrong—but what?

"Your Royal Highness!" Esterházy fluttered her hands to her breastbone in dismay. "You must not touch! And, please, no first names."

Elisabeth was taken aback. No one had told her about that particular rule. She'd had her fill of others: this fork for one thing and not another, this type of bow for one noble and not another. Elisabeth tried to smile through the ridiculousness, nodding at Esterházy to end the lecture.

The next stop on the tour was Elisabeth's dressing room— the largest, brightest dressing room in the whole world, as far as she could tell. Dozens of gowns in rich colors and intricate patterns hung on petite dress forms. There were cream-colored jackets with intricate pink embroidery, teal gowns that swept out at the waist like a raging sea, a skirt as yellow as a sunbeam. Half a dozen other people were in the room, and she was quickly introduced: two seamstresses, four lady's maids. Six more names she would struggle to remember. Elisabeth's chest tightened— excitement at war with the staggering scope of it all, the thought of needing so many people for such a small thing as dressing herself.

"These are the latest fashions from Paris, Saint Petersburg, Milan. I chose everything for you myself." Sophie ran her hands along the dresses as she spoke.

The other women spread out through the room, admiring lace cuffs and puffed sleeves, yards of fabrics in rich red, snow white, deep-sea blue. Elisabeth's eyes were drawn to where two rows of shoes stretched along in an endless line of soft orange, soothing purple, and a hundred other shades. There must have been more than a hundred pairs. Enough shoes for every woman here to take ten.

"So many." It was overwhelming.

"An empress can never wear the same shoes twice," Esterházy explained. "They will be thrown away at the end of each day."

The pride in her voice turned Elisabeth's stomach. "Thrown away? But that's such a waste."

Her mind drifted back to the people at the gates. Some had been barefoot, many threadbare. Why should she—who never loved shoes to begin with—throw away perfectly good pairs? Not to mention that new shoes pinched and rubbed and scraped at the skin. If she had to wear shoes, she wanted her well-worn riding boots or the traveling shoes that had bent themselves to the will of her feet already.

"It's tradition, Your Highness." Esterházy shrugged.

The casualness of the gesture chafed at Elisabeth like each of these new shoes inevitably would. Elisabeth had only been in the palace for a couple of hours and already it was overwhelming. She'd already memorized so many foolish rules, and now there were more.

She longed for Franz then. She hadn't come here to talk about shoes or try on pretty dresses. They *were* pretty, and something in her wanted to be pretty in them—to see his face when she walked into the room in the crushed velvet or the blue silk. But that desire was swallowed by the stronger need to hide away in curtains with him and feel his lips soft on her skin, his breath warm on her neck. The stronger need to be alone so she could say out loud what she'd only put in letters: *I love you. He* was the point, not the gowns.

Something tapped lightly against her leg, and she opened her eyes. The other ladies were all examining shoes and dresses, distracted. Elisabeth raised an eyebrow, lifted the silk skirt, and found—

Luzi.

She smiled—bright, real—feeling lightness tug at the anxiety that had started to descend on her during the tour. It was just the kind of game Spatz would enjoy too: hiding from the grownups under a cascade of silk, pretending fairy magic had made her invisible.

Elisabeth winked at Luzi and then dropped the silk before he was discovered. Another confidence between them. And a relief. Because it was a reminder: Franz wasn't the only one in the palace she was fond of. Luzi would be here always, reminding her of Spatz whenever she missed her. And Maxi was a sort of friend—even if he was also a rogue.

Her soul settled a little.

Elisabeth looked for something else to focus on, her attention landing on a spot of sunshine sparkling off the dresser. Jewelry, she realized. In a glass case, sparking like flame in the sun. It was a necklace hung with orange-yellow gemstones—old, elegant, regal.

"Do you like it?" Sophie emerged from the group, joining Sisi at the jewelry case. "It's been in our family for hundreds of years."

"It sparkles as if it were alive," Elisabeth answered.

Sophie took the necklace out of its case and placed it gently against Elisabeth's skin, fastening the clasp at the back of her neck.

There was something tender in the gesture, motherly. Elisabeth wondered if Sophie, with so many boys, hadn't had many moments like these, if Sophie felt the warmth of it as acutely as she did. Elisabeth's own mother had spent whatever small amount of tenderness she had on Helene. Elisabeth hadn't gotten a single drop. And the gentle way Sophie placed the necklace on her skin made her want to cry.

Elisabeth's heart, already lighter since finding Luzi's hiding spot, lightened more still. She hadn't realized how much the last months had worn at her. How long she'd been waiting for one of the women in her life to feel that sort of protective love. The kind that placed a necklace carefully around a neck. The kind that listened when she spoke. The kind that forgave. Elisabeth lost herself in the relief of having it from Sophie—even if only for a fleeting moment.

When Sophie was beckoned away by a servant, leaving Elisabeth in the so-called capable hands of Esterházy, Elisabeth felt the loss like an ache. And she missed her sister more than ever.

FORTY-SIX

FRANZ'S CONCENTRATION HAD GONE TO HELL. ALL HE wanted was thirty minutes, fifteen—five even—alone with her. To breathe in her scent, press his face to her hair, feel her body warm and soft and strong against his. That almost-kiss, outside the carriage. He thought he might come apart with the wanting, with the tension of holding back. She'd said once that she wished he was a tailor, and oh, how he wished it for himself today. If he were a tailor, no one would be watching. No one would expect him to follow protocol. No one would have separated them for *months*. Months! The longing was pain and pleasure all rolled up together.

And now she'd been whisked away yet again. This time for dress fittings or some such thing. He pictured it in his mind's eye: seamstresses unlacing Elisabeth's dress, letting it fall from her body. Her naked. Her laced into another dress. Then naked again. His whole body flushed and straightened with the image.

He needed to be fully present for this meeting, this conversation about the fate of Habsburg. He forced himself to focus, to think of anything but Elisabeth. The purple marble columns, the sea-green walls, the long table set with a map of Europe and ringed by important men in uniform—and his mother standing seriously across from him.

"France and England have officially entered the war against Russia. The Russian army near Odessa has been under fire since yesterday," one advisor said.

The news sank heavy into Franz's heart. Every new move and countermove of their neighboring nations made the war harder to stay out of.

Echoing Franz's own concerns, the advisor spoke again. "Your Majesty must take a side, or a side will be chosen for us."

Franz cast his mind back to one of Elisabeth's letters. She had been clear on one thing in particular: You had to stand firm in your convictions. Otherwise you had nothing. Franz had never met anyone like that. The court was full of people jockeying for position, vying for his attention, changing their convictions to get what they wanted. There was a purity in how Elisabeth saw the world, and it was how Franz wanted to see things. She believed he had the strength necessary to stay true to his convictions. He hoped she was right.

Around him, his advisors were still speaking, a general pressing his hand to the hardwood table they were all arranged around. "It's imperative that we strengthen our forces."

Von Bach, Franz's financial advisor, chimed in. "If I may, sir, this year's military expenses have already placed a heavy burden on our budget. Entering the war would leave no money for anything else."

Von Bach cast a significant glance at Franz, and Franz knew what it meant: There would be no money for the plans Franz had quietly, secretly been making to improve Habsburg. Plans for a railroad—a way to connect the empire from end to end. No more multiday carriage rides over bumpy half-finished roads. He'd build those up too—the roads. But the railroad—that would be his crowning achievement. He could feel the greatness of it in his bones, the way it would measurably improve so many lives. Solve the hunger problems, ease the unrest. He wasn't naive enough to think it would fix everything in an instant. But it would show the people that he was making a start, that he was serious about change.

And Elisabeth—he couldn't wait to tell her. He'd been holding back in his letters because he wanted to see her face when he outlined the grandeur of the plan. Wanted to see her face when he told her it was all because of her. He'd had vague notions about how to improve Habsburg before, but it had been Elisabeth who'd made them feel real to him. He didn't want anyone to feel the kind of unfulfilled longing he'd been suffering for so many months. The railroad was an answer to that. It would bring people close, connect them across the miles. Connect them to each other *and* to the things they all needed. Food for their tables, wood for their hearths.

It was yet another reason to stand strong against the war.

One general raised a sarcastic eyebrow at Von Bach. "What do you need the money for this time? A home for old widows?" Laughter rolled through the room.

"Gentlemen," Franz broke in, his voice stern. He was gratified when the laughter died immediately in their throats.

The warmongers tried another tactic. "Your Majesty, what could be more important than the defense of the empire?"

A tired argument.

"You want to *attack*, not defend," Franz replied. Did they really not see the difference?

"I recommend waiting." A moderate man held up a hand. "The situation is still too confused, the right course of action unclear."

And then, Maxi's voice broke in, tinged with a disdainful sort of laughter. "Confused? Please." He stood from where he'd been lounging, his navy coat unbuttoned over a blue-and-white vest with a lavender-gray neck bow. With everyone else in uniform, he stood out in exactly the sort of way he loved most.

Everyone went quiet as Maxi simplified the situation with a smattering of fruit on the map they'd all been poring over. Figs were French ships, strawberries British steamers, grapes the Russian infantry, each placed strategically. Maxi tossed a grape into the air and caught it in his mouth, smacking loudly. Ever a showman, never with a conviction about what was right.

"As you can see, the tsar will be destroyed with or without us." He motioned to the map. "So, we should look to the West. We could learn something from the French and the English."

Sophie stepped in, then, her voice silencing even Maxi. "We shouldn't go against Tsar Nicholas. Our alliance with the Russians safeguards our position in Europe. We must stand *against* the West."

Everyone turned to Franz: tiebreaker between mother and brother. And yet—not. Because Franz was not going to enter this war. He summoned Elisabeth's conviction. "Getting involved on either side is a waste of money and—more importantly— lives. I have bigger plans for Habsburg."

After a long pause, one of the generals raised a hopeful hand. "I implore you to reconsider, Your Majesty. The envoys from

Paris and Saint Petersburg are here for the wedding. They want to know which side Habsburg will take."

"You have my answer." Franz stood firm and then dismissed them all. He wondered what Elisabeth's expression would be when he told her what he'd done. He'd already faced off with his mother about his marriage, and his heart was lighter for it. Now came a greater test: the fight to keep them all out of an unnecessary war.

Von Bach waited outside the room and followed Franz as he left, the clip of their footsteps on the tile floor echoing off burnt orange walls and marble side tables.

"I fear your mother hates me," Von Bach said.

Franz almost laughed. "Don't worry about it. You're one of many."

"When should we tell the cabinet and archduchess about your plans?"

Franz felt the familiar push-pull of excitement and dread. Dread because there was still so much standing in his way. Still ways the war might force itself upon him. But excitement because if he could pull it off, the railroad would change everything.

Of course, it would be only the second time he'd done something without his mother's involvement. It felt somehow both wrong and daring to keep her out of it, but he didn't want anyone—especially her—to shatter his dream. Now she and the cabinet were pressuring him to take a side: Napoleon or the Russians. They'd see the railroad as a distraction. He'd defend his plans when the time came, but he wanted to wait until it was ready first—everything in place, no piece of the plan unfinished and open to critique. He'd engage his experts, map the routes, and then share his plans with his mother and advisors.

Franz stopped, faced Von Bach. "We tell them when everything is perfect."

And after he'd told Elisabeth. He wanted to tell her first, to see how she'd react. He wanted her to know she had inspired the whole thing. He wanted to tell her before anyone else.

Von Bach nodded, turned to go. "As you wish, Your Majesty."

Franz was back in his sitting room, at his desk, when a knock sounded on the door: Franz's next meeting, and one he wasn't looking forward to. The excitement of his earlier railroad conversation had been fully replaced by the preemptive anger of this one.

Theo ushered Maxi into the room, hands in his pockets. Cool. Casual as ever. A sharp contrast to the formality of the room itself—decorated with the busts of historic men, the golden crests of centuries-old lineages.

"Brother." Maxi stepped to the desk where Franz was sitting, elbows propped against dark wood, fingers steepled. "You wanted to see me?"

"Maxi." Franz steeled himself for what was coming next, leaned back, and let the disapproval in his heart show fully on his face. "Are you taking your role at court seriously?"

"What does that mean?" Maxi narrowed his eyes, irritation bleeding through the casual facade. "I've been your advisor for months. Though I know you only have ears for that ferret Von Bach."

Franz took a long, slow breath and directed his eyes to the other man in the room, sitting quietly against the dark green wall to his left. Lieutenant Krall—a tall colorless man with close-cropped hair threaded through with gray. His eyes were serious, lines etched into his face by war and hardship. He'd lost an arm in the revolution, lost worse more recently. When he had come to Franz earlier that week with his story, it had taken days for Franz to look at Maxi without wanting to strangle him.

"Lieutenant Krall gave his arm for the empire during the revolution." Franz motioned to the man and he stood.

"How nice." The indifference in Maxi's voice made Franz want to shake him.

"The lieutenant has two daughters. Agnes and Emilie."

Maxi's casual mask slipped, his face paling. *At least he remembered their names*, Franz thought wryly. It would have been worse—the indifference more sickening—if he hadn't.

Franz continued. "Agnes got pregnant by a young man who had no intention of marrying her. She died in childbirth. The child is orphaned."

Maxi stared.

Franz shook his head. "Emilie fell prey to the *same* young man. Consumed with grief and heartbreak for herself and her sister, she threw herself from their barn and has been living in a sanatorium ever since."

The lieutenant's eyes filled with tears, and he stared at Maxi, chin quivering with something between rage and disgust. Maxi grew smaller in his gaze, pulling his hands together and twisting at the gold rings on his fingers.

Franz's jaw tensed. "As we do not know the young man's identity, we can only make sure the lieutenant and his family are compensated. A noble title and a yearly pension. Do you agree?"

"Yes." Maxi nodded, solemn as he should be. Franz clenched his fists.

"That is, so that the lieutenant can forget this story and no longer feel compelled to tell it." Franz hoped his full meaning was clear to both the lieutenant and Maxi. The family couldn't afford to spend their time embroiled in scandal when war and unrest were already wearing away at the edges of the empire.

Franz turned to the lieutenant then, nodded.

"Thank you, Your Majesty." The man inclined his head, rose from his chair, and left the room. Maxi flinched as he passed.

As the man's footsteps echoed along wood floors into the distance, leaving Maxi and Franz alone, Maxi turned to his brother, ghost white. "Believe me, I didn't know they were sisters."

"And that makes it right?" Franz shook his head, incredulous, then stood, leaning toward Maxi, pressing a clenched fist to the desk. "We talked about this when you agreed to be my advisor. You must abide by the rules!"

Maxi had spent months chiding Franz for picking Elisabeth, telling him how he'd ruin her, how he'd destroy her life. And all the while Maxi was—as usual—treating the women around him as if they were objects, forgettable and easily discarded. Franz would never enter into an affair knowing he was going to hurt someone, let alone so many people. It made him sick. This was Maxi's worst offense yet, and it had cost not only hearts, but two lives. Even Maxi shouldn't have been capable of such cruelty.

"You have to stop this. You undermine us all, undermine everything we've built, with your reckless behavior. What if he hadn't been willing to take the title, the money? What if he kept spreading his story around court? How are you supposed to be my representative on diplomatic missions, in war councils, if this is how you are known?" Franz appealed to his brother's love for Habsburg. God knew his love for Franz wouldn't stop him. And his conscience certainly wasn't doing the trick.

Maxi's eyes sparked with anger. "So you threw me to the wolves, exposed me instead of talking to me?"

Franz's frustration was a steaming kettle. He *had* tried talking to Maxi; it never worked. The situation was impossible: keep Maxi in court and be seen as complicit in his scandals or send him away where he was sure to do more of the same, only with no one to pay off the next grieving father with titles and pensions. Franz didn't know which was worse..

Maxi slipped his indifference back on like a familiar suit. He gave no indication of whether he planned to change. He simply bowed. "Brother."

Franz motioned toward the door, and Maxi disappeared through it.

FORTY-SEVEN

ELISABETH HAD NEVER MINDED BEING NAKED, BUT SHE'D also never had so many people in the room watching. Her ladies-in-waiting hadn't shuffled out during bath time, but rather positioned themselves around the room. Some stood. Some sat. One leaned suggestively in front of a mirror and admired her own dress. The maids removed Elisabeth's clothes, and she wrapped her arms around herself, over her breasts, as everyone looked on as if she were an animal in the circus. A bird in a cage. A thing trapped.

One of the girls helped her into the large copper tub, and Elisabeth sank gratefully into the hot water, the edges of her hair floating around her like seaweed. Esterházy instructed her not to wash herself, so she leaned back and let the ladies do it. They reached in with sponges, brushes, brass carafes of warm water. It was strange and uncomfortable, and Elisabeth tried to pretend she was back home instead, Helene the one helping to wash her hair. That image hurt in a different way, longing for a sister who'd rather tear out her hair than wash it. A frown tugged at Elisabeth's mouth. How long would her sister be so close and yet so unreachable?

"She has such beautiful skin—like moonlight!" one of the ladies cooed.

"I bet the emperor fell in love with her eyes first."

"No, it must've been her lips!"

Elisabeth's nose crinkled involuntarily. Or Franz had fallen for her cleverness. Her wit. The way she spoke her mind. The spark in her soul. The idea that his love was a purely physical thing sat uneasy on her heart. The dukes with their undone trousers may have been purely physical beings. But it was an insult to include Franz anywhere near their category.

"I wish I had hair as long as hers," another added, wistful.

Discomfort tightened further around Elisabeth's throat and across her skin. Why were they talking about her like she wasn't in the room? Or worse, like she was a thing instead of a person. A painting they were all admiring and critiquing and judging.

Esterházy raised a cruel eyebrow. "Perhaps the whole mane will have to go, and we'll put her in a wig."

She was saying it to scare Elisabeth. At least, Elisabeth was pretty sure they wouldn't really cut her hair. But still, the horror of the suggestion was the last one she was willing to endure.

She took a deep breath and slid slowly below the water, letting it distort and erase the conversation. There, the words were only sounds, songs almost. Hums and murmurs, bass and treble, lifts and drops. She didn't have to parse out their meaning.

Elisabeth held her breath for as long as she could and coughed when she finally emerged, the women around her exchanging concerned looks. She wished them all away, wished she could be alone with the soothing heat of the water, the light echo of the room, the spots of sunlight coming in through the window.

Well, not completely alone. With Franz. She'd been longing for him so long, and the few minutes they'd had so far weren't enough. She was a drought-stricken land craving rain, a flower needing sunshine. It was frustrating, the aliveness of her skin screaming for his touch and finding it nowhere. She'd expected something else. Not a dozen women watching her bathe, speculating about her lips and hair.

As the ladies dried and dressed her—skirt twice as wide as she was used to and slightly too long for walking without tripping—Elisabeth tapped impatient fingers against impatient hip. She needed to get away. If she couldn't see Franz—and her multiple inquiries had resulted in insistences from Esterházy that it was *impossible*—she needed to be alone. In forest or garden or muddy hill. She needed to *move*, to let the pent-up electricity spark off her.

When she could take it no longer, she announced she was going for a walk and simply marched through Esterházy's outstretched hands, through the grand double doors and labyrinthine corridors, and onto the grounds. Her ladies followed, flustered. Well, if they could keep up, let them. If they couldn't, Elisabeth would find her solace in a forest grove. She might even lie down in it. She giggled to herself at the thought; Esterházy might collapse if she returned with her sunshine-yellow blouse streaked with mud and shards of wet brown leaves. Elisabeth would think it art, Esterházy an abomination.

These grounds were much more extensive than the Kaiservilla, and she felt immediate relief as she explored the maze of walkways. She almost laughed at how she'd thought the Kaiservilla was grand. From there to here was the difference between a bite of perfect cheese and a perfectly executed cheese soufflé. The intricacy of a feather compared to the intricacy of the whole bird. The villa had been one sprawling, beautiful building on equally sprawling, beautiful grounds. But this? This was a beautiful, sprawling *city* of buildings, surrounded by cobblestones and gardens stretching as far as the eye could see.

Elisabeth followed the perfect lines of manicured shrubbery, her heels crunching against the white gravel pathways. The sweet earthy smell of a sunny day after rain rose up to greet her. If only she could be barefoot, feel the softness of each fallen leaf directly on her skin.

The ladies walked behind her in perfect unison, hands clasped politely at their waists. Elisabeth amused herself by turning quickly down each path and watching the group rearrange itself to follow.

As she turned one sharp corner, she noticed an unusual bird standing in a patch of grass between the paths. It was regal, tall—taller even than herself—and bright white with a scattering of black feathers at the end of its back and an orb of orange red on its forehead tapering down into a sharp blue-gray beak.

Elisabeth approached through the grass, leaving all her ladies except one behind, none of them wanting to leave the path and dirty their shoes. She lowered herself into the grass, her violet skirt spreading around her.

"Have you ever seen such a thing?" she marveled.

"He's looking at you," Leontine said.

"Well, that's because I'm new here." Elisabeth tilted her head, wondering if the bird could tell humans apart.

"Not the bird, Your Highness." Leontine leaned over beside her, hands pressed against her sky-blue skirt. "The archduke." Leontine motioned with her eyes toward one of the hedges.

There, a surprise: Maxi. Elisabeth had barely noticed him when she arrived; she'd been so wrapped up in Franz. But now seeing him was a relief. Someone else she knew, who understood her jokes, who liked her, who wouldn't gasp or laugh at her if she asked a foolish question or did a foolish thing. She smiled, stood, and took a step toward him, and he returned the grin. His own smile was exactly as she remembered: charming and fun with a little mischief at the edges.

"It's nice to see you again." Maxi spoke first.

"I'm happy to see you too." Elisabeth meant it with her whole heart.

"Well, you can see me anytime now. Like tonight at my soiree." Maxi pulled an invitation from a pocket and handed it to her, tilting his head toward the winding paths. She tucked the invite into her waistband to read later. "Shall we walk together?"

The yes on the tip of her tongue tripped over itself. There were so many rules here: Could she walk with Maxi? Would she accidentally cause a scandal? The very thought was exhausting. She'd been here only hours and already she was second-guessing herself. Father's warnings from the carriage came back to her, then. This was another chance to prove him wrong, to act like herself and let the chips fall where they may.

She took Maxi's arm and followed him through the maze, past quiet flower beds and other walkers in high-necked dresses and fashionable top hats, carrying parasols or small black books. Elisabeth was relieved when her ladies hung back, perhaps far enough not to eavesdrop on the conversation. It was strange feeling like everything you said was something to be judged, repeated, or commented on. Perhaps with time, the ladies would become her friends, but right now, it was all—so much.

"You've changed since the engagement," Maxi said, one eyebrow raised. "You've opened like a little almond."

Elisabeth shook her head, laughed. She felt no sting. "How do you do it?"

"Do what?"

"You give a compliment, but actually it's an insult." She raised an eyebrow to match his.

He made a satisfied noise. "I'm teaching you."

"I don't need the lesson. I prefer a direct insult."

"Well, you *are* known for your honesty."

Elisabeth smiled. They continued, and the grounds opened before Elisabeth like petals peeling back on a flower. They were on a long, straight path beside a little canal adorned with rows of flowers and playful, dancing fountains. A smattering of people strolled ahead, pausing to admire the well-shaped calves of a statue, the well-shaped thorns of a tangled rosebush.

"It's beautiful," Elisabeth marveled.

"At first glance, perhaps." Maxi looked at her seriously, and she felt her smile falter.

"Are you trying to scare me?"

The tightness that had loosened in her upon seeing his familiar face returned.

"It's just the truth."

She returned her attention to the path and changed the topic. "How is the charming Italian baroness?"

Maxi laughed, and she felt that familiar sense of fondness, his attention fully, flatteringly captured by her.

"Excellent, so I hear," he answered after a moment. "She's engaged to a count."

"And you?"

"And I'm not."

Good for Francesca. Elisabeth had always liked her, and the countess deserved better than Maxi and his casual cruelty. Elisabeth hoped she'd found someone whose brightness matched her own.

"Elisabeth." Maxi stopped walking, turned to face her. "If I could give you some advice . . ." He leaned in, then, breath warm on the skin of her neck, raising goose bumps along it. "Stick with me and nothing bad will happen to you."

His voice was sincere, urgent in a new way. Part of her wanted to ask what he meant, but the ladies behind them had clustered within hearing distance. So instead Elisabeth raised an eyebrow yet again. "I have a feeling the opposite might be true."

FORTY-EIGHT

GUILT AND DELIGHT KNOTTED TOGETHER IN HELENE'S chest. Sophie had called for her—for *her* specifically! Not Sisi. Esterházy had delivered the message, asked Helene where Sisi's trunk was, and then taken it and led Helene into the corridors. Helene wasn't sure *how* she knew, but she *knew* mischief was afoot. Sophie wasn't just bringing Sisi's case to her new rooms. She wanted it for some other purpose. It was a violation of privacy, and Helene felt both darkly delighted and breathtakingly guilty all at once.

Esterházy led Helene to Sophie's rooms, and Helene was awestruck once again. Every spiraled column of the furniture, every swirl of gold woven through a burgundy rug, every delicate swivel of the hand-carved windowsills dripped beauty and power. And on a thick black velvet settee, Sophie reclined as if she had no worries in the world—every inch as grand as the room.

Esterházy placed Sisi's bag on a small table in front of the archduchess, and Helene wondered, fleetingly, anxiously, if

Sisi's diary was inside. It was the thing her sister would most want to keep secret. The thing Helene should want to protect from prying eyes.

Esterházy settled herself on a small settee, stiff in a blue jacket that Helene couldn't help but think—uncharitably—matched the veins in her too-translucent neck.

"Something is wrong with that girl," she complained, staring into the distance, lips tight.

Sophie frowned, glanced at Helene. "Countess, don't give Helene the wrong idea."

Helene curtsied. "Your Majesty, my lips are sealed." There was the guilt again, and the dark satisfaction. Helene didn't know how to banish either.

Sophie smiled. "A woman after my own heart. We all need to keep our secrets."

After her own heart? The words wrapped around Helene like a hug. After months of being ignored, being shuffled off to the side, it was a relief to be seen. If things had gone according to plan, this woman would be her mother-in-law. Yet another thing Sisi had stolen from her.

Sophie lifted Sisi's diary from the bag, and Helene's heart sank. So, the diary *was* in there. Helene handing the bag to Esterházy had been a greater betrayal than she'd realized.

As Sophie thumbed through the pages, tracing an elegant finger along the poems, moving the feathers Sisi used as bookmarks carefully aside, discomfort worried at the edges of Helene's heart. Sisi never let anyone but Helene read her poems. She'd be so hurt to know that Sophie was staring at them now, so much more hurt to know Helene was allowing it.

But Sisi hadn't cared about Helene's hurt. Why should Helene care about hers now? The fact that she *did* care made her even angrier. She wished she could just hate Sisi without the love constantly trying to fight its way back in.

Esterházy now had a book in hand. *The Sorrows of Young Werther*—a story about unrequited love. Helene wanted to laugh. As if Sisi knew what unrequited love was.

Esterházy tossed the book aside. "Did I tell you that she interrupted the fitting? And did you see how she greeted His Majesty?"

The memory cut at Helene. Both of them had looked so happy. Sisi had thrown herself into his arms. He'd looked at her like she was the only woman in the world.

"You have forgotten what it's like to be in love, Countess," Sophie answered, closing the diary. "And you already know my decision on the matter: my son has chosen his bride, and I will no longer fight him. We cannot change his mind. What we can do, *will do*, is ensure she becomes the empress we all need. You'll be firm with her about protocols, as will I. But we don't need to gossip about her failings in order to do that."

How Sisi would hate it—being forced to follow protocol at every turn. Helene's conflicted heart both worried for her and felt that it served her right.

"Helene," Sophie continued, looking at Helene now, "I brought you here because I wanted to tell you that you would have made a stunning empress. I hope you know that."

The flush of approval was back, warming Helene's shivering soul. It was everything she wanted someone to say to her. Everything she'd been longing to hear for months now. You would be a good empress. You deserved it. You are good. You are—

Lovable.

Loved.

Important.

Helene tried to bury her guilt in the comfort of those words.

FRANZ'S HEART WAS A STONE IN HIS CHEST. HE'D BEEN on his way to the ballroom, so ready to see Elisabeth, anticipating the dance lesson like a child waiting for dessert. He'd made it through hours of tense meetings—with the generals, with Maxi—and when he'd finally had a moment to himself, a few minutes before Elisabeth was due to join him in the ballroom, he'd stopped at an upper window to look out over the grounds. He was looking for her, and he found her: a bright-yellow-and-purple sunburst against the white-and-green maze of the gardens. His heart leapt—and then sank.

She was with Maxi. Maxi walking beside her. Maxi leaning in, too close. He paused there, so long, whispering something into her neck. Was this Maxi's endgame? Had his letters, as Franz darkly suspected, been laying the foundation for an attempt to steal her away—or at least undermine him? It wasn't that he believed Elisabeth would hurt him. But he did believe she might not see Maxi coming. He did believe in his brother's power to manipulate.

And he did believe that Maxi *wanted* to hurt him like this. Like Franz had—accidentally—hurt Maxi when he started his affair with Louise. Franz hadn't even known Maxi was interested in Louise. But that didn't matter. Maxi felt the betrayal keenly, no matter Franz's intent. And if his brother—who had already stolen the affections of one woman Franz had loved—could return the hurt now, Franz had no doubt he would.

Pull away, Elisabeth, Franz's heart whispered.

She didn't, though. Only stood there, still for another moment, before one of her ladies moved her along.

Franz's chest tightened, his stomach clenched. He turned away from the window, pressed his back against the white floral wallpaper of the hall. It was just a walk, just a whisper, but still he felt betrayed. He pressed a hand against his too-fast heart.

Why was his body reacting so strongly to such a small thing? He groped in the dark of his mind for the answer.

Fear. That was the revelation. It was fear that sent his heart racing over as small a thing as a whispered word. A tiny fear was starting to bloom larger than life in him. He was afraid he'd never touch Elisabeth again, feel the warm press of lip on lip, the electricity of hand on hip. He was afraid Maxi's manipulations would work, and Franz would have to spend his whole life watching her love his brother instead of him. Just like he'd spent his childhood, knowing Franz was the best-behaved boy, the oldest, the heir, but Maxi was the *favorite*—the king of hearts. Maxi liked to say that Franz got everything he wanted, but Franz knew Maxi's power over everyone, even if he didn't know it himself.

He hadn't realized how much he cared about that particular gift of his brother's until this moment. Maxi could have every heart in the palace, every heart in Vienna, every heart in Habsburg—except this one.

Franz knew it was unreasonable fear, but this was the tainted gift the assassination attempt had given him: any fear could be interpreted as life ending. The smallest drop of ink could bloom through water like an explosion.

Franz waited for Elisabeth in the ballroom, with its sun-bright circular windows two stories up, a lofty ceiling that curved into art at its center, and matching rose-gold chandeliers sparkling like raindrops.

In the moments between the window and the ballroom, his body had settled, but the agitation in his mind remained. What was Elisabeth doing walking through the gardens with Maxi in the first place? Hadn't Franz told her enough stories about his brother that she knew the danger? Didn't she know how foolish she made Franz look by traipsing around with his known rake of a brother?

Then the doors opened.

Her eyes were sparks, her face the sun from behind the clouds. The smile, the excitement, the quick steps. They were for him. Not Maxi. *Him.*

How foolish his fears looked in the brightness of that smile. He'd panicked over nothing. Maxi might want to hurt him, but his brother didn't have that power.

Elisabeth stopped in front of him, curtsied, and Franz's shoulders loosened, his heart speeding up again—this time with excitement.

They were together. Finally. Allowed to touch. Alone with only a couple servants and a pianist for company.

"Your Royal Highness." The pianist stood from the piano and bowed to Elisabeth as she stopped before them. "If I may introduce myself . . . I am Johann Strauss, composer. I have composed a waltz in your honor for the dance after the wedding."

Franz bowed slightly in recognition and the man returned to the pianoforte. Elisabeth's face was all hope and brightness, and, as the music started, she stepped into Franz's arms. She said nothing, but she didn't need to. The excitement at the corners of her eyes, shivering through her body in his arms, said everything Franz needed to know. He counted out the beats in his mind—one, two, three, one, two, three—and swept her into the dance.

As they moved, Elisabeth leaned in close, her breath hot and cinnamon scented on his neck, his ear. "Our composer friend looks like he has a stomachache."

She wasn't wrong. Franz glanced over his shoulder, where Johann was bent over the piano as if playing it was the worst thing that had ever happened to him. So serious. So agitated. So animated.

Something about the joke unstitched what was left of Franz's tension, lightness overtaking him as he waltzed her away from the piano, across the room. Laughter bubbled up then, and Franz could hear himself echoing off the high ceilings, Elisabeth's laugh joining his in their own symphony.

"It's good to hear you laugh; I can tell something is weighing on you," Elisabeth said, her eyes searching his as he twirled them around the room, following the familiar triple-step rhythm of the waltz.

His heart softened again. Even after so many months apart, she could still read him, see him, in a way no one else could. He'd been tense for so much of the day. Not just from seeing Maxi with Elisabeth, but from dealing with Maxi's indiscretions, the war council, the railroad. It had all sat so heavily on him. But now, the warm, steady weight of her in his arms made the rest of it feel so much less important. So much lighter.

He chose one of the many things tugging at his attention. "Everyone wants me to take a side in the war—and as soon as possible."

"And you don't want to." It was a statement, not a question. She understood simply from his tone that war wasn't what he wanted. He'd been a fool to think that Maxi had any power over what was between them.

"The truth is . . . I have other plans." He didn't expand—not yet. "I'll tell you soon."

She nodded, her eyes bright, expectant as the music swept them away together. Franz twirled them faster, smiling wider, letting the weight of the day slide off him like it was nothing.

Elisabeth's laugh was a magical thing, coaxed from her delicate throat over and over again. He basked in it as he released her waist and spun her around, then pulled her back to him, pressing her close against his chest.

He was breathless—almost dizzy—from the proximity. The feel of her heart beating against his, the heat of her skin where it pressed to his skin.

He twirled her again, watched the laughter spark off her, her smile bright, eyes brighter.

Then Elisabeth let go of his hand, and he watched her sashay away, turning to look at him in a way that shifted everything. From laughing to longing, a game to—

Something deeper.

She danced back and leaned into him. Automatically, he leaned into her, too, pressing his forehead to hers, drinking in the scent of her, the heat radiating off her skin onto his. From this angle, he could see each individual eyelash—perfectly curled, delicate.

He moved his hands up the featherlight edges of her puffed sleeves, felt her hands press against his waist and his body press against hers. He realized then that this was the closest to alone they'd get all day. His heart sped up, this time a fluttering, flying thing instead of an oppressive weight. Perhaps they could sneak away somewhere, find a voluminous curtain, a hidden grove, a dim doorway where hungry lips and exploring hands would go unseen.

As if she were reading his thoughts, Elisabeth tilted her head toward a small, decorative door, camouflaged along one wall, matching its wallpaper, its golden highlights. Her voice was low when she asked, "Where does that door lead?"

He raised his eyebrows in wonder. He knew where the door led:

To quiet. Reassurance. Possibility.

And her lips on his.

ELISABETH DIDN'T KNOW WHERE THE DOOR LED, BUT SHE knew what she wanted to do. What every inch of her body cried out for. As many minutes as they could find wrapped up in each other, skin to skin, lip to lip, hip to hip.

His mouth opened, soundless, looking from her to the door and back. She smiled, grabbed his hand, and ran toward the door, a portal to their own world. If anyone were watching, it would be a scandal. But the servants were busy with their own tasks, the composer swept up in his own moment.

Franz led her through the door and closed it behind them, the room a dim collection of furniture ready to be trotted out for the next event. A storage closet, really. Not so different from kissing behind curtains.

She stood between piles of chairs, and he stepped to her, their bodies close again. He tipped her face up with a gentle finger on her chin, studying her as he leaned slowly in.

Their first kiss was tentative—all laughter and smiles against each other's faces. The second: hungrier. Her hands pressed into his hair, moved slowly along the edge of his ears; his hands traced the curves of her. What would it feel like to have his hand there without the corset, the yards of fabric?

He pulled back from the kiss, slowly, traced the contours of her face with his fingers, from cheekbones to chin. She leaned into the sensation like a cat basking in sunshine. Why was this moment so much more *real* than any other moment of her day? It was like she'd been hearing everything underwater and now she'd emerged to a world full of sharp, distinct sound. Like she'd been straining to see through fog and now the sun had risen—bright—burning it all away. She could almost cry with the relief.

When Franz spoke, it was an echo of her thoughts. "When I'm with you, I feel like anything is possible." He kissed her on one cheek.

She paused, let her fingers linger in the slight curl of the hair at the nape of his neck. "You're planning something, I can see it."

"I am." His eyes were sparks.

"Tell me." Her heart was a fire.

"I've been waiting for this moment for months." He tucked a stray hair behind her ear. "It was so hard not to write about it in our letters. But I wanted to see your face."

She raised a curious eyebrow.

"I'm building a railroad." And as if those words had a broken a dam, the rest of his plans spilled out. He told her about his vision for a connected Habsburg, for faster food distribution, business expansion. He described the contours of the country-side the rails would cut through, the people they'd serve.

"No one will ever have to be separated as long as we were." He kissed the words into her neck, her jawline.

"Then our suffering will have been worth it." She ran two fingers along his hairline.

"Imagine how much more connected the world will be." His voice was breathless.

Her imagination soared with it, with the vastness of Franz's vision, the vastness she'd have her whole life to explore.

He was a marvel. Her mind wandered to one of her poems, and she recited it aloud:

> *And were it in my power,*
> *I would carry you to the sea;*
> *Then you would finally see*
> *Your splendor . . .*
> *The North Sea would be the reflection*
> *For you to look at yourself*
> *Where, in waves high and wild,*
> *You are building a new empire.*

The words were so true. He was doing it, really doing something new. Building a new empire. It was an echo of what he wrote to her in his letters—a man finding his values and standing for them. She smiled up at him, moved her hands to his chest, against his heart. "I love it."

She could see Franz's whole body exhale, shoulders dropping, expression gone perfectly light. He bounced on his heels, then laughed at himself. Giddy. Boyish.

"The whole plan was inspired by you." He blurted out the words and then laughed again.

She raised her eyebrows, teasing. "Ah, so when you think of me, you think *railroad*."

"My love," he teased back. "You don't think thousands of miles of steel beams represent you?"

"Well, I am both reliable and fast." She kissed his bottom lip.

God, she wanted him. She wanted every part of him. His mind, the way he met her jokes with subtle ones of his own, the way he was when he stood firm in his convictions. And his body, so close to hers and yet so far away, kept back by her thousand layers of fabric. Damned Paris fashions.

Franz must have been thinking the same thing because he pressed her back to the wall, took her wrists and lifted them against it, leaned in and kissed her again. She returned the kiss with equal vigor, deepening it, biting gently at his lower lip. Her body was electric, aching to be closer. So close that you couldn't tell where one person ended and another began.

"How did I get so lucky?" he murmured into her neck.

"You are a miracle." He kissed a little higher on her neck.

"A wonder." He dragged his lips higher still.

"A wild thing come in from the forest to nest in my heart." His lips were behind Elisabeth's ear now, pressing so soft against that tender place. Sophie had once called him unpoetic; it made Elisabeth want to laugh now. This man was a poet, and she was the poem. He traced the shape of her, kissed the words into her.

"You know"—she flashed Franz a wicked smile—"people here at court don't wear undergarments."

He raised an eyebrow as she disengaged her wrists from his grasp and wrapped her arms around his neck to kiss him again and deeper. He used his newly freed hands to trace the curve of her waist, tugging upward on her skirt, moving a finger lightly under—

"Ahem."

The voice was a shock in the silence. Silence Elisabeth hadn't realized had descended. The waltz in the next room had shut off like a light.

They pulled reluctantly away, turned toward the cough.

Esterházy, of course. She had a gift for timing—and ruin. She exhaled loudly, disapproval packed into the sound.

Franz shook himself, stepped back. Elisabeth felt the loss of him in every molecule.

"Your Majesty," Esterházy addressed Franz. "I apologize for the interruption. But the imperial bride must continue with her preparations."

Neither Elisabeth nor Franz moved.

"If you will follow me." Esterházy motioned for Elisabeth to move toward the door.

"Indeed, I will," Elisabeth said. "But one last thing."

And then she kissed Franz again, hand to his chest, lips parted against his.

They only had these stolen moments. She wasn't going to waste any of them.

FIFTY-ONE

THE PERK TO BEING INVISIBLE WAS THAT NOBODY tracked your movements. Helene could walk the palace halls to her heart's content. No one called her for dancing lessons. No one wondered where she was during tea.

It hurt, and it freed her. To discover every corner of the place—the imperial wing where Franz's and Maxi's rooms were. The simply furnished servant quarters where the sounds of a couple taking their pleasure had slipped through a wooden door. The seriously furnished studies of important men with their liquor cabinets and gold cigarette cases, where Helene leaned out of white-paned windows, stolen cigarette in hand.

Helene wandered a dozen hallways and overheard a dozen little conversations she normally wouldn't be privy to. A maid terrified of dismissal because of a surprise pregnancy. A cook dismayed because they were out of the archduchess's favorite sweets. Two ladies gossiping about how Sophie had never wanted Sisi for a daughter-in-law.

And the conversation she was listening to now, leaning against peacock-printed wallpaper with another cigarette in hand. Casual, invisible.

It was Maxi. And it was less a conversation and more a speech. Him practicing to himself or arguing with an invisible person, working something out as he paced back and forth across the star-shaped patterns on the wood floor. He hadn't even noticed Helene in the back corner.

He ran a hand through his hair and took an unsteady breath. "I shouldn't be this nervous. I'm *never* this nervous." He shook his shoulders as if he could dislodge the feeling.

Helene leaned deeper into shadow, curious, listening. This seemed so unlike the Maxi she'd encountered before, even the more sincere version in his letters to Sisi.

"He isn't for you." Maxi's voice grew softer, more vulnerable as he started, stopped, and then closed his eyes like he was trying to remember what came next. "He isn't for you. He isn't like us. You and me—we're the same."

His voice shifted from passion to tenderness, both emotions a surprise coming from Maxi. "We're a match. We fit. Just imagine us—together."

He stopped pacing.

"Elisabeth." He paused on the word as if it were sweetness itself. A prayer. A benediction.

Helene's heart bunched. Could she never escape from Sisi? If she wasn't so irritated, Helene would have felt satisfied knowing she'd predicted this: another brother in love with her sister. She wondered if Franz knew, if her sister knew—then realized she didn't care.

"He'll throw you to the wolves just like he did to me. He's not who you think he is—" Maxi turned, paced in the other direction, his brows knit together.

Bitterness rose like a tide through Helene's body. Sisi wasn't who people thought she was either. She had her own secrets, her own betrayals. She'd lied so easily. Helene hadn't had the faintest idea that Sisi was slowly pulling the rug out from under her.

Maxi stopped, ran a hand through his hair, then turned to the windowsill, staring out over the grounds. His voice was a whisper now, barely audible across the room. "The first time we met, I thought—I *knew*—you were made for me."

Helene quietly put out her cigarette in a stone ashtray on the desk she was poised beside.

"Not him." Desperation crept around the edges of Maxi's voice. "*Me.*"

Maxi took a deep breath. "He won't always be the one in charge, you know. We could rule together, you and I. *My* empress."

Now there was another surprise. Helene's eyebrows twitched upward. She had heard plenty about the unrest, the assassination attempt, both back at home and here at the palace. Was Maxi expecting his brother to be dethroned? But if the unrest was to blame, why would Maxi expect that he might rule instead?

Maxi answered her unasked question. "There's going to be a war, and Franz doesn't want anything to do with it. If he won't get involved, the generals will put someone on the throne who will. You need to stay away from him; he can't keep you safe."

Alarm spiked across Helene's pulse. She could feel it speed up in her neck, her chest. Bitterness gave way to something she hadn't felt in months: real, unfettered, untainted concern. *Fear* for her sister.

Was Sisi in danger?

It was one thing for Helene to want to see Sisi suffer from Helene's sharp silences, Sisi's various faux pas at court, the consequences of her actions. But it was another thing for her to be mixed up in whatever Maxi was talking about. He clearly wanted to keep Sisi safe; Helene could feel his sincerity from across the room. But if what he was saying was true, *could* he protect her?

Maxi closed his eyes and took a long, slow breath.

"Just tell her how you feel," he said to himself. "Tell her you love her." Then, nodding as if those last words had given him courage, he pushed off the windowsill and slipped out of the room, never noticing that Helene was there.

She stayed where she was for a long time, pulse still racing. And, for the first time, she wondered if it might be a good thing that she wasn't going to marry the emperor.

EVEN ESTERHÁZY'S PINCHED EXPRESSION COULDN'T
dampen Elisabeth's spirits. She could still feel Franz's
fingertips on the skin of her neck, feel the way his body
had responded to hers, pressing in as she deepened her kiss. She
was almost floating as she followed Esterházy through the halls,
reaching a hand out to run it along sleek wallpaper and over
gilded portrait frames.

Esterházy led Elisabeth back to her rooms, throwing open
the double doors and ushering her in. Elisabeth smiled at how
familiar it felt, even after such a short time in the palace. This
was her home now. These were her rooms: the diamond-
patterned wood floor, the doors a muted blue green, a bookshelf
full of new titles, and a cheerful little statue in white plaster
reaching toward the heavens.

Elisabeth wanted to reach up with her.

A strange collection of people stood around the room, she
noticed with surprise, some faces familiar and others less so.
The most expected were Leontine, another lady-in-waiting,

and some maids. Less expected was a man in a long, black coat and straight blond beard, balancing small, round spectacles on his nose. And then there was a priest—jowly and serious with a violently violet cap on his head and a matching drape over his robes. The color made his face look unsettlingly pink.

Esterházy motioned Elisabeth toward the bed. "You can keep your dress on, Your Highness. This won't take long."

Elisabeth blinked fast, the lightness in her body crashing back to earth. What did Esterházy mean? Of course she would keep her dress on. There were men in the room.

Esterházy waved her impatiently in, but Elisabeth stood still. "What won't take long?"

"Dr. Fritsch is here to confirm the imperial bride's virginity," Esterházy answered without emotion. "And her ability to bear an heir to the throne."

Elisabeth blinked again, her mind and body confused by the sudden shift—from love and light to something strange and unsettling. How would the doctor confirm her virginity? The question lodged in her stomach like a stone. Heavy. Unyielding. And why was Esterházy referring to her in the third person, as if she wasn't there? Something about that was unsettling too. Like the woman was distancing herself from Elisabeth. From whatever was about to happen next.

"It is an honor, Your Royal Highness." The doctor bowed.

Elisabeth only stared at him.

"Of course, the final decision about her purity and suitability for the throne belongs to our Lord. If she is impure, He will not bless the union." The priest stepped forward onto the thick green Persian rug in front of Elisabeth's bed, and Elisabeth's mind cast back to Father in the carriage.

These people believe God himself chose them, he'd said. It had seemed
a silly thing to care about at the time, but now Elisabeth felt the
full weight of his warning. He'd been trying to say that people
who thought God ordained them also thought that gave them
the right to do—anything else they wished.

"As of tomorrow," the priest continued, "you will be a vessel
of God's will."

When Elisabeth didn't respond, the doctor motioned toward
her bed. "If you would lie down, please."

Panic shivered through her, hot across her face and arms. She
wanted to leave, but could tell from the look on Esterházy's face
that she wouldn't be allowed to. Shuddering, she did as the doctor said, lying back on the bed, staring up at the golden curtains
hung above it. She'd thought them whimsical before; now they
felt heavy.

Beside her, the doctor washed his hands, the sound of water
hitting the basin strangely jarring. Louder than it should be in
her ears. The priest turned away, and her ladies placed themselves on either side of her, each taking a leg and positioning it
bent and . . . open. Vulnerable. They lifted her skirt and cold
swept over her entire lower half.

Was Elisabeth shaking from the cold or from the realization
of what was about to happen? She couldn't tell. The doctor was
going to look up her skirt—and what else? Her heart pounded
hard and heavy in her ears as the doctor's face appeared above
her, a large white funnel just visible in his hand. Was he going
to . . .

And then—the violation of it, the abrupt pressure and pain.
Elisabeth gasped, choking on the sudden, shocking tightness in
her throat. Was this the kind of thing Maxi had been warning

her against? That they would hurt her, humiliate her, quite literally reach inside her for their own purposes and without her consent? That the court was a danger in ways Elisabeth had never even imagined?

"The doctor will be done soon." Esterházy still managed to have no emotion over the violation she was presiding over.

Elisabeth pressed her hands to her cheeks, willing herself to focus on the pressure there instead of the pressure now inside her. She cast her eyes around the room, looking for something—*anything*—else to focus on. The dark wood headboard. The curled loops of the maid's hat. The fine lines of gray through the white marble of the fireplace.

Then, finally, "Everything looks healthy," the doctor said.

"Health is important, of course. But proof of innocence is what matters most." The priest spoke to the wall, still turned away.

"Yes, Your Excellency, I'm checking that now."

Innocence. The irony wasn't lost on Elisabeth. She'd never been with a man in the way they meant, but she knew there were ways around those unyielding rules, that so-called innocence. Ladies who wanted to maintain such proof simply opted for fingers and tongues. Elisabeth had stumbled into enough of her father's wild parties to know that much. There were a hundred things a woman could do without spoiling her chances of passing this test.

The fury of that irony broke through her numbness. The horror flamed into sudden rage. As the doctor returned to his work, another pinch sent Elisabeth's leg kicking into him, sending him sprawling to the floor as she sat up.

"Stop! Please, stop." Tears burned in time with the shame and the rage. "I am a virgin. I am chaste, I swear it."

What was wrong with this place?

The priest turned around then, staring her down as if she were a naughty child, and she hated him most of all.

"Your Highness, that is all very well but the doctor must confirm it." Esterházy's face was a blank space. Elisabeth wondered if it would look the same if it were her skirts lifted to the sky with a man and a funnel inside them.

"Countess, I actually couldn't see anything." The doctor sounded apologetic, and fear spiked through Elisabeth. A new fear—not of the violation itself but that it might be in vain.

That she would have allowed these men to hurt her and in the end, they would still declare her unfit. Still keep her from Franz. It all would have been for nothing. The months of longing. The stresses of court. And losing Helene. She would have lost her best friend and the love of her life over some anatomical thing she didn't control or understand.

"That cannot be." Elisabeth's voice was small, her heart smaller.

The room went quiet. One heartbeat, two.

Finally, Leontine stepped in. "Your Highness, you are an avid horseback rider, I believe?"

Elisabeth's mind scrambled to catch up. She didn't know why that mattered, but she nodded all the same. Desperate for Leontine—for anyone in the room—to take her side.

"Don't you know what that means?" Leontine turned to the doctor, raising an eyebrow.

"Indeed," he paused, "that is a possibility. Her Highness's hymen could have been torn during riding."

Elisabeth's stomach churned. She didn't know whether this proclamation was hope or doom.

"Without proof of innocence, there will be no marriage." The beady-eyed priest turned his back again as if that settled it. Elisabeth added him to her mental list of people in the room who deserved a funnel up *their* skirts.

You love Franz, Elisabeth told herself. *You love him more than anything. Do this for him.* Sick to her stomach and now visibly crying, she laid back down and grasped Leontine's hand, pushing her anger, her upset, the fear and the humiliation into that gesture. Leontine squeezed back reassuringly, and Elisabeth tried to send her mind somewhere else. *Fly away like a gull, fly over the sea. You are free. You are away. You are anywhere but here.*

So many long moments later, the doctor stood and made his proclamation. "I believe in the bride's virginity, although her hymen is not fully intact."

The ladies released her legs and Elisabeth sat up, clenching her hands in her skirts. The priest turned, expression smug, the huge cross around his neck flashing a sliver of light directly into Elisabeth's eyes. "May kings issue from your loins and make all the earth your subjects."

He bowed and left.

Elisabeth watched him go, watched them all go except her ladies, shock sitting heavy on her like a rain-drenched cloak. Her heart spiraled, a storm of hurt and disbelief and rage.

She stood, wobbly on shaking knees, and started toward the door. She needed to talk to Franz. To hold him. To cry, probably. He was the only person here she could trust.

Before Elisabeth could escape, Esterházy held up a hand to stop her, her voice all resentment. "We have so much more to do today, Your Majesty."

"No. We don't. We can't. I have to find Franz."

The woman only gave her an irritated look. "Majesty, that is not possible—nor proper. The emperor has important business this afternoon. And you must prepare for tonight's celebration. The maids are waiting with a facial treatment for you as we speak. You can't be looking exhausted tonight—or at your wedding tomorrow."

As if facial treatments could possibly matter now. As if Elisabeth wanted any other person touching her. Her stomach flipped and flipped again and then her mind snagged on Esterházy's last word.

Tomorrow. The word she'd reveled in just hours ago was sheer panic now. Tomorrow would seal her fate, trap her here at court forever. She loved Franz. She wanted him. She'd chosen this. But doubt stabbed cold through her now. If this was what court was like on her very first day, could she really handle it in the weeks, months, *years* to come? Could she really stay—even for love?

The idea of leaving was a horror, but so was the idea of staying. She felt frozen in place, all paths leading to pain and humiliation and being robbed of her very soul. Her father was right: she'd lose herself here.

She needed to see Franz, to hear him say that today wouldn't be what every day looked like, that he wouldn't let them hurt her like that again. She needed to see him dismiss the priest, dismiss Esterházy, chastise them all. Her chest tightened with the need for someone—for him—to share her horror.

"I need Franz. *Now.*"

"Majesty, with all due respect, that is not how this works." Esterházy took her by the elbow, her bony fingers cold and sharp as she led Elisabeth to the dressing room.

If Elisabeth knew where Franz was, she'd run. She'd leave Esterházy choking on the dust her feet kicked up. But she didn't know, and her knees were shaky, so instead she pulled her elbow from Esterházy's grip, ordered everyone out of the room, locked the door, and cried.

FIFTY-THREE

THE SETTING SUN CAST FRANZ'S SHADOW LONG ACROSS the marble corridor as he made his way to the party. To her. His Elisabeth. He hadn't seen her since the dance, and oh, how he longed to. He wanted to tell her more about the railroad, hear her say again that she loved it. *Loved* it. Loved him. They'd have hours together at the party. Surrounded by people, of course. But hours in the same room for the first time in so many months. They would find stolen moments just between them, he was sure.

He was lost in those thoughts when he heard the moaning, the rhythmic sound of movement through a doorway to his left. He paused, glanced into the room.

It was a rarely used sitting room full of last year's fashions: couches in pink and silver, curtains in dark purple with crest-like designs, the ceiling painted pink with white clouds. And against a windowsill, two figures intertwined. A woman pressed against the sill, throat tipped back, lips open to the heavens, an endless stretch of leg angled out from the side of her lover. A man—*Maxi*, Franz realized with a start—moving rhythmically against her in time with the soft moans escaping her lips.

Franz stepped back into the hall and away from the door, anger kindling. He'd *just* chastised Maxi for these kinds of casual affairs. His brother had driven one woman to death, another to madness, and did not even care enough to abstain for a single day. He'd be their ruin. Franz wanted to wring his neck.

Franz unclenched his fist, forced himself to breathe deeply. There was no reason to involve himself now. He'd only embarrass the woman. But he needed to keep a closer eye on Maxi. That much was clear. His brother was a bomb waiting to go off—still.

He passed the door quickly, hoping Maxi wouldn't see him, and clenched his jaw all the way to the evening's reception. But even there, Franz found no relief. He wasn't two minutes and one sip of Riesling into an attempt to relax when his mother started in on the latest political disagreement. Oh, how Franz longed for Elisabeth to arrive and give him an excuse to dance or toast or just breathe for a few minutes.

"The officials sent word and they need your answer immediately: Are we keeping Hungarian as the official language of business in the eastern part of the empire?" Sophie was all business, her own glass of wine untouched.

She'd had a brief meeting with a Hungarian delegate before the party, scheduled another equally brief audience with Croatia after. He didn't need to be in attendance, she assured him, since he'd previously asked her to help him minimize meetings on trivial issues so that he could focus on critical ones. But she did need his answers.

He was so tired of meetings like those. Who cared what the official language was when he was doing everything in his power to stay out of an unnecessary war? When there was unrest at Habsburg's doorstep, a brewing revolution that had literally stabbed him in the neck? It was exhausting.

"Franz?" his mother prompted.

Franz sighed. "What do you think, Mother?" Perhaps this would be his concession to her. He was standing against her on matters of love and war. Perhaps he could stand with her if she had strong feelings on matters of language.

"I say tell the Croatians you'll reconsider their proposal in a year's time once Napoleon has stopped sending you gifts to try to tempt you into an alliance."

He nodded, and she looked pleased.

And then—

Then.

Finally.

Elisabeth arrived, and the relief of seeing her was so overwhelming that Franz felt instantly drunk with it. How was it possible that every time he saw her, he was stunned all over again by how beautiful she was? She was in a yellow-and-olive dress with a pop of bright red in the collar framing her neck and shoulders, drawing the eye to her delicate collarbone and that perfect place where chest started to curve outward.

In the low light of the room, she looked ethereal. If only he could tuck her behind the curtains for a secret kiss. If only they were alone and he could do much more.

"There she is!" The first voice to speak was all sunbeams. He knew how they felt. Elisabeth lightened the whole room with her entrance. Everyone raised a glass to her before continuing their conversations.

She found his eyes then and held his gaze. He could live forever in that moment, just gazing at her across the room.

Then Elisabeth was pulled into a conversation, and Franz couldn't politely exit his. He watched her out of the corner of his eye, wishing he could take her into his arms, press his lips to her temple. She was so close and yet so far away.

FIFTY-FOUR

ELISABETH, WHY DON'T YOU COME OVER HERE?" SOPHIE motioned to her from across the room, warm and welcoming.

Elisabeth's heart sighed with relief. She could have cried, finally seeing Franz for the first time since the dance. She wished they were alone, but it was relief either way. Franz, who'd stood up to his mother for her, who was standing up to generals, standing firm against war. He'd comfort her. Stand with her. She'd tell him about the doctor, the priest, the shock, the pain. And he would help her, protect her, ensure that it was the last time any woman had to endure such an invasion.

Before she reached him, her heart bumped into a wall of shock. *The priest was there*, just now stepping into the small circle with Franz and Sophie, pontificating. "A war can also be something meaningful, Highness. It gets the rabble off the streets."

Franz looked as sour as Elisabeth felt. He answered, slow and measured, "War is a last resort, Your Excellency—not a pastime."

Sophie, eyeing the two men shrewdly, diffused the tension. "And we will give the people new hope tomorrow, in any case, will we not?" She smiled at Elisabeth, her gaze going motherly again.

Franz smiled then, just a hint at the corner of his mouth, as he reached for Elisabeth's hand and kissed it—holding it slightly longer than was proper.

"I assume you met the imperial bride, Your Excellency?" Sophie drew Elisabeth's gaze back to the horrible priest in his horrible violet cap. Her stomach turned again at the sight of him, her whole body tensing.

"We've had the pleasure, yes, Your Highness." He nodded at her, happy—as if this afternoon hadn't even happened. As if she would be *glad* to see him again.

He puffed out his chest. "I had the honor of determining the lady's innocence this afternoon."

"Wonderful." Sophie's tone was relaxed, as if this were a perfectly normal conversation.

Elisabeth pressed her fingernails into the palm of her hand, fist matching tight jaw matching tight heart.

The priest couldn't read her. He smiled wider. "It gives me pleasure to tell you, Your Majesty, that nothing stands in the way of an heir to the throne."

It was dizzying all over again, being discussed like she wasn't in the room. Or like she was *a thing*—in the room but incapable of her own feelings or reactions. A piece of furniture. A machine. A thing here to make a baby, nothing more.

Maxi chose that moment to join the group, sipping Champagne and looking curious. Franz nodded his head at the priest in a way that Elisabeth couldn't quite decipher. And Sophie lifted a glass, still shockingly cheerful. It was one thing for the men in the circle to act like the exam was nothing; it was another for Sophie—who had likely endured it herself—to call it wonderful. *Wonderful.* The word was a weapon. Confusing after Sophie had been so tender with her earlier and the hint of confidence just now.

The anger underneath the hurt slipped free as Elisabeth met the priest's gaze. "I'm glad at least it gave *you* some pleasure."

"Elisabeth." The word was a gasp as Sophie's expression dropped to shock. "His Excellency was just doing his duty."

Duty. Elisabeth had thought she could embrace it as long as it came with love. But this wasn't love *and* duty. It was being kept away from love for the sake of duty. It was isolation and violation and no quiet, intimate moments in between to make up for them.

"I'm sorry that the sacred ritual was uncomfortable for you." The priest smiled at her.

How dare they call something like that sacred? Elisabeth looked at Franz, his face etched with concern, and it gave her strength.

"A sacred ritual? Oh, please excuse my error. It felt like two men looking up my skirt."

Behind her, a tray of glasses smashed to the floor, the noise startling every person in the circle. Elisabeth turned and saw her mother, pale-faced, standing over the wreckage.

To her right, Maxi lost his composure, laughing incredulously and pressing a hand to his mouth. "Pardon me, Mother. Pardon."

The priest didn't let the conversation drop. "You seem agitated, my child. No need to get hysterical."

Another spike of anger arced through Elisabeth. "I'm not hysterical."

Franz put a hand out to her, his eyes worried. "Is everything all right, Elisabeth?"

Before she could answer, Sophie answered for her. "Perhaps the bride could use some rest."

Elisabeth blinked. Some rest? Was Sophie sending her away from her own party for telling the truth about this afternoon? For refusing to stand by and pretend it was all normal? She hadn't had power when it was happening, hadn't felt like she had a choice, but she thought she'd have her power back standing next to Franz. Thought that he liked that she spoke her mind. Thought that he would stand up for what was right.

She looked to Franz, eyes pleading.

"I don't think that will be necessary, Mother." His voice was soft as he studied Elisabeth's face.

Elisabeth turned to face the priest again, ready to demand an apology. "I—"

"Franz," Sophie interrupted, the tenderness of before long gone. "It was a long day for your bride. We want everything to go well tomorrow, don't we? Elisabeth should rest."

Elisabeth looked at Franz again, waiting for him to defend her.

Instead, he inclined his head. "It *has* been a long day. A little rest would do you good, Elisabeth."

Her heart twisted into a knot as her mind flashed back to the day Puck died. She'd stood there covered in blood and dirt, drained of tears, bled of hope, and Helene—then the most important person in her life—hadn't asked her if she was all right. Had prioritized the meeting with the duke over Elisabeth's feelings. And now? Now Franz was her most important person, and he was betraying her in exactly the same way. Couldn't he see that her anger had reason? Couldn't he feel her distress?

"No, please. I'd like—" She started but didn't finish. *I'd like to stay. I'd like to speak to you privately. I'd like to change this arcane ritual.*

"It's better you rest," Franz said again, this time firmer.

The knot in Elisabeth's chest grew tighter. It was always the same. Men behaved badly. They undid their trousers at dinner, told her that her dreams didn't matter, touched her without permission. And it was always she who was sent away. Punished. Silenced.

Is this what her life would be like—even now? Even with a man she'd thought really understood her. It would be just like home, but with a new set of keepers. Mother replaced with Es-terházy, with priests, with ladies, maids, and doctors with sharp funnels burrowing into tender places. Now a hundred people to hurt her instead of just one.

"But—" She tried once more.

"I insist." Franz closed the conversation.

He held a hand out to her, and she ignored it. She had to leave this room before she fell apart. Before the cracks in her fragile soul shattered her into too many pieces to put back together.

Maxi met her eye as she turned, and she saw something there that almost hurt more. *Understanding.* He had told her earlier that day that he was her ally at court, but she hadn't believed him. Now she did.

As the doors closed behind her, leaving her alone in the quiet, dim hall, the tears came quickly, doubts crashing down on her with each wave.

Had she made a terrible mistake? Should she run now and leave Helene to be empress if she still wanted it? And could she ever trust any of them again after this?

The only marriage she'd seen up close was her parents' and something ominous wrapped itself around her heart now, thinking about them. Was this how it started? A misunderstanding, dismissal, a refusal to see the pain of the person you loved—and the next thing you knew, all you could do was hurt each other?

When Elisabeth got back to her rooms, the first thing she did was write a poem on tear-stained paper:

> *Will the North Sea rumble,*
> *Tell me that I broke my own heart?*
> *The naive thing fooled me,*
> *And I hate every deception.*

FIFTY-FIVE

FRANZ EXCUSED HIMSELF AND STEPPED ONTO THE balcony, staring out over grounds flickering with lamp-light. Elisabeth's refusal to take his hand stung. Sending her away stung too.

Stung and worried him.

It had seemed like the right solution—telling her to get some rest. Not because he wanted her to leave. All Franz had wanted the entire day was to be near her. But she was upset, and his mother was upset, and allowing things to escalate in front of everyone was out of the question. These were the kinds of upsets that needed to happen in private, be dealt with behind closed doors.

Not for the sake of the priest. Franz didn't know exactly what the man had done, but Franz had no love for him. No need to defend him.

It was Elisabeth, Mother, the family, he was worried about. There was already too much unrest outside the palace. Too many ways Maxi was creating enemies within it with his own scandals. Franz couldn't allow anything that made that worse, made them more enemies, made things more dangerous for them all.

But Elisabeth had ignored his hand. And that meant she didn't understand.

The thought worried at the edges of his conviction. Had he been wrong? And if he wasn't wrong, could she still forgive him? Perhaps even more importantly: Could she change?

Franz ran a finger across the rough iron rail of the balcony, bit his lip. He loved that Elisabeth spoke her mind, that she was so perfectly herself. He loved that she'd shown him how to be himself again. But could they find the balance? He wanted her to be herself, and he needed her to know when to handle things in private, how to hold her words back—not forever, just for a little while.

He pressed his finger harder against the rail, as if he could push the worry into it and leave it behind him. Maxi had accused him over and over of ruining Elisabeth, trapping her. But this was the first time Franz wondered if it was true. Would he break the magic in her by needing her to learn to hold her tongue? Would he ruin the things he loved about her by asking some of them to stay secret, to be just for the quiet moments between them?

He could hear the party in full swing behind him, piano music seeping out the balcony doors, glasses clinking together in celebration. And he knew he couldn't stay away long. Part of keeping the peace was not allowing public upset, and part was showing his smiling face, shaking hands with generals and ministers, accepting congratulations.

Franz almost wished he and Elisabeth could trade places—his mother suggesting he was too tired and her staying to shake hands and make nice.

He took a deep breath and tried to press the worries to the back of his mind. There was nothing he could do now. He couldn't leave; he couldn't call her back. He could only accept a parade of matching congratulations and try not to wish that he was holding her instead.

FIFTY-SIX

E LISABETH'S HEART WAS A SHARD OF GLASS LODGED IN
her chest.

If only he weren't the emperor. If only he were a tailor! She had never wanted court, never wanted formal dinners,
dresses, dances. Certainly never wanted *anything* that had happened today. It had hollowed her out, the reality of it, how very
much coming here, saying yes, was surrendering herself—her
will, her very body—to the empire.

Tears blocked her throat, and a headache nudged at her tem-
ples. She loved Franz. Loved him like trees loved rain, like flowers loved sun, like a horse loved the wind through its mane. Her
love was a visceral, physical thing—rainstorms, thunder, shooting stars. But what was Franz's love? What was his love worth
when he'd sent her away?

In just a few minutes, he'd erased her certainty that he was the
rock she'd hoped for, the great love of her poems, her dreams.

It's not too late, Helene had said after the engagement. Sophie
had said it to Franz. Maxi had said it to her in a letter. Maybe
everyone was right.

Maxi. There was someone who would talk to her, someone whose face had flashed concern and understanding instead of alarm when she'd spoken up for herself. He had invited her to his soiree tonight. She still had the little card. And now, she knew she had to go. She wasn't exactly sure whom or what she would find there; she only knew that she didn't want to stay here, crying herself to sleep in the shadows of her doubts.

Elisabeth re-dressed in her bedroom, thankfully without the aid of six ladies, whom she'd asked to stay in the adjoining sitting room. She pinned her hair up in two messy buns. She felt so much more herself like this, her hair wavy and comforting as tendrils brushed against her exposed neck and ears. A white lace top was gauzy against her skin, a deep-blue vest offering contrast. She kept the necklace Sophie gifted her around her neck and added others in varying lengths—jewels upon jewels. Making these little choices about what she wore and how she styled herself was like taking something back. It steadied her, drove away the tension in her throat, the knots in her stomach.

Her ladies followed as Elisabeth left her rooms and made her way through quiet nighttime hallways to the soiree, held in another ballroom on the opposite side of the palace from the formal party. Maxi's festivities were in full swing, and there was something soothing about the chaos—all hookah smoke and Champagne giggles and people talking with their hands. Short skirts, experimental fashions, women with secrets in the arch of an eyebrow, men with questions in the turn of a lip. There were men in sailor suits manning the door with their midriffs showing. A man in a full beard and yellow ball gown swept through the center of the room.

And no one was staring at Elisabeth.

The freedom of it was intoxicating. She felt like dancing on a table. With no one telling her what to do, no one explaining another rule. In fact, no one here was behaving as if they were at court at all. No bowing. No formalities. Maxi had released an entire room of people from court's invisible, ever-tightening bonds.

The room was full of tapestries depicting scenes from Paris, London, the Alps. Between them, pearl-colored statues of nude women reached to the heavens or stared into space. It was a very Maxi place to hold a party. It said something about him, about the depths behind his rakish grins, the sharp wit. It wasn't just a party. It was a portal to another world. To Maxi's internal world, perhaps.

As Elisabeth moved through the room, soaking it in, she felt she understood him in a new way.

"We should go back," one of her ladies-in-waiting said, hesitant, from behind her. But another spotted a famous pianist, and Elisabeth was delighted when they scattered toward him, still near her but no longer attentive. She leaned over the piano and let the music—so much more exciting than anything she'd heard before—wash over her. How alive she felt here, how much more herself against a backdrop of experimental music instead of a waltz.

Then, in her ear, a familiar voice, the tickle of hot breath on her neck. "Are you having fun?"

Maxi. It was shocking how well he fit there, how the room lit him up from the inside, how the shadows added depth to his eyes, definition to his jaw. He was handsome, she realized. She'd not noticed before. The moonlight, the lantern light, his casual necklace made of shells, the shocking expanse of chest—this was Maxi truly unbuttoned, unperforming, for the first time since she'd met him.

"Don't worry. I didn't invite that creepy priest."

It was like he'd read her mind, seen the thing she had so desperately needed Franz to see, and *cared* about it. She wondered, for the first time: What if she had fallen in love with Maxi instead of Franz? This boy who'd somehow released a hundred people from the confines of court. Who loved travel, who spoke his mind. Helene would have been free to love Franz, and—

No. Her stomach turned over. She *hadn't* fallen for Maxi. Even toying with the idea hurt her heart. Her love for Franz was a precious thing, a poem, a song, a sparrow. Not a *what if*.

"Is Franz here?" She still needed to see him, to tell him how much he'd hurt her, how uncertain she felt.

"Not that I know of. I invited him, but he's always busy, our Franz." Maxi glanced around. "Is that a reason to leave?"

"No." Elisabeth wanted to see Franz, yes. But she also wanted to revel in the freedom of this place, the euphoria of it. The release.

"Good." Maxi's voice was soft. "In that case, may I introduce you to my good friend, Franz Liszt?" He motioned to the pianist. "Maestro, this is our future empress."

The man reached across the piano and kissed her hand, slowly, informally. And that was a relief, too. It was like court was one world and this was its distorted mirror. You still kissed a hand, wore a gown, danced to piano music. But here the kisses lingered, the gowns deconstructed, the piano transported you to another world.

"A song for you, Your Highness." The pianist inclined his head, long hair falling loose over the shoulder of his embroidered collar. Then, with elegant, practiced fingers, he started to play.

The song was playful and somehow sad. It was the sun coming out to comfort you when your mother said your smile wasn't pretty enough, your waist unseemly. It was romance and heartbreak in a forest grove. It was a window into her soul. Elisabeth wondered if this was the magic of a true musician: that they could see inside a person so completely.

As she watched the composer's hands slide effortlessly across keys, Maxi leaned close to her ear yet again. "Down here, the music follows you, not the other way around."

Her heart was full of the idea and the words themselves. It was poetry. And it had come from Maxi, of all people. Who would have thought both brothers had so much poetry in them?

Elisabeth longed for a cigarette. It was scandalous for women to smoke, and she felt scandalous in this space. She wanted to revel in it.

As if he'd read her mind, Maxi held one out to her. "Some relaxation for the bride-to-be. Or, if you prefer, there's hookah. I got that one from Constantinople." He motioned to a hookah behind them. "It's made of real gold."

Constantinople. Elisabeth's heart leaned into the idea. What would it be like to be able to pick up and leave like that, go wherever you wished? Constantinople, Geneva, Greece, Hungary. The places he'd told her about in his letters. The cage of court hadn't kept Maxi in. Perhaps he was the one who could tell her how to be here, be with Franz, and yet escape court's confines.

Elisabeth reached out and took the cigarette, let him light it for her.

"How do you do it?" she asked, watching the end of the cigarette smolder into life.

"Do what?" He put out the match.

"Travel. Live. Joke. Retain your sense of self here at court. Free all these people from their courtly confines for a night. Every time I think I know you, you turn out to be something different. Jokester in Bad Ischl. Traveler in your letters. Something even more expansive here. Please, tell me your secrets."

He shrugged. "I'm but a lowly second son. Being the family mascot doesn't come with as many expectations."

She frowned. Was that the answer, then? Did position dictate everything? Had she chosen hers without understanding what it meant—just like Mother said?

"I'm glad you came tonight. I knew you would." Maxi smiled, a real smile again, none of the performative arrogance he put on during court proceedings.

"Will Franz come later?" she asked. She needed to see him more than ever.

Maxi raised an eyebrow and shrugged dramatically. "Apparently he has something better to do. And on the eve of his own wedding!"

Her disappointment must have shown on her face because Maxi handed her his untouched Champagne. Feeling reckless, she downed it all at once. If she couldn't find Franz and couldn't get any useful answers out of Maxi, at least she could try to relax, enjoy the one not-stuffy thing about court. Maxi looked impressed and snapped his fingers at a servant to bring them two more flutes.

Elisabeth took a long, slow drag on her cigarette and let it wash over her: the room, the party, the people, the alcohol, the nicotine. Her body settled into itself, a skin-deep sigh of relief—though she could tell the panic was only temporarily calmed. A glass of bubbles didn't solve what had happened today. It didn't solve the problem of a court that was already suffocating her.

She downed another glass.

"Do you know where he is?" she asked after a beat.

Irritation flickered across Maxi's face, then disappeared behind good humor once again "Franz? He mentioned some late-night meeting. Trying to be a man of mystery, but I doubt it's anything interesting. Probably has to go watch Croatia and Hungary insult each other all night. You'd be shocked at how boring even fighting is when it's political."

So, Franz was away. Not in his rooms, even if Elisabeth could get their location out of Maxi and slip away to find Franz herself. She took another drag on her cigarette, the pleasant warmth of two glasses of bubbles dulling the disappointment and sparking something else: hope. If Franz was at a meeting, perhaps he would still make an appearance at the party. She'd wait for him till then.

The next hour passed in a blur. Maxi introduced her to a dozen people she couldn't now remember. She sat on a settee and let the lively music carry her away. She danced with strangers. She laughed until her sides hurt. Her ladies-in-waiting—to her delight—acted like normal people. Not babysitters. She learned another of their names. A *first* name. Amalia. Who would have thought remembering names would feel like delicious rebellion?

Maxi eventually joined her on the cream-and-gold settee. She smiled, happy to see his friendly face, the dance and drink and smoke and freedom still sweeping her away. He reached across the space between them, lifting the gold-yellow necklace gently from the top of her vest.

"Do you like it?" she asked. "Your mother gave it to me."

"It belonged to our great-aunt, Maria Antonia." He dropped his hand.

"Marie Antoinette?" Elisabeth tilted her head.

"She was wearing it when she lost her head to the guillotine."

Elisabeth's nose wrinkled involuntarily. Why was he telling her this? And just as she'd started to relax? The danger—the edge—of court intruded again on her joy.

Maxi released the necklace, his tone turning dark. "My family has a talent for using pretty things for ugly purposes."

"Franz said you had a dark side."

He raised an eyebrow. "You will too if you stay long enough. A storm inside you, ripping you to pieces."

So few words, and yet she felt so exposed. Her heart *was* a storm, and it had only taken one day to make it so.

"Why are you here if you despise the court so much?"

"I've tried to leave many times." Maxi turned more serious, let the ghost of a troubled expression flit across his face. This was the Maxi from the letters: earnest, honest.

"Elisabeth." There was something wild in his face, a rawness. And in his voice: a tremor. "The first time we met, I . . . I thought you were made for this life. That you were made *for me*." The words were unexpected, the force of them even more so: sure and wild, a crashing wave, a whipping wind.

"Maxi, I'm getting married tomorrow." Even as she said the words, she wasn't sure she believed them. Was she getting married tomorrow? After everything? Would she still choose this life, even now?

"It's not too late." Maxi leaned in, his eyes caught on her lips. He reached for her, and Elisabeth felt—

Nothing.

There was no spark, no gasp, no goose bumps. No recognition soul to soul. And it was the absence of that spark that brought her back to herself. Reminded her what she and Franz had.

Something magical.

Something unmatched.

"No." She pushed Maxi away.

Hurt flashed across his face. Elisabeth had never seen a man so diminished. Like he was a small boy who'd lost his last friend, a sailor marooned on a lonely island.

A heartbeat passed, then another. And then a curtain dropped over his pain so fast and so fully she thought she must have imagined it. Now you see a boy who loves you; now you don't. And he won't. And he never did. She blinked twice, kept her hand up between them, pressed against the warmth of his arm.

"You should see your face." He laughed. "You thought I was serious?"

He wanted her to feel foolish, she knew. But instead she felt sad for him. Covering up your hurt with a dart aimed at someone else's heart wasn't a strength. It was a weakness. A mask. A lie.

"You've never felt true love, have you?" She said it with pity. And then, "I love your brother."

"And yet"—he leaned in again, this time no longer tender—"you're still here."

He reached for her one more time, and this time she stood. He was right. Franz wasn't coming, and it was time for Elisabeth to leave.

FIFTY-SEVEN

H ELENE WAS TWO DRINKS IN AND WATCHING SISI FROM across the room, trying to sort through her emotions. The bitterness and anger were still there, but so was the worry that had taken root when she'd stumbled upon Maxi earlier. The protectiveness she used to feel for Sisi all the time crept around the edges of her rage. And so did an old fondness. For her drunken, laughing, twirling sister, who looked so much like herself here. All messy hair and unguarded joy.

Helene had been watching her sister for an hour now. Watching as she soaked in the piano music. Watching as she danced. Watching as Maxi had come up behind Helene, leaning over her shoulder and whispering in her ear, "I know how it feels to be passed over."

Helene had moved a half step away, lifted her martini glass like a shield, her confused heart tripping over the words. Maxi made her nervous, especially after what she'd overheard. But the words themselves had been a thing she wished someone would say to her, a small comfort.

"It would be nice if people would stop avoiding me," she'd admitted, guarded.

It was strange how even speaking to someone she didn't fully trust had been cool relief. It had been so long since she'd had anyone to confide in. Mother was a terrible confidant, all sharp opinions ready to stab you. Papa was just as bad: dismissive and ever prepared to laugh at your pain. Spatz was a baby. The horses couldn't talk. And Helene couldn't say any of it to Sisi, not when she'd been the one who'd caused the hurt.

"Don't worry. I've been suffering from severe rejection for years now." Maxi lifted his flute and touched her glass, a gentle toast.

Helene's face had twitched with an involuntary smile. She could finally see how all those girls got into trouble. She knew Maxi was dangerous, and yet she felt the pull of him. The flattery of the attention. The relief of feeling seen. The nameless charisma that radiated off him in waves. She didn't believe for one second that he actually knew what rejection felt like, but the show of solidarity still felt like a cool compress on a hot fever.

It would have been so easy to give in to that. If Helene hadn't overheard him just hours ago practicing a declaration of love. If she hadn't just watched him flirting with Sisi over the pianoforte.

Helene had leaned away from Maxi, pointed her glass at Sisi's twirling form. "You're playing with her." *And me.*

He'd raised an eyebrow. "I'm playing with everyone."

"That I believe."

He'd smiled without teeth. "Life is a game. You might as well play."

She knew it was meant to be charming, but the words had felt ominous. Was that what he was talking about earlier? Was it all a game to him? Emperors rising and falling. Replaced and reigning. The concept itself was full of danger; seeing it as a game felt even more dangerous.

Helene had been glad when Maxi tipped an invisible hat and left her—once again heading straight for her sister. She should warn Sisi about him, she'd thought then, the protectiveness pulling tight across her skin. But she'd held herself back. *Sisi never protected you*, she'd reminded herself, though the usual fire in the words, her righteous sense of justification, hadn't been there.

Now Sisi pushed Maxi away and rose suddenly from the couch, stumbling toward the door—toward her. Helene pointed her eyes resolutely at the ground. She might not be feeling her usual rage, but she would punish Sisi in her usual, silent way.

To her surprise, Sisi stopped beside her, voice threaded through with grief, desperation. "Will you really never speak to me again?"

Helene had been reveling in her sister's desperation for months, soaking it in like a sponge whenever she could see the hurt in Sisi's eyes, the way her silences landed like blows. But now, suddenly, it brought her no joy. Only the guilt that had been lapping gently at her all this time. Only a sense that she should be *protecting* her sister and wasn't.

Still, Helene wasn't ready to speak. Wasn't ready to give in to a momentary change in feeling. She twirled the olive in her glass, ate it.

"How many times do I have to apologize? I'm sorry! I'm sorry! You know I'm sorry!"

"You're drunk." Helene kept her voice even.

"I know."

"That's not how a future empress behaves." Her silence had been a dam, and now it was open—all her uncharitable thoughts spilling out.

"Helene . . ." Sisi's voice was soft, fragile, a snowflake melting at the slightest touch. "It just . . . it hasn't been an easy day."

"I'm sorry you thought it would be easier."

There was a malicious kind of justice in it, watching all of Sisi's chickens come home to roost. But who had Helene become? A woman stirring her martini and smiling at a sister destroyed and hopeless? The malice and guilt wrestled for her soul.

Sisi turned to leave, but Helene had one more jab for her. One more cruelty broken free from the dam of her feelings. One more victory for her malice. "You always do that, you know, when things get hard, you run away. It's time to grow up, Sisi."

Sisi's own hurt spilled over, aiming Helene's cruelty back at her. "You know who you've become?"

She paused.

"Our mother."

Helene watched as her sister disappeared around the archway, down the hall. Was it true? Had she become as small and cruel and petty as their mother? Was Helene training herself to leave her softest feelings behind and aim all of her hardest ones at the people around her, the people she was supposed to love?

Then Maxi was back again. His breath sweet with grapes and liquor, tickling her ear. "I give their puppy love three months. What do you say?"

And there was the familiar anger. But this time, to Helene's surprise, it wasn't pointed at Sisi. It rose up, hot and powerful and familiar in her chest, aimed at *Maxi*. At Franz. At Mother. At the court. All this time, she'd been punishing Sisi and herself—but there were so many other places that anger should live.

It should live with her mother's lies: do the right things and you'll be rewarded! It should live with Franz, who could have told her at any time that he was in love with her sister, his pretense never necessary. And it should live with Maxi, who was knowingly toying with her—and her sister. Who used their hurt against them. She let the anger sit on her skin, burn down the careful walls she'd kept around her real opinions, burn through the shame and guilt that had been lapping at its edges. She'd been ashamed of her anger. But now she realized that it was protective. Powerful, even. She'd just been aiming it at the wrong places.

Maxi lifted a hand to run it along the bottom of her bobbed haircut. Helene's eyes were flint, her heart fire. She leaned ever so slightly toward him, eyes narrowed, and flicked her gaze to his.

"I'm not your consolation prize."

Her anger was hers to wield.

She shoved her empty martini glass onto a small wrought iron table, turned her chin upward, and left Maxi standing there, under the archway, watching her go.

The night had unlocked something in Helene. She'd been holding back the tide, and it was time to let it through. Flatten the levee, burn the bridges, and damn the consequences. She felt a little like—

Elisabeth.

She went after her sister. Elisabeth wasn't in the hall, but Helene knew where her rooms were. She only hoped she was right that Elisabeth would go back there now.

For the first time in months, Helene's heart reached out for her sister, unencumbered. How had she been so foolish? She'd thought all the hurt had been caused by Elisabeth. But that wasn't true. Wasn't even close to the truth. Mother. Sophie. The Habsburg court. They'd torn Helene from her best friend in the world. It wasn't just rejection from Franz that had bent Helene into a new shape; it was the loss of the person she actually loved most.

Helene swept into Elisabeth's rooms without knocking. The bed was empty, the dressing room too. But she knew her sister better than anyone in the world. She knew beds and dressing rooms weren't the only places to find her, weren't even the most likely places. Dew-soaked grass under an open window. Tree branches too close to the house. Hidden in the folds of a heavy curtain, listening to your every secret. These were the places to look.

Helene found her curled up inside a cream curtain on the far side of the bedroom, face wet with tears, skirt spread around her like a puddle.

Helene moved down to her sister's level, studying her bleeding makeup and puffy eyes. "Are you all right?"

"It must make you happy, seeing me like this." Elisabeth's voice was broken, and Helene's rage wrapped itself protectively around it.

She reached through the curtain, wiped a tear from Elisabeth's cheek. "I thought it would, but it really doesn't."

It was the truth. The newest, truest truth.

After a pause, Helene bridged the space between them with a jest, the corner of her mouth twitching upward. "You smell delicious, like old Champagne."

Elisabeth's own mouth twitched to match Helene's. "You too."

Then, a smile, a real one, and Elisabeth whispered, "I like your short hair. You look beautiful."

Helene's chest expanded, settled into itself. How was it possible for one compliment to feel like it had mended a fissure so bone-deep? Helene's anger was cooling into something new: Release. Relief. Her skin tingled with it.

"I'm sorry for what I said."

"Me too, Néné."

"Please say I'm not like Mother." Helene pressed a hand to her heart in exaggerated dismay.

They both laughed, then, Elisabeth sitting up and leaning forward past the curtains to wrap her arms around her sister's neck. "I promise, you're not!"

Then they were both hugging, crying. A tear traced slowly down Helene's cheek as she pulled away to look her sister in the eyes.

There was something raw in Elisabeth's expression as she whispered, "Néné, I hope he's worth it."

Helene smiled again, hoped it was comforting. "You'll get used to it. The circus will calm down."

Elisabeth exhaled her surprise. "That wasn't what I meant."

Helene tilted her head.

"I meant losing my best friend over him."

Helene closed her eyes, opened them slowly. Their hurts were the same. Losing each other. Losing the kind of friendship only sisters could have.

But they hadn't lost it. Only—

Delayed it, caused it to skip a beat.

"You didn't lose me."

Elisabeth leaned forward and Helene met her halfway, their foreheads pressed together. And then the other dam in Helene's heart burst—her hurt, her fear, her desperation to talk to Elisabeth spilling forth. She told Elisabeth about Maxi, about standing by while Sophie went through her bag. Guilt pinched through the anger, the sadness.

"I'm sorry," Helene whispered, tears tracing cool tracks down her face as she pulled back and pressed her hands to her eyes. "I'm so sorry."

Elisabeth took her hands. "I forgive you."

They sat like that a long time, both sticky with tears and runny makeup. Hands held, eyes searching.

When Elisabeth spoke again, her voice was still raw. Vulnerable. Small. "What if I was wrong, Helene? What if I can't do this?"

Surprise flickered, then more anger. At everyone who'd made Elisabeth feel as Helene had felt for months: *not enough*.

"He loves you," she said, taking her sister's hands and squeezing all her reassurance into them. "I've seen how he looks at you. Forget everything else. You were right. You were right all along. Love is what matters. It's what will carry you through."

"What if the court breaks me? What if our love can't protect us?"

Helene pulled Elisabeth's hands toward her and pressed her face to them, kissing hard. Fierce. "You are the strongest person I know. If anyone can survive this court, it's you. I was wrong before when I said you wouldn't make a good empress."

She laughed then, surprising herself. "*No*, actually I was right. You won't make a good empress."

Confusion flickered across Elisabeth's face.

Helene squeezed her sister's hands. "You'll be a *great* one."

Elisabeth smiled, squeezed back. "I just wish I could talk to Franz. They've kept me away from him all day."

The anger carried Helene to her feet, pulling Elisabeth with her. Now that was something she could do. Her own private tour of the palace had included the imperial wing.

"Then let's get you to him."

FIFTY-EIGHT

NÉNÉ WAS A MARVEL, A FIRE, HERSELF AGAIN. *HERSELF*. For the first time in over a year. Elisabeth's heart reveled in it. The playfulness. The anger. The righteous indignation. Elisabeth emerged from the curtain, washed her face, and joined Helene at the door. Helene took her hand, leading her through the corridors, confident in her sense of direction. Her big sister was saving her again, capable of anything. Oh, how their mother would hate it.

Elisabeth's heart soared.

When they finally made it to Franz's rooms, Helene was the one who knocked. A sleep-ruffled Franz answered, and Néné stepped aside. She kissed Elisabeth on the cheek, whispered, "You are enough," and then left.

"Franz," Elisabeth breathed the word like the relief that it was.

"Elisabeth." Her own name fell from his lips like a blessing.

She started to cry again, her heart so fragile, and he pulled her into the warm, clove-scented solidity of him, wrapped his strong arms around her. Safe. Loved. Herself again. The three things she could be here in his arms. And yet . . . was she completely safe? He'd sent her away, and the hurt of it was still there, tucked under the relief of the embrace.

He led her to the settee, lowered her onto it, keeping an arm around her shoulders, now holding her hands in her lap. "My love, tell me what happened."

So she did. Told him about the indignity of the day, the anger, the hurt, the helplessness. Told him about Sophie going through her things, how violated she felt. Told him how much he'd hurt her by sending her away, by siding with the priest. And how deep her doubts had seeped into her soul.

"It broke me," she whispered. "It broke me to think you would send me away instead of listening to me, talking with me."

He held her and he cried—the tears, more than anything, convincing her that he finally saw how hurt she was, how much it mattered what the doctor and priest had done.

"I'm sorry," he whispered into her hair. "With all the tension in that room over other things—war and language and Maxi and Mother—I thought letting you rest would be better for everyone. I was so afraid of making enemies with a public scene that I didn't stop to think . . . didn't realize how it would feel to you. I didn't know what they'd done to you. I'm so sorry."

Elisabeth breathed into his chest, pressed her face hard against the strong warmth of him. "I need you to promise you won't do that to me again. That you won't just send me away without asking why I'm upset. I can't live like that—cut off from even you, fighting my battles alone."

He pulled back, looked her in the eyes. "I promise."

He took a deep breath. "I love you."

It was the first time he'd said it aloud, and Elisabeth's heart settled with the truth of it. "And I love you."

She'd practiced the words so many times, but nothing compared to the look on his face when she said them aloud. She leaned her head into his chest again, felt his hand move to run fingers through her hair. He kissed the top of her head. Twice. Three times.

She almost laughed with the relief of it. She'd seen her parents argue, hurt each other, and it had always drenched the whole house in despair: her father off to get drunk and seduce someone, her mother looking for someone else to lash out at. Their disagreements and missteps had made them the worst versions of themselves. Somewhere, deep down, that's what she'd feared this was. A breaking point. A battle. The moment their relationship would become an echo of the pain she'd seen in her parents' marriage.

But this wasn't that. Not even close. There was *love* between them, not disdain. She and Franz were tearing at the things keeping them apart, not building those things up. Franz wouldn't run from her pain when he really saw it; he'd feel it with her, hold her through it.

"Before I met you, I felt like everyone here just wanted something from me," he whispered. "Everything was duty. People wanted war or peace. They wanted power, a place in my court. They wanted an heir, pressured me to marry. Even marriage was duty. The one thing that should have been my own—love—I dreaded."

Elisabeth held her breath, listened, felt his heartbeat against his rib cage.

"But you—you wanted everything and yet nothing. I can't explain it. You wanted me, yes, but just as myself. Not as a tool for power or war or peace." He laughed, then, softly. "You wanted me a tailor, a lover."

She pulled back from his chest, looked in his eyes, closed her own when he swept gentle thumbs across her cheeks, wiping away the tears.

"I'm sorry I let you down today. You saved me. You were the one person I could tell about the nightmares, the one person who understood me without asking me to change. I want to be that for you too. The person you can come to. I'll do better."

Elisabeth's restless heart settled, stretched out toward him, this man who saw her, knew her, *trusted her*. He'd saved her too, just as she'd started to believe that her great love might not be in the cards.

He kissed her on the forehead, painfully tender. "There's a reason you made me brave. You were worth it, are worth it. And I don't care how much we have to fight this court for our happiness. I won't give up on it. Ever. Here, look—"

He stood, pulled her gently to the window, unlatched it, and gestured over the grounds, the buildings, to Vienna, sprawling under a midnight sky. It was a symphony of lights, thousands and thousands of candles and lamps—blue, white, red—flickering at the sky.

She stared, entranced.

He lifted her hand and kissed it. "They're for us—the lights. Austrian colors and Bavarian ones."

She laughed in surprise, delight.

"We're not the only ones who are happy. Don't lose sight of that. Vienna itself is welcoming you."

Helene's words returned to her then: *You'll be a great empress.* And Elisabeth's heart expanded across the darkness over Vienna, to every candle and lantern flickering its hope into the sky. They'd given her a gift by believing in her. And she was going to fight this court as much as she had to for them—and for Franz. For love. For the line she'd drawn in the sand so long ago.

She'd have great love or no man at all. Now she understood what that promise to herself had truly meant. She'd thought her promise was love over duty. But now she knew that her great love would come *with* duty, come with a fight. But she wasn't fighting alone. Not any longer. Franz was there. And so were a thousand tiny lights flickering to welcome her home.

Elisabeth turned to face him and pressed her hand to his cheek, watched his eyes close as he leaned into it. And her breath caught in her chest as she realized that they were *alone*. After so many months apart. The quiet stretched around her, lamps turned down low in the room, casting everything into romantic shadows across the burgundy couches, rust-red rugs, golden sconces. They had the thing she'd been craving so long: a whole night to themselves. Only Helene knew she was here, and she would keep their secret.

Franz realized it, too. She watched his eyes flick open with the knowledge, his eyebrows rising.

He closed the remaining space between them, turned her chin up with a finger, and kissed her softly. His lips found her cheekbones, jawline, eyelids, and she melted with each touch. His hands wandered soft across her neck, through her hair, down to her waist—not rushed this time, not urgent. Exploring.

Finally, finally, *finally*—her whole body and soul cheered, danced, sang. She loved him. He loved her. Tomorrow, they'd fight together; tonight, they'd love together.

She reached up and undid the buttons of his collar, kissed his neck. One side, then the other. Another button gone, another kiss along his chest. And again. And again. With the last button, she pushed both hands along the smooth skin of his stomach, up his chest, and over the shoulders, pushing his shirt off, marveling at every curve of lean muscle, the spicy scent of his clove cologne stronger, so close. It was a scene she'd imagined a hundred times, but it was so much better now that it was real.

Elisabeth's body was light as air, aware of his every movement, every touch. Lanterns lit up the city to invite her home, and her body lit up to invite *him* in.

He unlaced each tie on her dress with care, traced each new exposure of skin. She kissed every line of his scar. He kissed every curve of her body. And when she was finally naked, he gasped—the sound a perfect thrill.

Then he was touching her, fingers tracing sparks across her once again. His mouth lingered in the curve of her neck, the slope of her breasts, the tender place on each inner thigh. By the time he pushed farther, Elisabeth was aching with need, longing for more, for the feeling of pressing deeper into each other, knowing him in every way there was to know.

Sex. It was everything Elisabeth hoped—and nothing she'd expected. She'd been told there'd be pain, but it wasn't like that. It was her whole body gasping oh! And then: *oh.* An oh that echoed through her, settled down inside her, sighed with happy relief at connecting with the person she loved most in the world.

"Do you like it?" he'd asked, breath warm on her face. "How do you feel?"

"Yes." Her voice was breathless. "Keep going."

She felt—unexplainable. Happy in a way she hadn't been before, with no worry lurking at its edges. She was immersed in the moment, tingling with it. Her skin, her heart, her body fully engaged. Vulnerable and loved. Beautiful in a new way, a way beheld by someone else.

She reveled in each sensation, how different the press of lips felt from fingers, how different fingers felt from—

Tongue was the one that left her gasping for air, shocked, pleasured. He'd taken his time and she'd sunk into the bed, felt her body arch without her trying, twisted her hands in silk sheets.

They explored for hours, pressed against each other, into each other, and then, as he gasped in a new way, hands grasping harder at her hips, another feeling emerged.

"How do you feel?" he asked again, now lying beside her, skin to skin as they both let their heart rates slow, as she marveled at it all, replayed it bit by bit in her head.

"Happy," she answered. Then, after a moment had passed, "Safe."

Another heartbeat. "You're what I've been waiting for my whole life."

He interlaced his fingers with hers. "Me too, and I didn't even know it."

It was worth every battle she'd ever fight in court. He was worth it. *They* were worth it.

FIFTY-NINE

FRANZ HAD GIVEN UP ON TRUE LOVE, BUT IT HAD FOUND him anyway. Found his laughter and his heart, the most hidden parts of himself, the ways in which he needed to be seen and known. They'd fallen asleep pressed together, silk sheets caressing them both. Before that, they'd talked: railroads and roadways, big dreams and small ones. Freedom, travel, horseback riding. She wanted to visit Hungary; he wanted to take her.

And now he'd get to. She'd get to. They'd get to together.

Now it was their wedding day.

He stood at the front of the church in a newly starched uniform, next to a priest with a basset hound face. He wondered if that observation would make her laugh later: them married by the basset hound priest. Patron saint of the dropped beef bone.

She'd left the palace in the glass carriage: it a snow globe, her the princess. Empress. The only time he'd seen her more radiant was the night before, as they lay together after. *After.* Her eyes had been stars, her laughter the unbridled joy of a babbling brook.

Today's beauty was a different kind. Eyes glittering with mischief through the glass carriage, lips rouged red, hair interwoven around a silver crown. She'd reached out to touch the inside of the glass when she saw him. He'd reached out to touch the other side, pressing his hand to it until the coach was whisked away.

As the ceremony began, he saw her again and held his breath. The intricate white beading of her dress hugged the curve of her chest, draped dangerously off her shoulders. Beaded flowers covered part of her neck and draped down her back. The skirt of her dress was starlight, shimmering as she moved toward him. Franz's heart tripped and stuttered, excited. This was it. His match. His person. The one he hadn't even been looking for. Wild and beautiful and *his*.

The priest spoke. "The emperor fights for us. He fights for our holy empire. He shows us the way."

Franz promised his heart he would fight for *her*.

"With strength and wisdom, the emperor protects us and our empire from the dark forces that want to tarnish it."

Franz promised his heart he would protect *her*.

"He protected us from the devils of the revolution who wanted to destroy our future."

At the front of the pews, his mother and Maxi stood and watched Elisabeth's approach. Mother's face was worried, Maxi's angry. But their feelings couldn't touch him. Not today. Not now. Maxi would drown his sorrows in the ladies at court; Mother would learn to trust his intuition, he was sure. The court would learn to love Elisabeth, too. And he—Franz—would step in if necessary. He'd fight for Elisabeth, even if he had to fight the whole court, the whole world.

"And now the almighty God has sent him a bride: Elisabeth."

Her name was blessing and benediction, spark and fire. She was closer now, winked cheekily at him as she ascended the steps to the altar.

"She must be like an island in the middle of a thunderous storm."

She was the island, and he'd live on it. She was the storm, and he'd gladly drown in it.

"In her lap, our godly emperor shall find safety."

Franz smiled wickedly at that one; Elisabeth raised an eyebrow.

"This bond—Franz and Elisabeth—will protect us, will shine, for all eternity."

Franz took Elisabeth's hand, slipped the ring from his pocket onto it. She returned the favor: ring for ring. Gentle touch for gentle touch. Promise for promise.

"By the grace of God, I hereby pronounce you husband and wife."

Franz held back a laugh of delight. They'd made it. They belonged to each other. And what God had joined, the priest had always told him, no man could separate. No man, no mother, no brother, no empire. He was all hers.

H USBAND AND WIFE. TEARS ROSE BEHIND ELISABETH'S eyes as Franz leaned in and kissed her tenderly. His lips were so familiar now, the smell of him still so intoxicating. To think she'd been so scared she'd almost given him up yesterday. Now she couldn't even imagine it.

As she stepped back from the kiss, she saw Helene clapping in the front row, tears of her own tracing curves down her cheeks. She was happy for Elisabeth, *really* happy. Elisabeth's heart soaked it in, full to bursting. So much happiness around her: Franz glowing like one of their lanterns, Helene smiling love through her tears, Spatz clapping enthusiastically, Mother bouncing on her heels, her smile self-important now that she had an empress for a daughter. Papa looked more reserved, but Elisabeth knew he'd come around. Franz just had to corner him with a good cigar and a description of his railroad dreams. Her father would love it.

Franz and Elisabeth left the church together, hand in hand. The people outside pressed in.

"Elisabeth!" they cheered. "Elisabeth, we love you!" The sound made her heart swell.

The sun danced down, warming them through. And they both boarded the same carriage. It was time to go home.

Home.

The palace was her home now.

No, that wasn't exactly accurate. It wasn't the palace. *Franz* was her home. Wherever he was, that was where she'd fortify herself to love and fight and defend. Here. Bavaria. The moon if necessary.

When they reached the palace, the party was just beginning: glittering chandeliers with a thousand candles overhead, Champagne on the terraces, mushroom tarts sweeping by on trays.

"What happens now?" Elisabeth whispered to Franz as five couples graced the dance floor and bowed formally to each other.

"The court will dance in our honor. We only dance at the end of the evening."

She grinned, the jokes bubbling up. "Oh, didn't they tell you? Our dance is canceled to save your honor."

He laughed. "I'm not that bad."

"Well, we didn't practice as much as we should. We got . . . a little distracted," she teased.

"You know you're an incredible distraction." A kiss behind her ear, her whole body alight with him again.

A tug on her skirt tore her attention reluctantly away, and she looked down to see Spatz, eyes bright.

"I'll be back," Elisabeth said to Franz, as she turned and let her little sister pull her onto the terrace.

Once outside, in the cooling twilight air, she dropped to her knees and kissed Spatz on the forehead. Her little sister was dressed in a dark, stormy sea-blue gown with gold embroidery around its edges. A tiny, perfect thing. Elisabeth almost laughed at herself: two days at court and she was starting to appreciate the intricacies of gowns, the intricacies of beauty.

Spatz leaned in, whispering and wide-eyed. "You look like a fairy princess."

Elisabeth nodded solemnly. "Fairy *empress*."

Spatz's eyes grew wider.

"You're the one who looks like a fairy princess." Elisabeth reached out to tug gently at Spatz's skirts. "Or a water nymph, perhaps."

"I am the ocean goddess," Spatz said, serious, twirling so that her skirt billowed out around her.

Elisabeth laughed. Indeed, she was.

Spatz glanced back at the ballroom, at Franz, then at Elisabeth, a small line appearing between her now-serious brows. "So . . . does he?"

"Does he what, baby sister?"

"Does he satiate your soul?"

Elisabeth's mind cast back to that day just a few months ago. She'd told her sister that she wanted a man who would satiate her soul. She'd dropped through a window and ridden away from a man who would not and could never. How her life had changed since then.

The answer was so easy, even if the road there had been hard.

"Yes." Elisabeth widened her eyes. "Yes, he really does."

Spatz giggled, threw herself into Elisabeth's arms in a hug.

Elisabeth pulled her sister close and kissed the top of her head, pressing her face to it. "I hope you find that someday too. A person who satiates your soul. Remember that—you never have to settle."

It was hope, and it was blessing, Elisabeth pressing her own joy into her sister's tiny frame, kissing it into the top of her head. Joy that was hard-won—and would keep being hard-won, she knew. Elisabeth still might not know which rules to break and which to bend to, or which new challenges the court would throw at her.

But she did know that whatever challenges came, they were worth it. Entirely, wholeheartedly, absolutely worth it.

For Franz. For herself. For Habsburg.

For love.

And for every soul that that inspired.

ACKNOWLEDGMENTS

LET'S START WITH VERONICA PARK—MY AGENT, A BONA FIDE badass, and an author herself. You believed in my work before anyone in the industry and fought tooth and nail to get me here. There's no one I'd rather have on my side. Thank you.

To my editor, Caolinn Douglas: from the very first call, I knew you'd be a pleasure to work with. Thanks for your insightful guidance, superspeed turnarounds, and reliable kindness throughout the whole process (especially when I was tagging you with line edit questions every day).

To my writing community—cheerleaders, joke makers, friends. This book was a closely kept secret, but I appreciated every encouragement, word count celebration, and wildly incorrect guess about what I was working on (Sami, I am sorry to disappoint your dreams about the Roosevelts). Thank you especially to Chandra Fisher (sex scene whisperer), Scream Town (keepers of screams), A. Z. Louise (keeper of word counts), David De la Rosa (keeper of my sanity), Lani Frank (my cubicle mate halfway around the world and my gut check on all things grammar), Sarah Rana, Daniela Petrova, Elizabeth Brookbank, Zoe Wallbrook, Jessica Lewis, A. Y. Chao, Gladys Qin, Emily

308   • *Acknowledgments* •

Varga, Sami Ellis, Amanda "Sexy Stuff" Helander, Kate Dylan, Angel Di Zhang, Vaishnavi Patel, Natasha Hanova, and the entirety of the No Drama Zone.

It goes without saying that this project would not have been possible without Netflix (with special thanks to Joe Lawson and Cindy Chang) and the rest of the team at Zando: Molly Stern, Tiffany Liao, Emily Bell, Andrew Rein, Nathalie Ramirez, Chloe Texier-Rose, Sierra Stovall, Sarah Schneider, and Evan Gaffney.

Finally, RJ, thank you for letting me be your messy big sister, the Helene to your Elisabeth. I wish for you a love that satiates your soul.

ABOUT THE AUTHOR

GIGI GRIFFIS writes feminist historical fiction often featuring little-known histories and unruly female characters. She lives in Europe with an opinionated Yorkie mix named Luna and spends her free time hiking the Alps, cycling around small villages, and eating as much French food as she can get her hands on. Her work has been featured in *WestJet Magazine*, *Get Lost Magazine*, and *Fodor's Travel*, among others, and has been translated into French, Italian, Portuguese, and Estonian. *The Empress* is Gigi's adult novel debut.